GW00401043

Killer à la Carte

Gerry Galvin

Doire Press

First published in 2011.

Doire Press
Aille, Inverin
Co. Galway
www.doirepress.com

Editing: Lisa Frank
Copyediting: Maeve Richardson
Cover design & layout: Lisa Frank
Cover image: Toya Legido
Author photo: Christopher Hirsheimer

Printed by Clódóirí Lurgan Teo.
Indreabhán, Co. na Gaillimhe

ISBN 978-1-907682-07-0

Published with the assistance of Galway County Council.

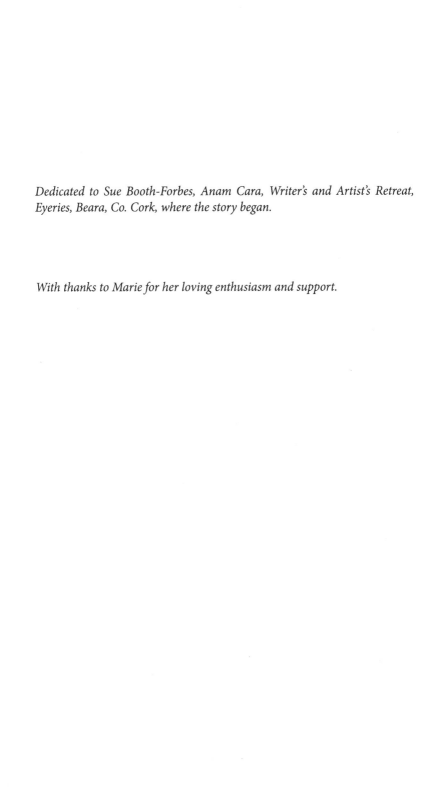

Dedicated to Sue Booth-Forbes, Anam Cara, Writer's and Artist's Retreat, Eyeries, Beara, Co. Cork, where the story began.

With thanks to Marie for her loving enthusiasm and support.

Food saves, food destroys, there is no enemy like food.

— Indian proverb

Good food is always a trouble.

— Elizabeth David

Chapter One

James dined regularly at Le Gourmet. It was not his favourite restaurant in London, not at all, nor did he expect to be surprised by Bruno's plats du jour. He knew them all: Fried Fillets of Sole in Almond Butter every Tuesday for years, Osso Bucco on Wednesdays, Navarin of Lamb Thursdays, Bruno's Bouillabaisse Fridays, et cetera, et cetera. Happenstance? Hardly. He dined there because of its convenience; his house was just a block away. Whatever about the food, the music was regrettable, wall-to-wall Piaf.

Maître d' Bernard greeted him. "Your special table, Mr G." Rarely was he addressed as he saw fit, James Livingstone Gall, for most a mouthful too far. "Mr G" was his moniker among restaurateurs, its snappy familiarity a token of distrust under the pretence of mutually beneficent exchange. Fact was they hated his guts. When it boiled down to it, he was a critic and the conventional assumption was that he had the power to destroy reputations as easily as he might gild the lily. They feared him and fawned. Butter was their stock-in-trade and Bernard spread it well.

James ordered the sole with a side dish of spinach and a bottle of Chenin Blanc from the Loire, serious and redolent of new mown hay. He had a keen nose. Lone dinners did that for a man. Solitariness he saw as a catalyst of understanding and assimilation in matters of the arts and music. Bernard was waspish as ever, breathing sweet poisons in his ear. He burnished James' ego with gossip about rivals and their restaurants. "You hear about Carlo?"

"Carlo Morelli?"

"His wife and the sous chef." Bernard made a play with hands and fingers to demonstrate an adulterous act.

"Not at all surprising, Bernard. The lady merely makes up for lost time. Carlo's been laying waste to waitresses for years."

"But he's a man!"

James swallowed more wine, suddenly recalling the childhood taste of his mother's skin after an Atlantic swim. So, so cold. The memory made him tremble and he consciously pushed it away, scanning the room for interesting faces. As the night's custom peaked, kitchen clatter and called orders mingled in a rising clamour. To James the noise from a well-run kitchen was not noise, it was music composed and orchestrated by the chef. At best it brought to mind Strauss, one of the younger's frantic polkas.

Parties of businessmen shared lubricated opinions, couples sought hands across tables in flickering light. He was the only lone diner, drawing glances that showed interest and then slipped away. Like it or not his was a formidable presence, not your caricature, corpulent, sage-gone-to-seed food critic, not in any shape or form. He was, he would have us know, the handsome exception, his early middle-age in charge of itself; he had his hair and his height, six foot at a stretch; when he opened his mouth, heads turned; submitted to the surgery of his pen, they rolled.

A waiter went by carrying a tray of food aloft: oysters in the half shell, a bowl of soup and a still tumescent soufflé. His identification clock clicked on: oysters, the flat Galway Bay variety; soup, tang of curry, coconut, coriander; the soufflé, ego food, puffed-up and erect with goat's cheese, egg, flour and butter. It paid to be right. He believed he had that quality, rare among men, of picking up the most ephemeral scents. It was essentially an animal phenomenon: bulls drawn aggressively to the inviting odours of cows; cats and dogs, however tamed, connecting to coded smells of genitalia in heat; a sexually-aroused human giving off smells of the sea not unlike that of crustaceans and fish. Ruminating as he drank, his eye was drawn to the couple just arrived at a table for two, Bernard seating them, male facing him.

"No!" The woman was emphatic. "You know I like my back to the kitchen."

As they changed places she looked across the room, straight at James, lingered for a moment too long while an outstretched hand accepted the proffered menu. His look lingered too. Whatever he saw there focused him with an involuntary jolt. Ever on the qui vive, he sensed he was on to something. He looked up again and at that precise point she did also. Bernard reappeared with what he believed to be a flourish, blocking James' view.

"Rognons sauté, sauce Madère," the lady said. "And a glass of Malmsey on the side."

"And after the kidneys, madame?"

"It's not listed, but I'll have osso bucco."

Bernard stiffened, head inclined. "Apologies madame, osso bucco is Wednesday, may I suggest tonight's—"

"Osso bucco!"

Bernard, contrite, turned his attention to her friend. "And Monsieur Felix?"

Her interjection brooked no indecision. "La même chose!"

Bernard scuttled to the kitchen, the lady's certainty snapping at his heels.

Her companion, a man of James' age, buttered a bread roll and sipped Madeira wine with sly, practised ease. James signalled for another Port. "Not '87. Is there a decent Cockburns in the house?" The quiver besieging his lower lip modified to an imperceptible tic under the influence of an imperious Cockburns '55.

The woman didn't quite finish the kidneys but her dispatch of osso bucco was swift. She lifted the stripped calf's knuckle to her mouth, sucked out the marrow and, glancing in James' direction, brought a napkin to her lips, dabbing them in slow motion: once, twice, three times. She then turned to her partner, brandishing a smile that donated all of her attention. James stifled a belch, his buttocks clenched and separated, emitting a sound that blasted ambient air in unison with Edith Piaf's highest note, regretting nothing.

He stood, steadied and made for the gentlemen's lavatory. A few closeted moments of sharp pain and relief, followed by consultation with a mirror renewed him. Back at the table he summoned Bernard. "More Blue if I may and a Port."

"Naturellement, Mr G."

He bisected the cheese, separating the varicose pieces, calling sharply to Bernard, who came at speed, muttering asides to unhearing minions. "Bernard, my man, an immature Roquefort is not good enough." He took a knife to the offending curd. "Look, it's virtually virginal. You can do better than that!" As the plate was removed, he bowed a gentle bow in receipt of the woman's unspoken approval.

She chose Floating Islands in a lime coulis for pudding, the unification of opposites. For once James was poised for spontaneity. Over the years he had learned to his cost that lost opportunity rarely showed up in the same guise twice. She stood up, flowing like her hair, a catwalk strut, upper body veiled by something pink and silky that clung to breasts without revealing them. By his table an almost imperceptible pause, the merest shimmy. He became aware of confluent essences in the perfumed zephyr of her wake.

Bernard materialised.

"Do you know the lady?" James asked.

"Very beautiful." His obliqueness irritated James. "But yes, she is a regular guest." Bernard hesitated, allowing space for innuendo. "You like?"

Sensed rather than seen, she approached from behind and this time she almost halted. The same silky pinkness enveloped waist and thighs, stretching fine fabric over a round, fleshy bottom. She had returned to her table when he noticed the card by his side plate: "Claudia Catalano'" simply scripted and her mobile number. He studied the card and turned it over.

Call me now!

Their eyes met again. He noticed the phone beside her left hand and heard it ring. She didn't give him an opportunity to speak. Turning outwards from the table, crossing her legs, she said, "Hello Louise, good of you to call. Sorry I couldn't make it this afternoon."

Pause, as her head did a smooth half turn towards him and then away again. "How about tomorrow?"

Pause, while she gave Felix the once over, which he must have noticed but chose to ignore, head bending in contemplation of an empty plate.

"Perfect, seven o'clock at The Butcher's Arms."

Pause.

Felix rose from the table, flicking imaginary crumbs from his lapel and straightening his tie.

"Yes, me too," she said. "Look forward to it."

James had a date.

Chapter Two

A smudged blackboard declaring "Today's Specials" straddled the bar counter. Lasagne Verdi (sic), Chef's Curry, Shepherd's Pie, Bangers & Mash, Liver & Onions, Maggie's Homemade Tart, Jelly & Ice Cream and other revered staples identified the market niche of The Butcher's Arms, as clearly as the smells of human frailty that an excess of disinfectant had failed to subordinate. James enquired of the barmaid if the lasagne was green or of the operatic kind.

"Yes dear, pasta, you'll love it."

Having been here before, he should have known what to expect. He had once crossed swords with the owner, Manny Johnson, a very dangerous man. Why here, he wondered. Why would a sophisticated woman of the world choose this down-at-heel pub? Suspicious, yes, but his overriding mood was of determined laissez-faire. She, not he, would be more discommoded in these insalubrious surroundings. Bangers & Mash at The Butcher's Arms, whatever the company, seemed to encapsulate measures of danger and opportunity that he could not possibly resist. The sausage hogging the limelight of peasant cooking, not only for its phallic associations but also for its symbolism of repression, challenged him; an encased amalgam of disordered parts that squirted and spat when heated, expanded to brazen firmness as it cooked, something James could identify with. He needed a drink.

His nose detected her before she came into view. He stood and they shook hands formally. She seated herself opposite him. "Drink?" he asked.

Without hesitation she said, "Guinness, a pint of Guinness."

James could not hide his astonishment. Guinness, and a pint to boot, the first choice of one of London's most sophisticated women. Mouth open, he did a double-take, pivoted to hide his surprise and went swiftly to the bar. He felt outflanked already by this self-assured woman in her low-cut designer dress. Gorgeous and Guinness. This woman, whom he had mentally categorised as assuredly of the méthode Champenoise, at the very least a Chablisienne, but the black stuff put her in a very different league. Terra incognita. He'd have to watch his step.

Bending to the glass, savouring the clerically-white collar on top of the dark body of beer, she took a moment to taste and then to lick its foam from her lips before facing James. "Why?" she said, licking her lips again and repeating, "why?"

"Why?"

"Yes, why did you arrange this?"

"Me?" James gasped. "I responded to your—"

Pointing a finger at him she said, "You made advances."

"Advances?"

"Very obvious."

"I could say the same for you, my dear."

"Call me Claudia."

"James," he said, bowing slightly.

"I know who you are, your fame precedes you."

Flattery always has a shopping list, James thought, noticing the single diamond hanging by a gold chain around her neck. "And your stance?" he queried.

"My stance?"

"Yes, your position on matters that concern us both."

"Such as?"

Not quite sure where this was going, his retort was authoritatively curt. "Culinary affairs."

She paused, taking a long draught from her Guinness, searching the air for explanation. "I admire your public stance on the scandal of G.M. food, intensive farming practices that put profit before taste and quality, and the acceptance of low standards in ... places like this, for instance."

"Why meet here then?"

"Very simple, James. I wanted you to myself. I wanted somewhere we would, neither of us, be known or disturbed."

"Are you propositioning?"

"Not exactly, not yet. But I do want to pick your brains."

"In that case let's order." He was curious. Of course. A beautiful woman and a fan to boot. Whatever her intentions, he would set the pace: encourage and challenge, draw her in, let her run, draw her in.

She passed the bangers test with flying colours, masticating the charred pigmeat, swallowing it along with mashed potato and gravy slop without a hint of distaste. At one point she looked up, cheeks bulging with sausage.

"How's yours?"

"Leather and onions."

"Tough!"

He laughed, she laughed.

Claudia was a few years his junior, no more than thirty-five, well-built and maintained. He had already noted her fragrance and the blonde hair that swirled about her face, half-hiding high cheekbones, a nose with the slightest upward tilt, lips that could only be described as full, rounded chin above an alabaster neck and eyes. Ah, the eyes! Black pearls to transfix with. He watched her walk across the bar floor accumulating stares of unconcealed lust and felt the least bit proprietorial. When her long legs returned her to him, it was as if they had vaulted an obstacle to intimacy. He felt a prickling sensation in the groin and pushed it away.

"Jelly or tart?" He had to regain some control.

"Cognac," she replied. Cognac after Guinness, she continued to surprise.

The top shelf hid a Remy Martin, Fine Champagne Cognac, behind a gossamer of cobwebs.

"Consistency of olive oil, extra virgin," he mused, studying the amber liquid. "Depth, extraordinary, holding up well."

Their eyes met and lingered as they had done at Le Gourmet.

The pub began to fill with evening trade; a pall of fetid fumes settled in a cloud above their heads. Fine brandy helped to create their own island in this heaving sea. He regaled Claudia with deliberate pedantry, well-worn anecdotes that put him in a favourable light. She listened for a long time with an attitude of reverence, imbibing slowly, brows knitted. "We could work together." She leaned towards him revealingly.

"How, pray?" James said almost in a whisper as he too leaned forward.

"You and I, James, as a team."

"You have something in mind?" James loosened his collar. All evening had been leading to this.

"Look, I read your reviews and columns, listen to your interviews, observe you at work and—"

"I work alone. Anyway what would your husband say?"

"He has no say," she insisted, running her fingers through her hair.

"Come, come, what could I possibly offer you, a woman of obvious means, a husband—"

"I told you, he has no say. We live separate lives."

"I watched you dine with him."

"Occasionally, publicly, we have dinner, but I can't bear to be alone with him for long."

"Children?"

"None."

"Do you share a home?"

"A large house by the park. I have a private apartment on the second floor, separate entrance. I come and go as I please."

"Financially—"

"Independent. I inherited my father's fortune. Sergio Catalano, you may have heard of him."

"You're Sergio Catalano's daughter?" James stiffened.

"The one and only."

"My mother knew him," he said in a tone striving for detachment.

"I know, James." Claudia hesitated, her dark eyes piercing his. He stared back, unsure of what was coming. "In fact, she knew him very well indeed, as we are both aware. Your mother, Grace Gall, was the last person to see him alive."

He waited, but she said no more, her chin snapping upwards in anticipation of his response. "What do you really want from me?" He hoped she did not sense his unease.

"Your ruthlessness, James. I want your ruthlessness and your cunning."

"You knew Grace too?"

"Enough, I know enough. They had dinner together on the night he died."

His lower lip quivered. They sipped brandy, and when she put her glass back on the table, he replenished it. She had a habit, he had earlier identified, of shaking her head in a curt clockwise motion. As she did it now, her features revealed themselves fully; those eyes were not merely beautiful. Looking into them he remembered clearly his mother's version of events the night Sergio died.

When Sergio Catalano's body was found in the summer of 2000 on a beach beside the villa he owned on the Adriatic coast of Croatia, he was, at seventy, retired from active involvement in the hotel and catering empire he had created. He was known to be a very private man, seen rarely in public since his wife died five years before. Every summer he spent at the villa near the town of Orebic, where he attended Mass and dined at local restaurants with visiting friends. The sudden death on a beach of an elderly man, even as rich and successful as Catalano, would not have hit the headlines were it not for the fact that beside his body lay another, that of his full-time maid, local woman Renata Boras.

The cognac bottle stood empty on the table between them. They should have been drunk but were not.

"Natural causes, Claudia. They died of natural causes, verified by the Croatian state pathologist and, if memory serves me right, confirmed by an independent medical expert invited as an observer by the Croatian authorities."

"Your mother was there at the time."

"Interviewed and cleared of anything nefarious. She was a friend, visiting, nothing more."

"She killed them, James. I know it, you know it."

"What is clear and proven, Claudia, is that my mother and your father were lovers, that she was a regular guest at the villa and that she discovered the bodies on the beach. Master and maid, dead side by side. Extraordinary, I grant you, grotesque, but accidental nonetheless. They were lovers, Grace and Sergio, I knew how devoted she was. She adored the man."

"She killed him!" She hesitated for effect, looked askance at him and continued briskly, not giving him a chance to protest. "They had a substantial dinner that night, prepared by Grace herself; it was Renata's night off. Hors d'oeuvres of Prsut, the locally-cured ham, with Parmigiana, and the olives and peppers the Croatians pickle so well. The fishing is so satisfying along the coast between the islands, as you know, James. I read a piece of yours once to that effect ..." She had her eyes fixed on a point somewhere beyond his head and he realised that she was talking to herself as much as to him. "They collected octopus, crab and sardines from the quay at Loviste in the afternoon. Grace had such a way with seafood, such invention, such flair. Sergio just adored his fish. Grace cooked it exactly as he liked it: lots of tomato, oil and garlic to remind him of old times. Grace's ragoût, he called it, nothing like Grace's ragoût. He had that Italian habit of pronouncing the "t" at the end: Grace's ragoût. A lot of fish, many ingredients: *the presence of alcohol and a variety of undigested seafood and diverse condiments in the stomachs of the deceased* was how the coroner's report put it. Torta, one of Renata's homemade marmalade cakes, for pudding and four bottles of wine, local stuff, you know the dark, heavy Dingač. Papa drank it all the time, he was no connoisseur. Four bottles empty …" Claudia swallowed a deep breath and exhaled venom.

"There was no evidence to show that all the wine had been consumed at one session," James said. "Sergio, as you have admitted, drank Dingač all the time."

She was not listening. "She got him drunk. Renata returned unexpectedly, delivering her homemade cake perhaps. Grace fed her also and, whether intentionally or by drunken chance, she poisoned them both."

"Natural causes are natural causes."

She continued, "Grace killed Sergio when she found out about his affair with Renata and in the end she got two for the price of one."

"Top marks for fantasy, Claudia."

"No, James. In this case the experts erred, outwitted by a devious and vengeful woman. I've done my homework. Remember the late Percy Livingstone Gall, James?"

"My father died many years ago. I do not see the relevance."

"She poisoned him too."

"Ridiculous!"

"He had the sweetest tooth, did he not, a glutton for sugar your dad? Meringues, vacherins, chocolate mousses, crumbles and fruit pies, sorbets and ice creams. How do I know? You told me yourself."

"I never—"

"An article for *Vogue* a couple of years ago: 'Family Food' you called it, a revealing piece about Mum's virtuosity and Dad's sweet tooth."

He had enough of her speculation. "You said you wanted to pick my brains."

"I do."

"Cards on the table then, Claudia. What exactly do you want?"

"I want you to help me kill my husband."

Chapter Three

James picked up his briefcase, left the apartment and made his way to the corner shop two streets away, as arranged. Claudia's black Jaguar awaited and he slid in beside her.

"Sercat Central? You can't be serious, James. Everybody knows us there."

"How very perceptive. That's just what the occasion demands. Nothing to hide, Claudia. I speak for myself, of course, clear conscience, clear as consommé."

"I see. Very public, very innocent."

"There is no reason why James Livingstone Gall and Claudia Catalano should not meet for coffee on any given Monday morning, is there? What better venue for this unremarkable engagement than Sercat Central, flagship of the Catalano hotel empire?"

"You could interview me."

"With the greatest pleasure, my dear. I have some pressing questions." He did not tell her then, but since she had taken such pains to attract him at Le Gourmet and The Butcher's Arms, he had spent several hours researching her father and his empire.

Sergio Catalano, like many an émigré after the war in Europe, brought with him to England a fierce desire to succeed. With a fellow

Neapolitan he had met on the Dieppe-to-Newhaven ferry, he rented a market stall in London's East End, where they established a reputation for handmade ices in summer and pizzas the rest of the year. Business boomed. Families in post-war Britain had come to accept the virtues of thrift and the suppression of appetite. They were ready for Sergio's liberating innovation and, when he split from his partner to open his first café, he knew he had the secret to success. He had too that blend of opportunism and imagination which, added to an intolerance of failure, drove him on. Like arrivistes everywhere, he was an apt mimic of respectability. Money encapsulated it. The bottom line was always about money and how he might make more of it. From cafés he progressed to restaurants and gradually he built up the Sercat hotel chain, insisting that each of his hotels paid architectural tribute to the country of his birth. Over a period of twenty years, versions of Roman, Florentine and Venetian landmarks with the Sercat prefix rose to dominate the downtowns of America and the grand avenues of Europe.

As Claudia drove through the great arch to the pre-lobby, James felt a quickening of the pulse. Sercat Central's lobby was a perfect replica of the Colosseum. James watched as Grant Percival, long time General Manager of Sercat Central, greeted Claudia like a beloved relative, kissing her on both cheeks and chiding her in tut-tut-semi-seriousness for "abandoning us for so long," even though she was in and out of the hotel every week.

"I'd like you to meet James Livingstone Gall."

"*The* James Livingstone Gall? I *am* honoured." James sensed that something other than honour caused him to assume a more formal attitude. "Welcome to Sercat Central. Business or pleasure?"

"James wishes to do a piece about me, Papa and the hotel. He may want to talk to you too, for all I know."

"Wonderful, I must tell chef. You know our executive chef, Gunter Gruber?"

James knew Gunter.

"Somewhere quiet, you don't want to be disturbed. I know just the place. Come, I'm going to put you in the Da Vinci room. Lots of hiding places."

Grant deposited them at a table towered over by a marble male nude in a miniature forest of greenery glistening from recent watering. They were given menus and had begun to study them, when they were plucked out of their hands by an oval-shaped Pavarotti figure in chef's whites, "Gunter Gruber, Chef de Cuisine", emblazoned in red and gold where his heart should be.

"Madame Claudia, you are so very welcome." She extended her right hand and he bowed to graze it with his lips. James stood and was engulfed in an enforced embrace, which he made a pretence of reciprocating. It was like fondling overcooked ham.

"My surprise," Gunter cried, "you will try my surprise." He left in a prostatic shuffle towards the kitchen.

"And you, James, do you have any surprises today?"

"Does your husband know you're here?"

"Of course not, I told you—"

"Yes, yes, you are not beholden to him, financially, emotionally, whatever. For all intents and purposes you are free as the air. Why then would you want to get rid of him?"

"You wouldn't understand. How could you, James, you in your ivory tower, caring for nobody but yourself?"

"It seems to me, Claudia dear, that I have a rival in you. You care so much for your spouse that you want him dead."

"I don't love Felix, can't love him …" She appeared suddenly pale and unsophisticated. "He hates me and humiliates me. I found him with two young thugs in our bedroom."

"But you have your own life. Why not leave him?"

"He insists we keep up this front, even though most of his colleagues in banking are just as deviant as he. Nobody faces up to anything."

"I sympathise, Claudia, but not to the extent of becoming an accomplice to …"

Within hearing a waiter fussed with cutlery, condiments and wine. James extracted a pad from his briefcase, asked Claudia some innocuous questions about Sercat Hotels and made a show of preparatory note-taking.

Gunter's surprise consisted of three subtle enticements: an oyster each, raw, in the shell, decked out in a cloud of foaming horseradish; demi-tasses of gazpacho with peeled muscat grapes and tiny queen scallops; twin lollipops of chocolate-coated foie gras. James had to admire Gunter's deft touch. Germanic but deft nonetheless. Amuse-bouches set out a chef's stall, an indication of style.

"Rather an excess of horseradish froth, don't quite see the point of it," he said, peering at Claudia for indications to her mood as she slurped an oyster from its shell. "And as for the lollipop, the only appropriate response has to be from the Concise Book of Americanese: it sucks!"

"He threatens to go to the police if I leave."

"Hardly a case for the police, a domestic issue."

"He has an incriminating tape."

"Come, come, Claudia. What have you done that is so incriminating?"

"Sergio not I. Matters he got involved with in the States when he first went there, the Las Vegas hotel."

"Las Vegas?"

"He had partners at the start to help him raise funds. Papa always said he bought them out a few years later, when the hotel broke even and he was in a position to expand on his own."

"So, what's the mystery?"

"That's my problem, James. According to the tape Felix has in his possession, the mystery surrounds one of those partners who disappeared at the time and has never been accounted for. Felix gave me a copy. It's no fake."

Through a mouth full of Gunter's surprise, James asked, "This tape, what does it prove?"

"That Sergio Catalano hired an assassin to kill his former partner."

"You believe Felix, that he's prepared to expose this?"

"I have no doubt."

"Have you tried to—?"

"I've tried everything. I wouldn't be telling you this if I believed there was any chance of reasoning with him."

"Sergio is no longer around, the scandal would blow over."

"I'm still on the board of Sercat Hotels. Trading has been difficult, particularly in the States since the recession, the business is vulnerable. I'm vulnerable. Make no mistake, this would not just blow over."

"I'm not convinced. What you ask requires considerable reflection. Not quite up my street, Claudia, although I must admit to a certain vanity that you should think I might be up to such outrageous mischief."

She leaned sideways to retrieve a document from her bag: a slight folder enclosing several typed pages with the title imprinted on the cover.

"Recognise this, James?"

Book Review by James Livingstone Gall.

"Lethal Recipes" is Carbery Dawson's best book since "Fingered Food" (Hamline 1998), a veritable Pandora's Box, which had food commentators, even up to government ministry level, in a flap. They had, in their blind orthodoxy (envy too from some predictable quarters) misread it. It was not a poisoner's manual at all, rather a singular gastronome's postulation that food is intrinsically baneful. Who could argue with that? As we eat so we dig our graves, each mouthful a marker of diminishing time.

Having read the first paragraph he leafed quickly through the rest of the review, noting that somebody (Claudia presumably) had underlined words and phrases throughout the piece in red: *the colonisation of our intestines by arcane foods of unexplained provenance … vegetables dragged from their homes to summary executions … toxicity in rhubarb and wood sorrel … excessive use of some foods may be fatal … I felt the blood on my hands, muscular odours of wine, spice and softening flesh permeated the house.*

Out of context these quotes made his disclaimer in the first paragraph irrelevant. Be wary of what you eat, it said, and be especially wary of James Livingstone Gall, who knows exactly how food can kill. James cleared his throat, shrugging nonchalantly for Claudia's benefit. "You think I'm capable of killing your husband on the evidence of selective quotes from an old book review?"

Claudia sat there with a fixed grin, nodding. James was about to excuse himself when she leaned over the table, tugging and caressing his tie. "I've been on your case for some time, Mr G. That's your moniker in the trade, James, isn't it? You'd be surprised what turned up in conversation with a nice nurse at the hospital where your mother died. You were so solicitous with mum right to the end. Alone, she said, nobody else in the sick room when Grace breathed her last. Sheila, that was her name, wasn't it, James? Pretty girl, said your mum went surprisingly fast. Bouillabaisse you cooked for Grace, before she had to be rushed to the hospital. Bouillabaisse, the doctor who treated her was absolutely sure. Strange, is it not, that seafood should be such a repetitive ingredient in the deaths of people we know?" Pause. "You don't have to explain to me James, I know. And if I have to, I can prove it," she said, letting go of him and sitting back as he gathered himself.

His lower lip quivered, he looked at her with unchecked fury, breathed in and out, looked away and then back again, managing a short forced guffaw. "Let's keep these little fantasies to ourselves, shall we?"

"Your fantasies as you call them are safe with me, James, as long as you help me kill Felix."

He excused himself brusquely, using this impasse between them to pay respects to the chef in his office overlooking the vast kitchen of Sercat Central. He thanked Gunter for the surprise tasting. "Grapes in gazpacho, that's new to me, and horseradish, punchy, interesting."

"Not sure yet about the horseradish. Too German, much power for the oyster, you tink?"

That was exactly what he thought and told him so. James believed that there was, among cooks like Gunter, a search for essence that was destined to be forever beyond their reach. The really surpassing chef, aware of this ephemerality at the heart of cooking, still continued the search but with that sense of fatalistic acceptance that fuels all art.

Gunter would not let him out of his little office without showing him his collection of cookbooks and magazines, drawing attention to a file identified by a picture of James on the cover. "I'm your big fan," he said, waving the file in front of him. A few pages fell to the floor and, as he bent to collect them, the title page settled on top of the rest. Like an accusation, it read: *Book Review by James Livingstone Gall*, the same one that Claudia had shown him. Gunter saw James hesitate, peered at the heading himself and chortled. "Ja, dat was a good one, a real killer." The chef's belly laugh pursued James out of the kitchen, back to the dining room.

James found Claudia talking to Grant Percival, who ushered them across a vast hall laid with crimson carpet to revolving doors big as a fairground carousel. "Back soon, I sincerely hope, Claudia."

She hesitated, glanced at James and turned to face Grant. "It depends on James. I'm not sure if he has uncovered enough in one interview."

"Yes, Grant," James chipped in smartly. "It remains to be seen if the story merits elaboration."

When Grant left, James shook hands with Claudia. Then he ordered a taxi and watched her walk away towards the Jaguar, purring in wait, flunkey in attendance. Knee-high boots below the tailored executive suit and snowy blouse, frilled over cleavage, bespoke power and privilege. As James' cabby slowed towards the hotel entrance, Claudia's car accelerated across his path, forcing him to brake suddenly. To his string of curses she responded with an expansive wave.

Chapter Four

Claudia had watched him for years, even before her father's death. James Livingstone Gall, the mere mention of the man's name in Sergio's presence was enough to plunge the household into a limbo. Sergio Catalano, in a bad mood, fluctuated between volcanic eruption and growling inarticulation, the latter by far most upsetting to his daughter. At least when he shouted she heard the very worst of his reaction. "That cat's testicle, Gall, what the fuck does he know about hotels?" The rumbling undercurrent of his ire served only to fire her imagination. Papa did not like to be crossed.

James had written several reviews of Catalano hotel restaurants, none of them in the least complimentary. Claudia knew that James would be flattered that she knew some of those reviews by heart. Of the London Sercat he wrote:

No mini-Niagara in the lobby, no two-foot thick oriental carpet, glittering chandelier, triple-king size bed or body shop in the bathroom can excuse this hotel's disregard for the fundamentals of a simple three-egg omelette!

Sergio wanted to sue him for defamation, but his legal people advised against it; the review itself was bad enough, drawing extra attention to it in the courts would only prolong the hotel's exposure to offensive journalism.

Consequently she also disliked James, so when Sergio hooked up with his mother, Grace, that was the last straw. What had until then been peripheral grew into an obsession, which consumed her completely after Sergio was found dead on the beach and Grace hung around behaving like a disconsolate widow. Meeting the man face to face had become a must. She would make him pay. Pagare!

She contrived to set up a crossing of their paths in Le Gourmet and the subsequent rendezvous at that horrid pub, setting in train a process which relied on intuition as well as planning. She was aware that the territory was pocked with pitfalls. James was cunning. She could seduce him. But, to be absolutely honest with herself, she was afraid, afraid of entering this alien territory, in which men like James bent all the rules in practised self-interest. This much was clear to her now: any proof she could produce would not be enough to nail James for Grace's murder. James didn't know that and she was not going to let him find out. Whatever mistrust persisted between them, she knew she would continue in the conviction that James' fatal talents inclined to her advantage; he was available and the activating button was hers to press.

Chapter Five

From a young age James knew that his mother loved him mostly for his ability to show her in the best possible light and that was, he believed, the reason that she taught him to cook as soon as he stopped throwing spoons out of his cot. If he had begun to display some respect, however minimal, for the implements of cooking, then it was possible that he was ready for the pursuit itself. In his dear mother's eyes there was no more worthy aspiration. At two he could tell if an egg was free range (that was a time when free range meant something) by the depth of gold in a cracked yolk. The road to his mother's affections was littered with broken eggs and how they might be rehabilitated to a form of edible usefulness.

"Rule one, James, we waste not," Grace said. It was her persistence and intolerance of failure that endowed him with those very same virtues. The body remembers: shoulders locked in pain from prolonged whisking, knife scars, fat-spat blisters on tender skin. And his mother's unwavering assessment. "Why can't you, why don't you?"

Of course she cared in a material sense. When his father died shortly after James was born, she fed him, clothed, educated him, and showed some kindness too. His fifth birthday present, *From your adoring Mother*, came in the black leather case he still used to this day:

a set of Sabatier chef's knives. He cut himself with every one of them, each wound a notch in the upward ladder of learning.

The aforementioned whisking recalled his first attempts at a zabaglione. Mother listed the ingredients and one by one presented them to him: eggs, sugar, Marsala wine. "Now James, separate the eggs and whisk like a demon with wine and sugar until the mixture peaks." She handed him a deep stainless steel bowl and a balloon whisk.

"Peaks, Mum?"

"Hills, darling, soft hills just like Mummy." She fondled her chest in illustration and he nodded his understanding.

Whisking gnaws at shoulder and wrist muscles; pain concentrates like migraine. Chefs' muscles learn to absorb the ache; numbed, they behave like mechanical devices. His untested limbs flopped after five minutes, unable to continue even if the viscous liquid in the bowl showed no enthusiasm for peaking, softly or otherwise.

"Beat, beat, beat, James!"

He did as she bade him and flopped hopelessly a couple of minutes later. Tears fell from his face into the bowl and his whole body sagged in defeat. She looked at him, the whisk and the bowl. "Didn't I tell you to whisk the yolks not the whites, silly?"

Zabaglione, the very word resonated like tinnitus ever after. French kitchens have their own term. They call it sabayon, which he liked, not as harsh sounding, more descriptive of soft peaks.

Grace was an obsessive foodie before the word was invented. Obsessive and unpredictable. For one whole winter everything had to be à la Normande: apples and calvados for weeks on end. She had what she called "My Pasta Period", some time in the late seventies, which James remembered mainly because it coincided with the time between the arrival and eventual departure of Federico. Avuncular and hearty though Federico was, James suspected from the beginning that his mother's interest in him was pragmatic; Federico was passionate about Mediterranean ingredients. They had met at an Italian food fair, at which he manned a stall, and it seemed entirely fitting to her that, if she intended to immerse herself in the food of the region, Federico would be the perfect catalyst. He stayed for some time, a couple of months or more, his presence marked by a procession of generous dinners. He showed James how to make pasta and a ravioli James had never bettered. James never saw Grace so happy. She loved Federico's cooking and him too, his brawn, his sweet tongue, his smooth sincerity. And then suddenly Federico disappeared. James missed his bustling good humour and did not understand why he did not even say goodbye, when all his comings and goings up to that point had been markedly grandiloquent. When James enquired about him, Grace said, "He taught me a profound lesson, James."

"Yes, Mum."

"The dangers of being taken in by propaganda." She shivered as if caught by a chill wind.

"What's propaganda, Mum?"

"He was, Federico, the epitome of it. He lied, lied about everything. Healthy eating, he called it, all that polenta and pizza and pasta." She paused to fuel her anger. "I've put on pounds, James, look at me!"

He admired her ability to carry her heaviness; he loved to brush against the protrusions of her upper body and the bulge of her tummy, more pronounced, it was true, by the vigour of Federico's cooking.

"The truth, James! My bottom, is it bigger?"

From then on she poured scorn on the Mediterranean diet, a volte-face that she considered courageous. She became a born-again butter addict, the flip side of which was antipathy to olive oil. "Butter is smooth and soothing, olive oil makes men hairy."

"But Mum—" he tried to interrupt.

"I did love him for a while but his simplistic devotion was, to say the least, over-zealous. He thought he could stay with us forever."

There were others, men not unlike Federico, loners, fly-by-nights who lived with them for weeks at a time. In the narrow orbit of their concerns, James might not have existed had mother not pushed him to show off his culinary skills. Without exception they liked him for his cooking. Crucial to these passing liaisons was sex. One night when a bad dream drove him fearfully from his bed, he went to her room. Federico-of-the-moment lay on top of her, his nakedness covering hers. Unseen, James watched their frantic exertion culminate in toe-curling orgasm.

Sometimes between resident male friends she would cut James off completely, shutting herself up in her room with pills and liquor for a couple of days at a time, from which she would emerge as if from a rehabilitative retreat.

James developed mechanisms of evasion that permitted him to behave as he liked. Only on the subject of food did she insist on superiority, even later when it grew obvious that the pupil had outstripped the mistress. Grace was a great cook, lacking only in ruthlessness. How should he explain it? She inherited the fundamentals from her Alsatian mother; a béchamel, for instance, that had the texture of fine silk. And those plum pies: luscious, rounded hillocks leaking veins of purple juice through buttery pastry. And yet she baulked when another glass of red might have raised her carbonnade de boeuf beyond the realms of a pedestrian stew. Her summertime gazpacho, however subtly enticing, lacked that icy ferocity the genre demands.

At school James got A's in everything except obedience.

"Discipline has to be self-imposed to be of any value," she told him. "You can be who you want to be, James. Don't let anybody stop you, not even your adoring mother."

When at seven or eight he came upon a dead cat on the road, James discovered he was different to other boys. Dead things terrified them, whereas he had grown up with quotidian executions of birds and animals: killing and dismembering a rabbit or wild duck were necessary steps before cooking and eating.

Once on the way home from school, a group of them came across a dying puppy. His friends recoiled, tiptoeing around the animal in a kind of timid dance, while James stayed with it, prodding its extremities with a stick.

After dinner James took one of Grace's canvas shopping bags, collected the now-dead animal and hid it until she left the house on some errand. Skinning it was no more difficult than a rabbit, the vital organs similar also, particularly the unblemished liver and kidneys. Back-passage blood-loss seemed localised, a blood vessel shattered by the impact, he guessed. So small when skinned and jointed, its flesh shone and felt tender to his touch. He dipped the puppy pieces in seasoned flour and sealed them in sizzling butter. They fitted easily into a big stew pot with chopped onion, garlic, celery and carrot, barely covered with water and a glass of German Riesling. As soon as the first signs of a boil rippled the surface, he dropped in a bouquet garni—parsley, thyme, bay leaf—along with a handful of stoned prunes, pepper and salt. When the simmer returned, he skimmed the grey-brown scum from the surface, adjusted the heat and put a lid on. It tasted as succulent as any young flesh gently stewed.

Grace complimented him. "That's quite good, James. Rabbit is it? Less gamey than usual, I'd say, and lacking some je ne sais quoi ... a blade of mace, grated nutmeg. But not bad, not bad at all."

He liked to test her. They had roast cat on one occasion, which he described as baby chicken.

"Not sure I like that, odd taste for chicken." She picked at a piece with her fork, nibbled the pallid flesh, swallowed and digested thoughtfully. "Fish!" she cried in triumph. "Decidedly fishy, James. Don't tell me you're playing games, trying to outwit me. This is fish, fowl it is not."

She deserved some credit. The cat happened to be one of a cluster of strays that loitered behind the fishmonger's. Roast cat, sustained on a diet of fish entrails and bones, was sure to retain a tell-tale fishiness.

In his last year at school James had become quite the self-assured young man, well able to maintain high exam marks, surpassing most of his peers. Confidence, he had begun to understand, fed on feelings of singularity. He had every reason to feel different and although he would have wished to share the excitement of his secret projects with a special friend, discretion kept his mouth shut. He had girlfriends but nobody special after Janice.

Janice lived two streets away from his home; they walked to school together every morning and sometimes studied together in school or in her home. He was seventeen when he suggested to his mother that he would like to cook Sunday lunch with Janice Worth as his guest.

"If you must, James, but I warn you. There is not a shred of sophistication in that lot. If cooking lunch for her is your tactic for seduction of the fair Janice, you will get absolutely nowhere. Charm and refinement are wasted on her type. Take her to the back row of the Stella if you want to get into her pants."

In spite of his mum's disapproval Janice came to Sunday lunch. Mum mixed Pimms. He kept it simple: sage and onion soup, roast lamb and baked apple for pudding. When Janice sniffed the aromatic soup she cried out, "Stuffing, it's just like stuffing!"

"So you're partial to stuffing, dear?"

James stared with pity at Janice, easy prey for Grace's sarcasm.

Main course passed without incident, but he was increasingly wary of his mother's drinking. She had opened a second bottle of Bergerac, having accounted for much of the first bottle herself. Janice, after a glass of wine, relaxed and appeared to enjoy the food. He had made a custard sauce to accompany the baked apple. When he passed the sauce boat to Janice, she studied it briefly before replacing it on the table untouched. Grace pounced.

"Don't you just love James' sauce?"

"It's, it's spotty, Mrs Gall."

"Don't worry, Jan," he reassured her. "The spots are from the vanilla. I used a real vanilla pod in the sauce."

"Oh, deary me, I thought something had got into it." Tentatively she helped herself to a spoonful, as Grace leered at her across the table.

James was at pains to keep his mother at bay and at the same time encourage Jan's enjoyment. "I, we like to use only authentic ingredients.

Mum is very particular, aren't you, Mum?" He had fallen into her trap.

"You wouldn't appreciate how careful we are, Janice. How could you?" A note of slurred menace had entered her voice. "Cooking is an art not much appreciated by the peasant class, but in this house our standards are high. High, yes my dear, high. We don't take short cuts, do we, James, not even for shortbread?" At this she doubled up, laughing uncontrollably.

"Mum!" He protested.

In drunken slow motion she looked at him, pointing an out-stretched finger in his direction as she moved her gaze to Janice. "See him, my beloved and only son. James takes no shortcuts." Chuckling at some private joke, she went on. "When James cooks salmon it's wild, when he cooks chicken it's organic and when he cooks dog it's only the finest free range puppy. Play along with James and you too Jan might one day partake of some of the finest stewed puppy in this fair land."

Janice was out the door before he caught up with her. He did manage to calm her and eventually convince her that mother was susceptible to nonsensical ramblings brought on by too much alcohol. But she did not come to their house again and no longer welcomed his attentions. He was loathe to confront Grace after the incident with Janice, kidding himself that it was a one-off without malice and because he sensed that they had reached a dangerous pass in their mother-son relationship. Then about a week later Grace raised the matter herself.

"Seeing the Worth girl still, are we?"

"Yes, of course," he lied.

"Don't be a fool. She's, pardon the pun, worthless."

Pent-up frustration exploded. "Bitch!" He roared at her and she flinched momentarily.

"You thought you pulled the wool over my eyes with that dog dinner. I knew all the time and went along with your little deception."

"What about the cat that you thought was fish?"

She was stunned, struggling to regain composure. That night she washed down a pack of sleeping pills with gin and, when he found her the next morning, the thread that held her between life and death was fast unravelling. Hospital emergency services intervened just in time. Intensive care at St. Michael's, the most exclusive clinic in the area.

"A hair's breadth!" That was how the doctor on duty described it. She recovered quickly, once cleared of toxins, but medical advice insisted on at least two weeks of residential care and counselling.

On the first day of mental clarity she peered benignly at him over the bedclothes. "Never let me do this again, James, promise me!"

"I promise, you will never do this again."

He was sure she did not appreciate the depth of that undertaking.

It was at St Michael's that Grace met Sergio Catalano for the first time. Their mutual attraction conspired to keep her hospitalised until he too was fit to leave after complicated surgery for a recurring hernia. When James saw them together, wheelchairs side by side in the hospital conservatory, they looked like a pair of smug royals recovering from a ski accident in St. Moritz. A copy of *The Financial Times*, half-drunk Bloody Marys and Sergio's Havana lay on a low table between them. Twin tartan rugs rested on their laps. They were animated in the way children and incipient lovers are: cackles, grins and body language loaded with intent. What differing physical specimens they presented. At that time Sergio still looked impressive: muscular upper body, cherub's face irradiated with his famous tan, and hair that had decided several years before to remain the colour of baked bread just out of the oven. Fully stretched in excess of six feet, he looked every inch the tycoon. What did he see in her? Had she seduced him already? Did Sergio know who this woman was?

Grace had aged. Weight loss accentuated the lantern jaw; it protruded more than usual and there were grey streaks through her hair, which she wore gathered in a tight bun at the back. Her wide face seemed wider, heightening the gap between her eyes. When she faced James, he could not tell whether she smiled or sneered.

Chapter Six

When James was eighteen, Grace sent him for summer work to an Alsatian restaurant she knew. "Eighteen and ready for total immersion, James, at the coalface. French flair and tradition can only be received at first hand. If you are to be a great chef …" By this time she had decided that cheffing was to be his chosen career. "… you have to start in a French restaurant."

He preferred to forget that experience even though Doctor Theo Hilfer, his psychiatrist, insisted at their first session that he recall and relate it in exact detail. Recall and relate? More like regurgitation, James thought. The long and the short of it was that he had "failed" (Grace's word) to adapt to the medieval tyranny of a French three-star kitchen, culminating in a regrettable scene involving a chopping knife, a bullying sous chef and blood on the floor.

James swore his stabbing of the sous chef was an act of self-defence. His "little performance" (Grace again) got him the sacking he deserved and a terror of commercial kitchens that had never left him completely. When James sank the kitchen knife into the ribs of his superior, for a split second he was euphorically touched and, as he extracted the weapon, the sheen of blood on the blade did not seem to horrify him. Rather, his feeling in the passing moment was of a mesmeric glow.

James returned from France with his Sabatier knives and a cargo of shame.

"Snap out of it, James!" Grace's disdain didn't help.

He had headaches that persisted.

"Go to the doctor, if you must."

The GP gave him extra-strength aspirin and took the time to quiz him a bit. He must have presented a sorry picture.

"Depression, James, nothing to worry about, but I think you might benefit from a visit to a specialist." There and then the GP phoned Doctor Hilfer's secretary to get an appointment. James resisted the need to tell Grace of his appointment with Doctor Theo Hilfer. He made it his secret.

James came to Theo's rooms with no great expectation. That he could trust the doctor, James assimilated subconsciously by some strange osmosis from Theo's opening, "So we have a little problem" to the conspiratorial "we're-in-this-together" raising of the eyebrows and the flat weight of his hand guiding him to the patient's chair, an upholstered cave into which he sank, body and soul.

James was gripped with confessional diarrhoea, spilling his fears at the psychiatrist's feet, encouraged by receptive silence. Some chronic lack had asserted itself. It didn't take Theo long to uncover a "mother neurosis" and dealing with it became central to his probings.

To say Theo had rooms was a misnomer: James was amused by the conceit from the beginning. There had always been only one, not very grand. It was ill-served in summer by claustrophobic brocade curtains, fully drawn, and in winter by the ancient gas heater stuttering in a corner. The fresh air and warmth came from Theo himself, chubby, astride a revolving chair, stroking his voluptuous beard as if it were the source of wisdom, eyebrows dancing to the lilt of some remembered ditty. The years had invaded the skin around his eyes in deep ruts but the eyes themselves, sparkling lasers in his head, showed no signs of age. He spoke with deliberation, giving thoughts time to gather themselves before he let them out.

Sometimes Theo would break off in the middle of consultation, directing James to continue speaking while he got up, walked to a sideboard and, with his back turned, mixed a drink. This he knocked back and, replacing the glass, pivoted like a performer on ice back into his chair opposite James. James was intrigued, tried to guess what the doctor was drinking, even as all his frightened energy focused on the strange process he was embarked on.

The first consultation ended with unexpected questions:

"What do you like to cook, James?"

"Did you learn much in France?"

"What's your kind of music?"

"Do you have a girlfriend, James?"

James lied about girls, pretending there were many at his beck and call. Theo sat back listening to the answers. He appeared to be a fan of French cuisine and its hierarchical practice. The subject of music was easy. Theo liked Chopin and Dylan too. As he was leaving, James asked, "Do I need to take anything, Doctor?"

"Yes, James, exercise. Take a girl for a walk and we'll talk again next week."

He was half out the door when Theo called him back. "Have you ever made that chilled soup called Vichyssoise?" James hadn't yet but did before the next consultation.

After that first session James felt a dichotomy at work: on the one hand an easing of tension and on the other definite restriction, of being caged in the way he imagined exotic birds in an aviary. Delineated freedom was new to him. He felt protected from the world and from himself.

When James turned up for his second appointment, he found the psychiatrist waiting in the small reception area where he had been met on his first visit by a secretary. This time there was no secretary. Doctor Hilfer was standing, more formal than heretofore. "A few things, James, before we go any further." He pushed his hands deep into his pockets, breathed in, looked intensely serious for a moment and then a slow smile took over his features as he said softly, "We can't go on like this, James." He went on to explain how he was no longer practicing as a psychiatrist; he had in fact retired early to concentrate on writing and research. The GP (a personal friend) had referred James because he guessed that the orthodox medical model was not suitable in this case. Theo said he would see James occasionally, but not as a paying patient. "What I propose is an exchange," Theo said. "We can learn from each other."

What James did not know was the GP's stated reluctance to submit the eighteen-year-old to a drug regime, the most likely course had he sent James to anyone else. "You see, Theo, young James' mother, Grace Gall, is a scary lady. If James comes home with a prescription for Valium, I would not be sure she wouldn't take advantage. She's a drunk and utterly untrustworthy. In my opinion what he needs is a dose of direction and advice, a father figure if you like."

Theo had huffed and puffed but eventually concurred. He had to admit that, on the evidence of their meetings so far, he quite liked the boy.

Chapter Seven

James felt almost unmanned by Claudia's proposition. It had to be faced. Music sometimes led the way when his conscious mind faltered, disabled by difficult choices; to finger a liquid nocturne on the piano did it, muscling through the grave thunder of Sibelius did it. For one whole day he did nothing else but alternate between Chopin and the Finn. Later he sat down, made a list, the pluses and the minuses, a technique to clarify the mind, initiated by Theo many years before.

I desire her. She's dangerous.

I'm awfully curious. She knows that.

The romance, the recklessness. I can play along. She knows that.

I *am* experienced. She needs that.

I could fall for her.

She could just be using me. Two can play that game.

She's rich and powerful. So attractive.

Tread warily, James.

James thought about her undisguised threat of blackmail. Was there any tangible evidence she could come up with to prove his involvement in Grace's death? All she really had was hearsay, from a nurse called Sheila and a doctor who hadn't a notion what bouillabaisse was. On the other hand, with regard to Sergio, could he be sure that a reopening of the Croatian case, even at this juncture, would confirm the earlier finding of Grace's innocence? Tread warily indeed, James told himself again.

Nevertheless what Claudia Catalano offered, whether she knew it or not, was what he needed most of all, to help him open himself to himself; let a light shine on the secrets he kept from himself; face the fact that more than her alarming interest, his curiosity or sexual opportunism, it was the prospect and buzz of the hunt that wheeled him gradually closer to the authentic James Livingstone Gall. An exhilarating flood bubbled in his veins. Tally ho!

James had been engrossed: up early for the market, baking, day-long mise en place. Pedro, James' jack-of-all-trades, came in the morning for a few hours: regular chores, laundry, cleaning, dusting.

"Special party tonight, sir?"

"Spot on, Pedro, tonight may be very special indeed."

"A lady?"

"A friend."

"Of course, sir," Pedro said. "Beg pardon, sir, I didn't mean to be nosey."

"The secret to a successful dinner is mise en place."

"What's that, sir?"

"Mise en place is a state of mind, Pedro. Someone who has truly grasped the concept is able to keep many tasks in mind simultaneously, weighing and assigning each its proper value and priority. This assures that the chef has anticipated and prepared for every situation that could logically occur during a service period."

"But you're not a chef, sir!"

"The relevant principles are amenable to universal application."

"I see, sir."

He didn't, bless him, James reflected. "Before you go, Pedro, check the glasses."

"Champagne, claret and water as usual?"

"A pair of brandy snifters also. My guest has a penchant for cognac."

"The silver, sir?"

"The silver, Pedro."

By mid-afternoon all the advance work was done. This was a dinner that allowed James' presence at the table for all but the minimum, last-minute garnishing; none of the final kitchen flourishes he sometimes employed to impress. He finished a report on Le Gourmet for *Restaurants, Critical Choices*, a new guide for which he had been prevailed upon to act as associate editor, and then walked twice around the Square, purloining the makings of a bouquet from a rose bush that spread itself invitingly over the railings. Home again, he ran a bath, fixed the music and cast off his working clothes. A melancholic cello left him defenceless, like an incoming tide rippling up and before he knew it, he was swept away.

James had two bathroom mirrors positioned to give a full-body view: to see himself as others saw him. The body was leaner than forty-four years had a right to expect: muscles disclosed gym work; flab modestly only around the thighs; his petit boudin nodded off in its undergrowth; buttock ovals showed some signs of slack; chest and upper back sported a fine fuzz. Grace's lantern jaw jutted out of his face, eyes wide apart like hers, ashamed, perhaps, of the misshapen nose. Mother and son, the resemblance was startling. He had a full head of brown hair, coaxed forward over forehead to distract attention from his nasal disappointment. Age and experience asserted themselves in pouches under the eyes and permanently furrowed brows. Naked, his middle-aged manliness stood its ground; clothed, it did much more than that. Conversing with mirrors cleared the head as well as giving the voice an opportunity to listen to itself: the melodious fluting that he considered his outstanding feature. Speech, orchestrated by floating palms and the percussive, background harmony of cough and pregnant pause, oiled the wheels of notoriety. James was heard. Unctions and the modern male failing for fragrance repelled him. A man ought to smell like a man, even when finely attired for dinner.

For this evening's engagement a note of purposeful informality was, he calculated, best struck by a white silk shirt, open at the neck, black satin waistcoat, charcoal slacks, burgundy suede slip-ons. Mirrors approved.

He took a probiotic yoghurt before dinner, convinced of its bowel friendliness and efficacy as a diuretic. One of Grace's maxims, "softly, softly", he took seriously in this context. Having suffered some irregularity on each occasion he had met Claudia, James yielded to another of his mother's prescriptions, that prevention is better than cure.

From the bunch of keys on his dressing table he selected a Yale, slipped it into a waistcoat pocket and went downstairs. Claudia had arrived, incognito as arranged.

"This damn outfit's heavy as lead," she complained as she doffed the ankle-length wax mackintosh and matching hat, a disguise as fetching as it was effective. "I took the underground to Victoria and taxi from there," she said as she shook her hair free of a confining headband. She did not recoil from a peck on the cheek, gave him the once-over, and said, "So good to be here, James. I just hate not being myself, that bloody mack made me feel creepy."

She went to the bathroom while he poured a couple of Tio Pepes and turned up the sound: a Chopin miscellany of preludes and nocturnes. Drinks in hand, he showed her around the house. He was conscious of her closeness, calculated he guessed. That perfume he remembered from Le Gourmet, precocious as before.

"An American Professor of Physics rehabilitated the place in the nineties. When he died his daughter inherited, had no interest, sold it to me lock, stock and barrel."

"Fully furnished?" As she spoke her eyes devoured him and the rooms he led her through, assessing the man by his possessions and his attitude to ownership.

"Exactly as it is now. I like the Shaker pieces, such a contrast to what

I was used to in Grace's old mausoleum of a place. I got rid of it after she went. No shortage of offers; sold to a developer."

"Miss it?"

"Good God, no! Too many memories." He hoped she didn't notice his involuntary shudder. "This is the music room."

Her eyebrows arched in disbelief. "You play?"

"I'm taking weekly lessons. My teacher says I have a lovely touch."

"But of course, James. I have a lovely touch too," she told him, as she sat down at the piano and played.

As they went in to dinner, Claudia stopped to inspect the Grandfather clock in the hall.

"Mother's, I confided in it as a kid, the only grandparent I knew."

Bending to look closely at the pendulum, she asked, "Ever married?"

"No."

"Currently attached?"

"Unattached."

"I like to know who I'm dealing with." She swung around and took hold of his hand.

"Me too." James felt the strength of her hand in his as he led her into the kitchen.

Claudia adored his Black Sea blinis.

"Many things have been said about caviar. It's overrated, too expensive."

"Beluga?" she inquired through a mouthful.

"Sevruga actually, considerably cheaper, bloody good value. Oscietra is cheaper again, about a fifth of the price of Beluga. Chefs use it for sauces and garnishing."

"What do you use it for, James?" This with a dart of the eyes and that curt shake of the head.

"To remind me of my good fortune."

On cue they drained their glasses and he poured more Charles Heidsieck, Claudia looking wistful as he poured. "Sergio believed in the best of everything. Caviar had to be Beluga. Substitutes terrified him, really. He couldn't cope with inferiority of any kind."

"Is that why he teamed up with my mother?"

"I left for the States before he came out of hospital that time. I did meet her on a visit to Croatia a year before the end, but to my deep regret I never took their affair seriously. Papa had a string of girlfriends after Mum died. Perfect physical specimens. I suppose I didn't want to know, resented every one of them, felt he let himself down. We never talked about it and it did open up a distance between us. Even so, I never stopped loving him, nor he me. There was no questioning that."

"The States, what did you do there?"

"I had my own ski shop in Aspen for a couple of seasons. That's where I met Felix, the scene of my greatest mistake. Charming, polished, he slid into my life, literally. We skied, skated and partied downhill all the way into a marriage that, once we came back here, cracked at the very first test."

"Thin ice!"

"I can't stand it, James, not for much longer. All he ever wanted was a trophy that he could put on display now and again. Fucking bourgeois respectability, you can do anything as long as it's not acknowledged or found out."

James reached across the table to take her hand in his and they sat in silence for several minutes. He stood to carve a couple of slices from the shoulder of pork that had roasted slowly for three hours through the afternoon. "You like crackling, Claudia?"

"Lovely, James."

"Do try the jelly, something sharp to counteract rich, fat meat."

"Wow, fruity but cutting, vinegary."

"Made from rowan berries, I make a batch every autumn. Changes every year, I play around with the recipe. I'm pleased with this one, it has an edge to it."

"Perfect for the pig."

"Indubitably, my dear." He used the ensuing pause to bring up Grace and Sergio again. "I had little knowledge of their affair either.

I knew that she and Sergio had something going on but my mother and I had grown apart by then. After graduation and a couple of years' apprenticeship, I was in the throes of establishing a name for myself as a foreign correspondent for *The Times*. A lot of African work: ongoing famine, bloody coups, British and American cock-ups, endemic corruption. Only met Grace for fleeting lunches. On one of my trips home I overheard a telephone conversation between them which surprised me: passionate declarations of mutual love, extraordinary."

"You packed in the foreign job?"

"I had to, hadn't the stomach for it."

"Then you wrote the novel about a food writer in Kenya, esoteric food practices of the Masai, relating mainly to wild food, odd combinations and flavours if my memory serves ..."

"You *are* well informed. Nobody remembers that slim volume. I went back to features, freelance stuff after that. Anyway I had to face facts. I belonged to the substratum of the rarely published. I felt cut-off. I had to make ends meet. One of the Sunday Supplements took several food and travel articles. I just wrote up on what I knew, so much raw material I took for granted." James paused and looked at Claudia, who said, "Do go on, James." He cleared his throat. "There was no eureka moment, I simply fitted into what I was good at: food criticism, restaurants, food health issues, organic farming, battery chickens, the celebrity chef nonsense. I took it seriously, wrote some fine pieces but there was always editorial pressure for lighter articles, food as entertainment. It came to a head when the then-editor refused a piece on famine in Africa. 'Don't go all heavy on me, James.' She actually said that. 'Recipes, James, for Christ's sake, give us some more of your quirky possibilities for sausages.' I told her impolitely where to go and promptly joined the editorial staff of *The Great Food Guide*, then in its second year and expanding. I travelled all over Britain and to Europe reporting on the finest restaurants. Two years on I had enough credibility to plough my own furrow. In between things I worked as a drudge in some of the best restaurants in Europe, a couple of weeks, a month here and there; had previous hands-on experience of that in Alsace, New York too, a stint with that Bourdain man. Seminal, I learned a lot. That's seven years ago now."

He had talked through cheese and petits pots au chocolat without interruption. Claudia sat opposite, nibbling langues de chat, expressionless except for a silent moue of solidarity at his treatment by the Supplement editor. "Come, Claudia," he said, "before the light fades. You must see the garden." He took her hand.

Evening air held the day's warmth in its breath, reluctant to let go. He valued his garden, so well tended by Pedro. A thick fuchsia hedge, dwarfed by mature lime trees, ran around the perimeter. The limes spread from the rear of the house on either side and met behind two identical sheds at the bottom to form a U, the only gap, a six-foot-high iron gate hidden from the house by the sheds.

"The river is just across the path here."

Claudia looked through the ancient railings.

"Very few pedestrians these days, cyclists have taken over."

"You don't do all this yourself?"

"Good God, no! Pedro, my man, comes in every day. He mows and weeds, sees to the herbs and the glasshouse vegetables, keeps the place in shape. That's his workshop."

"What's in the other one?"

"My sanctum sanctorum, would you like to see inside?" He opened the heavy lock with the key from his waistcoat pocket and ushered Claudia inside.

"Looks like a small kitchen." She pointed out a Sabatier cleaver among a battery of culinary implements suspended by hooks over a stainless steel worktop, adjacent to which stood a walk-in cold room.

"It is, in a manner of speaking, the equivalent of a garde-manger in a French kitchen, where I do basic preparation of game, rabbits, wild duck, fish too." He showed her the heavy-duty mixer, the liquidiser and the gas-fired ovens.

"You cook here too?"

"Accumulate bones, make stocks in one of those big pots and freeze them in batches; jams, chutneys, jellies like the one we had this evening, terrines, pâtés, baking."

Claudia cocked her head to one side while he was speaking. "Is that water I hear, the river can't be so close?"

"Yes it is. The river at some time diverted under the path a couple of hundred yards upstream from here. It runs below the gardens to this point, where it has cut out a channel back into the main course again. You hear it because we are right over it where we stand now."

"You mean right here beneath us?" She looked at her feet, disbelieving.

"Exactly." He bent to peel back the heavy sisal matting that covered the floor area between the worktop and cooker, exposing a three foot square manhole cover underneath. The rush of water was more audible now and, when he lifted the manhole upwards and to one side, a fast-flowing torrent came into full view. "Careful!" He caught her arm as she leaned forward to have a closer look. She reversed into him, gasping and holding on.

"It's frightening, James. Incredibly powerful."

"Quite a volume of water in a narrow channel, awesome in winter." James guided her outside, locked up and they sauntered back to the house, bringing the chill of dusk in with them. He lit the fire that Pedro had set in the drawing room, poured a quarter balloon each of cognac and joined Claudia on the sofa.

"You *are* a devil, James," she said, recognising the Fine Champagne by Remy Martin, a twin of the bottle they had demolished together at The Butcher's Arms. She nestled into him and he put a hand on her thigh. "Do you want to sleep with me, James?"

"Ever since I saw you at Le Gourmet."

Her skirt retreated upwards with an adjustment of her position on the sofa and his hand followed. Desire simmered in the warming atmosphere as they kissed, lingering mouth to mouth, eyes closed. As if rehearsed they drew back simultaneously.

"Business before pleasure, James?"

"Business without pleasure is no business at all, Claudia."

Her skirt slipped off easily. "Felix?" Claudia reminded him as they stood, almost touching, beginning to strip each other.

"Yes," he replied, as she lifted his shirt above his head. "I think we should inveigle him here for dinner some evening soon." His grateful penis throbbed in her hand. The smell of her invited him in; he clutched her buttocks, she wrapped her arms around him and they made love where they stood, shuddering to a standstill. Later, as they lay together in James' bed, the "business" they were now intent on occupied their thoughts.

With no mention of the mental struggle he'd endured since she first mooted the subject in The Butcher's Arms, he offered her now his pragmatism. "Somehow you will have to arrange it that you arrive here separately. Do you think you can manage that?"

"Leave it to me, James."

"Delighted. I think we can expedite the matter to your satisfaction with as little fuss as possible."

"Poison, is that what you have in mind?"

"That's a pejorative term. Think of it more as digestive malfunction, the logical last step in an inevitable progression of events."

"What do you mean?"

"Felix is not difficult to fathom: a thoroughly venal man, cruel to his wife, sexually deviant, distrusted by colleagues."

"Distrusted, how can you prove that?"

"I did some private research during the week, Claudia, among banker friends, financial journalists and contacts of mine in, shall we say, the nether regions. Rough trade, if you follow me."

"And?"

"Felix Underwood is an able banker, a reputable broker, quite ruthless, I gather. He has the grudging regard of colleagues but nobody likes the man. There's talk of illegal, under-the-counter deals."

"Why don't they sack him?"

"He knows too much. Banking has, as you must be aware, an ugly underside. Beneath the well-padded cloak of respectability the sharks of the financial world swim freely. Felix is one of the sharks. He knows who the main players are, who's playing by the book and who's not. Believe me, he wouldn't think twice of shopping them if it was in his own interest."

"Are you inferring that he would not be missed?"

"Not only would he not be missed, there are people in the city who would be very pleased at his departure. There is reason to suspect that he is being blackmailed by an ex-lover, who has not taken kindly to Felix's promiscuity, a most unsavoury individual with links to organised crime."

"Gee, James, you have been busy."

"Mise en place, Claudia, mise en place."

"Put in place?"

He explained the meaning of the phrase once again.

"If I can entice him to come to this house for dinner, ensuring that he arrives unseen, what then, James?"

"Then, my dear Claudia, we will have to be very cunning and resourceful. I will be depending on you to ensure that he comes in expectation of an interesting dining experience. Nothing else, absolutely nothing else!"

She was agreeable and totally in his hands. As indeed he was in hers. They made love again. Wrapped around her in the silk plushness of his own bed, he felt the pull of something new to him, an awareness that he could not quite capture. Claudia, the thought and feel of her, whatever her intentions, had pierced his protective emotional wall. He fell asleep before he could carry the train of thought any further. When he woke, Claudia was gone.

Chapter Eight

James learned early that all life is obedience, struggle or revolt. Obedience he rejected, aided and abetted by his mother, when he was still in short trousers. She was sufficiently short-sighted not to anticipate the inevitable backlash. Thenceforward he became entrenched between struggle and revolt, bogged down by one, fearful of the other. The appellation James Livingstone Gall was a weighty one, a millstone it was said. James didn't think so. Not since his Latin teacher, in an attempt to test his mettle, asked aloud before the whole class, "All Gall is divided into three parts: stones, bladder and unmitigated. Which one are you, James?"

He sensed a trap, as did the class, and hesitated before replying, "Probably all three, sir."

Instant cheers from his fellows and a compliant "Touché, James!" from teacher. Subsequently the name had served him well, attracting comment, mostly of a deferential nature. A fellow critic, who considered them rivals, had ascribed what she referred to as "excessive hubris" to his name. "That preposterous moniker which he trails after him like a performing hound. What gall!"

However much he regretted Grace's legacy, those pathogens of hers that quite arbitrarily asserted themselves, he strove to let go.

Ultimately he stood on his own, aware that all men were unique and that the import of inheritance was overplayed. They were, first of all and finally, themselves.

Grace's overdose and her affair with Sergio Catalano conspired, along with James' career in journalism, to keep them apart. When they met here and there to lunch together or on his few trips home, she took pains to keep him at arm's length. Her repertoire of sighs, pursed lips and long, demeaning looks was more pronounced, as if she had practised for his benefit. But a new note surfaced, disdainful of his opinions and the writing life in general. Food gave her a platform from which she released spiteful arrows.

They had just been seated in a restaurant he had chosen. "I've heard good reports of the new chef here," James told her.

"Chefs!" Her upper lip curled in contempt. "Imbeciles! Peacocks with egos as big as their ridiculous hats. Don't be taken in by the hype, James. There is profound ignorance about food, the ignorance of the public only surpassed by the so-called professionals, the chefs." She would not permit him cook at home any more. "It's not that I distrust you, James, but you must respect my desire to be queen in my own kitchen and I know you will agree that I am a better cook than you could ever be. Watch me, darling, watch and enjoy."

"You haven't forgiven me, have you?"

"What's to be forgiven, James? Be a dear and pass the salt."

The gap between them grew, a holding centre for all that was left unsaid: Federico and the others, her overdose, her alliance with Sergio. Although she denied it, that gap became a receptacle for distrust. If he cooked for her, what might he dish up? And Federico, what did James know, what did he suspect?

"You don't trust me, Mum, do you?"

She was impatient with his questions; for a brief moment a mad flame rose in her eyes. Just as quickly it was gone, not extinguished but on hold. She had regained control. The effort altered her appearance subtly; he felt the presence of a malign energy. She took a step closer to him and he backed off. Her hands rose together in a priestly gesture, moving up over her face and to the back of her head, where she disentangled and shook free the bun that held her hair in a tight ball. This she accomplished very slowly, deliberately, while all the time she never took her eyes off his. "Trust, James, I've told you before, is something to be earned." And then she turned away to attend to a pot bubbling on the range.

The incident left him convinced that his mother was more than a little mad. She burned with a fuel he could not name. His heart throbbed with the understanding that he did not know her anymore. Dinner that evening left him drained: a psychotic ensemble designed, he'd no doubt, to intimidate. A soup of fish in tomato broth looked interesting until he approached it with a spoon. The surface rippled around the edge of the soup spoon and, as he delved deeper, a miniature tidal wave exposed a section of epileptic eel fighting for its life in the pinkish liquid. Aware of her watchfulness, he stifled the gasp in his throat and dealt with the bisected fish, in the knowledge that it was well and truly dead, its contortions purely reflexive. Fish again for main course: a humiliated trout served up in its entirety, bloated with bread stuffing, suppliant eyes pleading with him as he carved and cut. Her banana mousse stank of rum and had, by the time he cleaned his plate, grown completely black, as if infected. She had made a basic error; he couldn't contain himself.

"For God's sake, you could have added lime juice, lemon at the very least."

"You had to find something to criticise, didn't you?"

Pretending levity, he said, "My turn to test your taste buds, next time, Mum."

"Is that a threat, James?"

During the night he became quite ill and a debilitating migraine stupefied him all through the following day. Unfit for strenuous activity, he spent the day slumped in Grace's geriatric deck chair in the garden.

She was overly solicitous, offering him lemonade and chicken broth, the mere mention of which made him nauseous. He attempted to read but could not; he got up occasionally to walk about and still the ache stuck like glue to his temples. It was late evening before the rumbling in his stomach ceased and only then his head cleared.

Next day he had an early flight to catch. It was still dark when he rose, showered and packed. He helped himself to juice and made toast. While coffee brewed he went to her room to bid goodbye. She wasn't there, she wasn't in the bathroom. He called but there was no reply. Looking out the kitchen window, he noticed that the cellar light was on, its exit door to the garden ajar. He found her in the cellar in her dressing gown, bent over a battered old chest. She looked like a scavenger on a rubbish dump. "I came to say farewell, Mum. I'm off now."

If she was startled she hid it well, but he could tell her lazy voice was lying. "Couldn't sleep, didn't want to wake you. Old clothes, James, meaning to sort them out for ages."

A couple of months later he arranged to meet herself and Sergio in London. At the last minute she cancelled; Sergio had to attend an urgent meeting in the Berlin Sercat and he wanted her to go with him. Perfect time to check out the cellar.

She had been true to her word. The basement that ran under the house from one gable end to the other was cleaner and tidier than it ever had been. The stench of disinfectant and damp that greeted him as he descended could not obliterate the smell of rotting flesh emanating from one corner, where cardboard boxes accumulated, one on top of the other, her wooden chest among them. As he disassembled the wall of boxes, the sweet and sour odour grew until he discovered two decomposing rats behind the chest. A sullen hum drew him to its source: a heaving blob of bluebottles feasting on the rodents. He watched, stunned, not because he was repulsed, but with admiration at the single-mindedness of the undertaking.

"I smell a rat," he said aloud, unsuppressed triumph in his voice.

The chest was empty. James studied it all over for signs of

secret compartments, running his hands over the wood inside and out. Nothing. He should have known. If there had been anything incriminating in it, she would have removed it by now. There was only one thing for it, open every box. He counted twenty-nine, calculating after examining the first three, that it would take about two hours to get through the lot. He set about the search for he knew not what. Boxes containing nothing more suspicious than clothes long out of fashion, shoes, well-thumbed cookery books and discarded bric-a-brac. He shifted, prised open, searched, resealed and reassembled as he found them. Standing back to assess the work, he saw, to his irritation, that he had not returned the chest to its proper place under a stack of boxes. It stuck out like a sore thumb in the middle of the cellar floor.

"Damn!" he cried, aiming a kick at it. On impact he heard a clicking sound; a slim drawer slid noiselessly out of one end of the chest, revealing files and sheaves of papers packed neatly inside. Under a pile of sepia photographs he found a dozen or so newspaper clippings yellow with age: *Wife interviewed by police after husband's death in boating accident. Wife inconsolable after tragedy. Grace Gall thanks emergency services. Describing the incident as a tragic accident, Detective Sergeant Maxwell thanked Mrs Gall for her cooperation and sympathised with her on the loss of her husband.*

A later piece in a local paper gave an account of the inquest and the coroner's report. The available evidence pointed to death from drowning while in an intoxicated state. Alcohol, a recently consumed seafood dinner and the fact that the victim was not wearing a life-jacket all contributed to the tragedy. Noted in the margin by "seafood dinner" were the words "My recipe". He recognised his mother's hand. Why had she not informed him of the circumstances of his father's death? Whenever his name was mentioned, she discouraged curiosity with typical, evasive bluster. "The love of my life, he should not have left me so." With a distant look she'd say something like, "Life's so short, James, shorter than we think."

News of the double death in Croatia did not reach James for several days. He caught a late-night flight from Nairobi to Rome, connecting to Dubrovnik, where he hired a car to drive up the coast to Orebic. The funerals of Sergio and his maid, Renata, had already taken place. Grace, a picture of controlled grief, withdrew to a cottage a few miles away in the village of Loviste at the tip of the Peljesac peninsula, making herself available to the continuing inquiry. Making a virtue of necessity, she vowed to remain as long as loyalty demanded. She visited his grave every day, depositing a single, lush sprig of rosemary on the fresh clay as a "symbol of my undying devotion, James, rosemary for remembrance." Being with her over a week, he was witness to a transformation. The untamed mother he knew retreated behind a shroud of grief, humble yet discreetly public also. She attended Mass each morning, walking up to the front pew, where she could be seen, head bowed, lips moving in prayer. She recruited him to promenade with her, arm in arm, along the seafronts of Orebic and Loviste. They dined al fresco in the restaurants she and Sergio patronised, surprising the waiters by her abstemiousness.

"No, Igor, thank you so much, no wine for me, not at this time."

Most surprising was that even in private she maintained the pose, so much so that he began to believe it. She even visited Renata's family "to show solidarity in our shared grief, James." It was difficult for her, he had to admit, although she was cleared of any suspicion in the case. A local woman had died in circumstances strongly suggestive of a ménage à trois, of which Grace was the sole survivor.

Stunning performance or not, James left to return to his duties in Kenya, with an appreciation of her strength of character. Perhaps he had underestimated her; he chided himself for being so dismissive; perhaps he had been wrong all along, his suspicions the product of an over-active imagination. He determined to keep in touch regularly and began to plan a holiday at home, to be with her for a while, just the two of them. A surprise!

It was one of those rare Sundays: hot but not too hot, windless except for an occasional breeze disseminating summer fragrances. He heard laughter as he reached the front door and quietly let himself in. More laughter, coming from somewhere at the back of the house. He followed the sound. Laughter and something else, a grunting that he realised was coming from the garden. He heard his mother shriek. At first all he could see was a male backside, trousers down around his ankles, shirttail fluttering with the motion of his hips. She wailed again, a wail of ecstasy. His glance took in the scene: Grace, mounted on all fours, wine bottles, unfinished food, discarded underwear, and the man James recognised as a local wine merchant, infamous, Grace had once told him, for cuckolding half the area's husbands.

He was able to pull back to the kitchen without being seen and blundered through the house onto the road at the front and into a field on the far side, where his legs caved in and he fell on the grass. Croatia had been just an act after all. How many had she killed? His father, Sergio, Renata and how many others? Lying there, looking up at an impeccable sky, he accepted with gravity that his mother was a monster.

Regaining his equilibrium, he drove down to the fishmonger's, and chose the range of fish he would require. By the time he returned to the house, he knew what had to be done.

She was alone, dressed and stretched full length on the sofa, reading a compilation of old recipes. No sign of her companion.

"James, James, it's you, it's really you. What a surprise!" She embraced him with such gusto that she did not notice his reluctance.

"Can't stay long, Mum, but long enough to celebrate. Look what I brought."

The sight of motley fish and shellfish banished her languor and her eyes lit up.

"I know, James, I know exactly! I'll make a bouillabaisse for dinner."

"No, Mum. *I'll* make a bouillabaisse for dinner!"

Chapter Nine

Felix Underwood met with a certain Manny Johnson in the full knowledge that Manny was a craftsman of shade and emphasis, not averse to using half truths, embellished truth or the whole truth, to his advantage. His coup de grâce was the admitted falsehood: "Ok, so I lied!"

Felix arrived in The Butcher's Arms ahead of time. All of life and especially banking was a game that Felix played to win. He prided himself on his timing and judgement, taking the calculated chances that caught the approving eye of his American bosses in the Bellingham Bank International. Bellingham, outwardly a conventional bank serving the public in all the usual ways, had, behind the respectable front, an arcane division devoted to money laundering, for which Felix had a special gift. Joe Haggard, Felix's immediate superior in Boston, spoke glowingly of "Underwood, our kinda can-do, will-do guy". Felix could do and would do anything to boost his standing in Boston, as long as there was also a pay-off for himself. He had also privately cultivated contacts of his own outside the bank. It had become almost de rigueur for formerly conservative bankers to consort with anyone and everyone in compliance with the "real-world" credo that banking's reason for being was the manipulation of capital for its own ends; all that touchy-feely pretence of supporting small business and emerging entrepreneurs merely soft-focus advertising for the woolly minds of the less well-off.

Manny entrusted large sums to Felix, investment money which the bank absorbed, diverted and cleansed. This was Felix's special talent: to satisfy client, bank and himself without attracting unwanted attention from regularity authorities. He had made millions for Manny and had been happy to take his cut. Now, however, it was time to call on the favour he considered his due, the accumulated cream. Manny owed him.

Impassive described Felix well; he sat, seemingly oblivious of his surroundings, taking short sips from his beer and making notes in a diary. He was clean-shaven except for a pencil moustache, black like the neatly cropped hair on either side of his bald pate. Dapper, in a dark suit, white shirt and muted red tie, he looked up from his notes and allowed his gaze to drift to a young man at the counter. With a sharp intake of breath he observed the slim-hipped, slick-haired youth, taking in the view of him as he might a landscape or a painting. When the object of his gaze left the counter to walk through the bar and out onto the street, Felix studied him every inch of the way and then he breathed deeply, exhaled, sipped his beer and went back to his notes.

As the young man left, Manny made his appearance. "Felix, my friend Felix, is this a pleasure or what?" The cigar that seemed stuck to his teeth inhibited his speech. Pleasure came out like leisure.

"Mutual, I assure you." Felix returned the compliment without warmth and they shook hands. He abhorred Manny's loudness, his plastered-down hair, his tropical ties and the suits he favoured, pinstripes as wide apart as railway lines. Manny was an exuberant moron with the instincts of a cat, but that did not intimidate Felix; business was business, manners and morals had no relevance. "Cash in the car?" Felix asked.

"Sure, in the car park. What's the soup, Felix?"

"You're not going to eat *here*?"

"Sure, why not? I own the place," he said, rising to inspect the blackboard on the counter.

"Help you, dear?" The barmaid rested her soprano's bosom on the bar counter as she leaned towards him.

"Lasagne Verdi, the house special, love?"

"Yes, dear, pasta. You know you love it."

"Add a couple of bangers," Manny ordered.

"Yes, dear."

In order to get to grips with the lasagne and sausages, Manny had to remove his cigar from between his teeth to a side plate where it lay like an oversized slug. Felix ignored it as he did Manny's piggish consumption while they continued to hammer out details of the transaction in hand.

"Usual terms, Felix?"

Felix stared hard at Manny. "I think I might be in a position to increase the dividend if a certain proposition pays off."

"Proposition, what proposition?"

"I'll be meeting a Colombian gentleman in Amsterdam in a few days. He has hinted that he may have a consignment for London we might be able to put your way."

"Could be interested if the price is right."

"The price will be right, if I understand him correctly."

"He owes you?"

"Like you do, Manny."

"You looking for action, Felix? Black or white?"

Felix winced, extracted a white handkerchief from an inside pocket and blew his nose on it, while Manny continued. "New club on the other side of the river. Lots of young black stuff. I could—"

"No, no, another time perhaps."

"Something else, then?"

"Something else."

"I'm all ears."

"There's a certain lady I have problems with."

"Lean on her a little, is that the idea, Felix?"

"More than that."

"Break a leg, two, maybe?"

"No, Manny, your indebtedness to me demands more than a couple of broken bones." He removed an envelope from a jacket pocket and handed it to Manny. "The details are all there: name, address, phone numbers, business associates, social contacts. Look after it, Manny, and remember, nothing connects to me. Understand?"

"Terminal!"

"And untraceable."

Manny guffawed, Felix allowed himself a smile thinner than his moustache.

It was not often Felix relaxed the grip of self-control that kept his demons at bay. Pike fishing gave him that freedom: solitude, being able to trust himself alone with himself, whether he caught pike or not. And he identified with the scavenger fish more than with any human being. When his meeting with Manny finished and he deposited the cash from Manny's car in a concealed floor-safe at his home, he drove to the pike river an hour or so away, thinking of Claudia and how he would need to work at a pretence of kindness to her for a change. For a limited period. He had married her for her money, calculating that his consort-to-Catalano role was one investment that had gilt-edged but purely short-term prospects. This arrangement had reached a point of diminishing returns. With deadly serenity he envisaged a life without her. Claudia knew too much about him. She was no longer a viable asset. Time to cash in.

Chapter Ten

Grace yielded before James' resolve to make the bouillabaisse, but she had to have her say. "What, no rascasse? Can't be bouillabaisse without rascasse."

"No weever either, Mum, but sufficient variety to capture the true spirit of the dish, call it a Med/Atlantic version if you like. There's lobster, dory, conger, crab, monk, mackerel, bass, whiting and gurnet."

"Poetic licence does not necessarily produce good verse, James."

"Without licence, Mum, we achieve nothing." His tongue yearned to add "you should know" but he held his peace. Just. He decapitated the fish, which were so fresh that they still thrashed in death spasms on the chopping board. The guillotined heads, fins flapping, plopped into the bin under the worktop and with them some of his anger fell away. A conger snaked about in layers of slime, which he had to wash off repeatedly in flowing water, snagging fingers on the rows of sharp teeth. Any fish dinner worth its salt took time to prepare: meticulous selection of the dead and dying, a brutally efficient cleaver, mercilessly-sharp filleting knife, implacable hands. He made a broth of fish heads with water and wine, strained and seasoned it. Then he sweated tomatoes, onions, garlic, thyme, fennel and parsley with a strand of saffron and a twist of dry orange peel in olive oil, cut the firm-fleshed fish and crustacea in equal-sized pieces and covered the lot with the seasoned broth, boiling it briskly, lid on, for eight minutes. After that he added the delicate fish, whiting and gurnet, with more oil and boiled again for a further five minutes. Breaking with tradition, his bread was a homemade soda and, with a bow to orthodoxy, he made a rouille sauce from mayonnaise mixed well with crushed garlic and pounded chillis. The preparation of this bouillabaisse asked for nothing less than total immersion, timing paramount. An air of lightness and expectation fed his daring.

"Soda bread with a bastard bouillabaisse! You break all the rules, James. I think I'm beginning to like you again. Hand me the Pernod, that bottle there behind the Campari." She made no attempt to hide her exhilaration as she filled a sherry glass with the anise aperitif, spread a layer of fiery rouille on bread and scooped a ladle of fishy broth on top. She had begun to eat and drink when he served himself.

"I was tempted to include a few potatoes, as they do in Perpignan—"

"Potato? Unforgivable!" Enjoying herself, she gobbled up the food. "That damn tuber is responsible for more dull dishes than anything else. Put it into Irish stew if you must, it is happiest in mundane surroundings. In bouillabaisse, James, no potato, please."

Grace was then, as she pontificated between mouthfuls, never more real to him. And yet he had never been so detached. Like a scientist peruses every fine detail of his experiment, James noticed every line and feature of her as if for the first time. Then in one wanton moment a voice that he wished to strangle wriggled into the ether. "I love you, Mum."

She threw him a corrosive glance and re-engaged with the bouillabaisse.

He might as well have raked the coals of a long dead fire in the hope of finding a flame. Now, more than ever, he was determined to see this day through. His mind had wandered. Revisiting the plan he had set in motion, all he had to do was wait for the symptoms to show and react as normally as possible.

She continued her frivolous harangue as he watched her every gesture and movement. "Chefs eat other chefs' ideas, they are all plagiarists; it is an essential tool of the trade. But they miss the point, James. To copy perfectly is an art rarely mastered. Only the very best achieve it."

"Yes, Mum."

James had drunk one glass of Pouilly Fumé to her three. Her earlier intoxication returned, carrying with it the grandiosity that gave free rein to resentment of all and sundry. At one stage, emphasising a point that had escaped him, she said, "All life is a lottery, dear."

"True, Mum, and very few winners." They finished the bouillabaisse, by which time the wine had made her drowsy.

"I think I'll lie down for a while, James, we'll have cheese later."

James' childhood was sustained on a raft of ritual, strongly evocative of season and his own metamorphosis: roasted leg of spring lamb at Easter, part of a whole side bought directly from a farmer and hung at home because the butcher could not be trusted; collecting the first wild greens, ramsons, sorrel, watercress and nettles for soups and sauces; summer mackerel fishing, when the shoals swarmed close to the coast; jam making, the consequence of hedgerow hopping; sloe-picking after early frost and the sloe gin his mother made, which he christened "fast gin" because of the effect it had on her; harvesting sea spinach, hardy from sun and sea spray on exposed beaches; foraging for fungus in deciduous autumn woods. Of all these rituals the mushroom hunt held most fascination.

"Don't touch, James. No, you can't pick that one either!"

"But Mum! You said we could pick chanterelles."

She took pains then to describe the difference between the prized chanterelle and the fungus he had bent to pluck from the mouldy ground, a poisonous variety which his subsequent research identified as *Cortinarius Speciosissimus*. Latin spun an aura that his reading developed further. Mushrooms were magic, its literature enchanting. Mycologists' tracts enthused about the thousands of fungi available and largely unexploited, peppering their texts with esoteric language that fuelled him. From books on the subject he copied whole paragraphs and read them aloud to himself as he trawled the woods: *A fungus consists of tiny filaments. In the process of growth they fall from the parent and are dispersed by wind ... To create a productive cell, similar mycelia of the same species bond in an approximation of a sexual stage.*

How right his mother was! James had come across the story of three campers in the north of Scotland in 1979 who cooked *Cortinarius Speciosissimus* in mistake for chanterelle. Within a couple of weeks they suffered renal failure, from which two of them died. Two weeks seemed to him a long time for the poison to take effect. He searched for other mushrooms of the deadly kind and found a couple whose toxicity took hold within hours of consumption: Death Cap and Destroying Angel. When he fed them in small doses to dogs, the results were dramatic: violent vomiting and diarrhoea and an accompanying agony that howled and yowled out of them until they succumbed. Subsequently he tried drying the deadly fungi in the garage, testing them months later on small animals: a cat, another dog and even a rabbit, which frolicked in a corner of the garden. The effect was the same. Then he cooked half a pound of mixed Death Caps and Destroying Angels over high heat, separating the juice that ran profusely from the solids and storing it in a sealed Kilner jar. When he added this juice to a dog's dinner, the original symptoms occurred along with much pain, which did not persist, and the animal recovered.

A similar juice, stored since autumn in a hideaway under the garage eaves, he had surreptitiously introduced to Grace's portion of bouillabaisse. In the circumstances they had to forego the cheese, a small wheel of Milleens, pungent with ripeness, to which she was usually partial.

"I can't, James, my head is splitting."

"Too much wine, Mum?"

"I don't entertain hangovers, you know that!"

"Rest a while longer then. I'll call you in a couple of hours."

She called him in a couple of hours, crying of abdominal pains, spasmodic and increasing in intensity even as she tried to describe them. In minutes she had begun to throw up all over the bed clothes partly digested bouillabaisse in a green ooze that gave off an acrid, alcoholic smell. He called an ambulance and went with her to the hospital. For twenty-four hours the pain and intermittent vomiting persisted and then gradually eased, leaving her drained and dehydrated. Nurses connected her to a saline drip.

"We did have a substantial bouillabaisse." He was responding to the doctor's query about Grace's most recent meal.

"Bewabase?" Medics are not regular students of gastronomy, James thought.

"A fish stew, doctor. A great favourite of ours, lots of fish, differing types in a stock with olive oil and saffron."

"Sounds like a dangerous concoction to me, if you don't mind me saying so."

"It never bothered her before, nor me indeed, for that matter."

"You had the same fish dinner as your mother?"

"Exactly!"

"Alcohol, had she drunk much? Definite traces there."

"Perhaps a glass or two too many, doctor."

"Likes her wine, does she?"

"My mother is something of a connoisseur, I'm proud to say."

"Connoisseurs don't vomit prodigiously, as a rule, Mr Gall."

James could detect the limitations of an overworked brain. The doctor was plainly annoyed. In his book she had drunk too much on a stomach already burdened with a gluttonous cargo of seafood. Hospital resources were stretched to capacity without the distraction of mindless self-indulgence.

"She's on the mend now I'm glad to report. Hope this unfortunate episode teaches her a lesson." As an afterthought he added, "We'll keep her under observation for a day or two. She's weak and at her age we can't be too careful."

"Thank you doctor, I'm very grateful." Precisely as planned, Grace was now officially in recovery.

On the evening of the second day he visited at seven o'clock, spoke to Sheila, the duty nurse and suggested that he would be happy to sit by the bedside for an hour or more. Grace was sleeping and he had a book to read.

"Have a break nurse, I'm in no hurry."

"If that's alright, Mr Gall, you sure?"

"Absolutely, do take your time."

As soon as she left the room he took the empty syringe from his pocket, pulled back the plunger, filling it with air. He attached the syringe to the drip feeding his mother, depressed the plunger to thrust a surge of air to her heart, causing an embolism to bring on cardiac arrest. He had another 10ml syringe in his pocket, which he manipulated in like fashion, disconnected it and rearranged the intravenous drip as he had found it. At most a two-minute operation. He felt completely calm, trusting in the determination of his desire to rid himself of his mother. By the time the nurse returned ten minutes later, Grace appeared to be sleeping peacefully. He put his fingers to his lips in a shushing gesture and they exited the room together.

"She looks so serene," he said, almost wistfully.

"She'll be up and about in no time, don't you worry. I'll look in on her in an hour or so."

"You're so kind, thank you, Sheila. Thank you so much." He walked casually through the reception area and out into the night towards the car park a short distance from the entrance. His legs responded with unexpected flexibility to the direction he had chosen for them and in his chest he felt the freedom of decisions taken and acted on. He picked up speed, head high with the bearing of a man in charge.

Grace lay in the coffin dressed as she would have wished in a flowing, velvet, party gown. For once in his life James was looking down on her. Her head, supported by a plastic prop, pushed her dead face upwards. This had the effect of forcing the chin to protrude even more than when she was alive, the chin that described her, sticking out like an aggressive promontory from the mainland. Afterwards the funeral assemblage paid muted respects in caring clichés and drifted away, leaving James face-to-face with a half-crippled pensioner.

"Good riddance!" the man said, running a pair of rheumy eyes over the grave. He hobbled straight up to James. "She did for Percy, you know." His tone was matter-of-fact.

"Percy?"

"My brother, your father. She was a smart one, got away with it, she did." He looked like breaking down but when James reached out in support, he shrugged him off in favour of stern self-propulsion towards the gates of the cemetery.

"No, she didn't," James called out in a firm voice, with a conviction that surprised him. But his father's only brother showed no sign that he had heard.

After the funeral James went to see Theo, who had offered to attend the service. But James had insisted he didn't. Theo knew so much about Grace but James stopped short of confessing that he'd killed her. That would not be fair to Theo, he decided. This pragmatic high-mindedness let him off the hook, drawing least attention to himself and being, at the same time, fair to the psychiatrist. Would he pass the information to the police or not? James couldn't place Theo in such an invidious position. Instead he availed of the opportunity to talk about his mother, as any bereaved son would.

They were seated as usual in Theo's rooms. Neither had spoken. James looked about him. Nothing had changed and yet everything was different. He was now a de facto murderer. He sighed deeply, resettling in his chair as he glanced at Theo, who posed behind arched hands, soft eyes seeming to say, "All you have to tell me, James, is all that you want me to know."

"I do feel sad, very sad," James offered as if in reply.

"You have just buried your mother."

"But I'm sad for myself too, that she's gone before we had the chance to …"

Theo, quite still behind his desk, prompted, "… reconcile?" From anyone else that word would have resonated with suspicion.

"Yes, but also to address the fact that I never had a father."

"You hold her responsible?"

With rising anger James replied, "Totally. She denied me that, that essential fatherly love and direction." James continued to bemoan the loss of a father in his upbringing, while Theo visited the sideboard for a drink and reseated himself. Pointedly Theo suggested that fathers go missing often out of personal choice, regardless of provocation.

"Not in this case, he had no choice. She got rid of him."

James spoke freely, unrestricted by consideration of the disposal of his mother. It was the account of one entranced by his own narrative. If he believed himself, Theo would believe, even though James was well aware of the deception. Theo didn't have to respond. Their presence together in these rooms was enough.

Later James took Theo to dinner in Le Gourmet. It was then, after a robust Claret and post-prandial Port, that Theo told James about his son who died at birth. James made a mental note of this but was not inclined to ask for more detail.

When James got home, he sat with a cigar and a notebook, attempting a clarifying list:

My mother is gone forever. I need fear her no more.

Claudia? Quite different to Grace but there are similarities.

Fantasy in such matters is useless, not to be indulged.

If Theo is family now, he has allegiances of kinship.

I believe he has a profound appreciation of all that entails.

I could be his son and that too carries responsibilities which I gladly accept.

Chapter Eleven

Claudia noticed a change in Felix. Not only did he call over after work a couple of evenings a week but his body language struck an entirely different pose, almost caring, she might have said if she were less distrusting. But this was no time to let softness divert her. Felix remained a fraud, regardless of mood change. A fraud who was about to get his just desserts, she thought, then smiled at the choice of words, realising that she was beginning to think like James. How to lure him unsuspectingly to James' apartment? That was the dilemma, her dilemma. She had to prove to herself, as well as to James, that she had the steel to see it through. Every so often she reverted to a state of enraged recollection, a kind of invited meditation on the events that had conspired to set her on this course. Without her anger she felt she might dissolve and disappear. She looked self-consciously around her at the other women working out in the gym she attended for an hour every morning. In the shower she felt her hardening muscles with approval. In this she followed her father's diktat: "Strong body, strong mind." And so to work. First Felix. Avanti!

An unexpected conjuncture of circumstances intervened to ensure the dinner for three could go ahead without any of the mind games she juggled in her head: Felix paid her a visit.

"Claudia, my darling, I want to take you to dinner."

"I'd like that, Felix. Anywhere in mind?"

"Anywhere, literally, your call."

"That's thoughtful of you." Did he notice the sarcasm?

"Well, Claudia, I should be more thoughtful. I've not been very attentive recently and I want to make up for it."

Lying hound, she didn't believe a word. "If you really mean it."

"I do, I do, I've been a complete shit and I don't want to lose you."

"You've heard of James Livingstone Gall?"

"The food writer, critic chap." He couldn't completely hide his spite.

"Yes, I met him at a Sercat fundraiser last week. He wants to do a profile of Sergio."

"So?"

"He invited us to dinner."

"Where and when?"

She gave him the details. He took out his diary and flipped it open. "Wednesday would suit me."

"Ok, Felix, I'll let you know." She accepted the brush of his lips on her cheek without flinching and called James. "You know, James, he looked so cocksure as he left. I saw the smirk on his face as he got into his car. I felt like getting a gun and shooting him there and then."

"That won't be necessary, your husband has handed us the initiative. It would be ill-mannered not to accept. I rather fancy something wholesome, meaty, comfort food to put everybody at ease. What do you think?"

"Not too heavy on the comfort."

Chapter Twelve

"It's Mr Manny Johnson on line two, Mr Underwood. He's called twice already this morning."

"I'll take it."

Manny's voice had an edge to it. "This Dago Martinez—"

"Diego," Felix corrected him.

"Dago, Diego, who the fuck cares?"

"You have a problem with Diego, Manny?"

"Right first time, Felix, he didn't show. I've been waiting at the airport, no sign of the guy or the goods. He's not on the passenger list."

"Must be a mistake."

"Right again, Felix, your mistake to recommend the deal, my mistake to take your advice."

"Leave it with me, Manny, don't panic. These are reputable people, no need to worry."

"My money, your guarantee. I'd be worried if I were you."

"I said leave it with me. This is still a very sound deal as far as I'm concerned."

"Let's say two days, Felix, two days to put it back on the rails." Manny hung up.

Felix sat looking out the window of his high-rise office building, his mind in a whirl. A jet passed within sight, slowing down on its approach to the airport. His phone rang again somewhere at the outer limits of his hearing. Manny did not make empty threats. He had to find Martinez. He checked his records and there, sure enough, transferred to his personal account in the Costa Rican bank he had nominated, still there in black and white, the 200k sweetener from the Colombian, on the strength of which he had persuaded Manny to hand over two million. "Safe as houses, Manny, foolproof, take my word for it!" So simple, a few imprinted figures on a computer. The sound of rapping on the office door interrupted his reverie.

His secretary, Miss Mitchell, "An Inspector Gibbons insists on speaking to you personally, Mr Underwood. A police matter, he says."

Felix assured the policeman he had never heard of Diego Martinez, despite what the FBI had to say.

"May well be an error, sir. The Americans are not always the most reliable but my informant is very persuasive. He says Martinez has been in custody for several hours and is singing like a canary. I'll call to the bank tomorrow if you can fit me into your schedule. Routine at this stage, but we can't be too careful, can we, Mr Underwood?"

A few minutes later Felix's secretary came to his door. "Are you unwell, sir, you look terribly pale."

Felix stared hard at Miss Mitchell for a moment, then closed his eyelids, behind which his eyeballs fluttered in frenzy.

"Your wife is on hold, Mr Underwood."

"Felix, is that you, Felix?"

"Yes, yes it's me. What is it, Claudia, what do you want?"

"Tonight is fine, seven o'clock at the address I gave you."

With a surge of self-will he brought himself back to the present, breathing deeply. "Tonight? Oh, yes, as agreed, I'll be there. Seven, you say?" Normality at all costs. He'd sort this out in his own way and in the meantime remain calm.

"Book me on the early flight to Amsterdam in the morning," he instructed his secretary. "And call Otto Frink, tell him to meet me at

Schipol."

Frink was Felix's link to the profitable mutual fund they had been skimming together for years. As an insider with the international banking consortium that owned the fund, Otto fed Felix lucrative information, at a price. Felix suspected that he was just one of many players in a much larger operation. Frink, when they met in Amsterdam or Paris or London, was forever taking calls from contacts all over the world. On one occasion he boasted to Felix that he had helped a colleague escape the unwelcome attentions of a gang in Miami.

"Dead meat, Felix. Got him a new face and passport just in time!"

Frink could do the same for him.

Chapter Thirteen

James did not have to understand something to feel it: his simmering emotional response to Claudia, beyond lust now; not love surely, but love of the chase? It was said that the pig lost all interest as soon as he uncovered a truffle; and avid anglers derived deepest satisfaction from the interrelation of mind, body and the elements, however insignificant the catch. These were the half-formed thoughts he awoke from and with a force of will he dragged himself from the bed, stretched the sleepy skin around his eyes, practised windmill exercises with his arms while simultaneously running on the spot. He went to the lavatory. Not without pain; there was always pain. Stay still and it passed; let limbs feel, get up, get dressed and advance into the day.

He had an early session with Theo.

"So, James, you like this woman, Claudia, and you want me to tell if you're in love. You should know I am not the one to decide. But I can say you will have to fall in love some day. Love, my boy, is the only hope for the sexually afflicted."

James, wide-eyed, responded, "And you put me in that category?"

Theo hesitated, choosing his words with care. "I'd say you have issues in such matters."

The ensuing silence permitted them to drop the subject. Theo had given up dissecting James' unsavoury side and James had neither heart nor stomach for it either. Nevertheless this was another occasion when James was made aware of the shallowness of his emotional exchanges.

Pedro came at ten and he walked the garden with James, discussing the siting of a bay tree, newly purchased and the table settings for that evening's dinner.

"The VIP drill again, sir?"

"Perceptive, Pedro!"

"You seem excited, sir."

"A banker and his wife, not very exciting I'm afraid."

"Rich people?"

"She is very rich, heiress to a fortune. You remember her, she was my dinner guest recently. His wealth I can only estimate but he does have lucrative connections."

"Including you, sir."

"Kind of you to say so, but we have little in common and I can't say that I anticipate a lasting relationship."

"You like the lady better." No question this. Pedro stated it as a self-evident fact. They exchanged man-to-man looks. "Will you be carving at the table, Mr G, or should I leave the knives in the kitchen?"

"Mr G"! It had always been a respectful "sir". "Mr G" rang bells of distasteful familiarity. James was not pleased and said, "No, I'll see to that later, just carry on as usual."

"Mise en place," Pedro proclaimed with a broad beam on his face.

Chapter Fourteen

Claudia dusted the portrait and pondered it for a long time before putting it back on the mantelpiece. Odd how this wedding photograph of her parents never failed to remind her that she was alone in the world. "Not odd, is it, Claudia?" she said aloud to herself, thinking of her parents and how her mother lived separated from her husband's rise and rise, always an afterthought as his schemes skipped continent to continent. She was the Italian Mamma in the background, alone with her daughter, not wanting for much except the love of her husband. And when she died giving birth to the brother Claudia never saw, she died alone, her baby dying with her. Claudia, then a teenager, inherited the duty of loneliness. She must not impose on Sergio; he had enough to cope with as a shaper of great events in the wide world of hospitality. While he embraced the universe, she remained steadfastly in the background, loving him desperately.

She took on the management of his funeral in the full understanding that he would want it so. Then she remained on the board of Sercat Hotels, determined to ensure the continuation of Sergio's intentions. In a very real sense his spirit guided her until the fateful meeting with Felix. Felix swept her off her feet with repeated declarations of love and the sheer weight of his attention. He opened her up to a new version of herself: spontaneous, loving, alive to all around her. She had no standard to judge him by, nobody to advise her. And when the magic waned, when she realised the extent of his deception, she sought and found again the consolation of detachment.

So far, so good. Felix had set his own trap. When she called him at the bank he sounded vague but confirmed the dinner date. At times she feared he might get wise to her animosity skulking behind the masks she gave it. But he had no idea, how could he in his self-absorption? That he saw none of it enraged her all the more, reinforcing her designs for him.

Chapter Fifteen

James loved planning a dinner party, believing that there is no greater liberty than the open mind, the gorgeous blankness and lively deference that are the primary ingredients of market shopping. One knows nothing and then, sure enough, the first course declares itself the first moment at the outer cluster of stalls, the anarchic jumble of lean-tos, barrels and buckets, supervised by owners hoist on the hysteria of seasonal abundance. So mused James as he filled his basket with watercress, baby spinach, radish, beet, sorrel, flowering borage, tomatoes, summer berries, and sauntered home in a jaunty breeze. From the garden he collected a dozen large rhubarb leaves, chopped and boiled them in sugar syrup for an hour, strained the liquid, boiled again until a mere tablespoon of thick syrup covered the base of the pot. This he spooned carefully into a jug to which he added half a bottle of champagne, mint leaves, ice cubes, sliced orange and crème de cassis, whisking thoroughly. He then prepared a second jug with similar ingredients, omitting the rhubarb juice. To the first jug he attached a gummed sticker inscribed "For Felix Only" and stored both on different shelves in the fridge.

He was washing salads when Claudia arrived.

"Looks so good," she enthused.

"Good dinners feed forgetfulness; lifetimes in themselves; bubbles of separation; happy, illusive interludes."

She raised her eyes to heaven.

"It's a quotation, Claudia, from a piece I wrote for *The Guardian* a few years ago. Pretty good even if I say so myself, don't you think?"

"Almost everything you say sounds edible."

"I'll take that as a compliment."

They prepared the dinner together, setting the table, brushing against each other as the work moved them from fridge to chopping board, table to cupboard. Accidental at first, but James wondered if there was calculation in Claudia's sudden sidles into bodily contact, her breasts rubbing his spine as she passed behind him, a loose hand momentarily trailed on his buttocks. Once he grabbed her from behind, brandishing a knife playfully beneath her breasts.

"Ooh, James, you're not going to stick that thing in me, are you?" she said as she turned, banging her backside against his groin.

They had everything clarified in order, except the primary purpose of the evening. Claudia could not restrain herself any longer. "How do we do it, James?"

"I wondered when you'd ask." He was play-acting, still several hours to go. "I have prepared a cocktail for Felix, a Mickey Finn Royale." With that he produced the labelled jug from the fridge, explaining its provenance and the toxic levels of oxalic acid in rhubarb leaf. "After a couple of glasses before the food, plus wine on top of that, I expect him to collapse, quite destabilised, at some point during dinner. And we will then carry him to the garden shed for the next stage." He explained how they would dispatch the comatose Felix and then he recapped, in answer to her step-by-step questions, the precise procedure from beginning to end. Her attention to detail, intelligent comprehension and riveted focus aroused him to such a force of passion that he wanted to take her in his arms there and then. Only an immense effort held him back. His upper lip began to quiver but she did not seem to notice.

Chapter Sixteen

When Felix arrived on James' doorstep, he looked like a fugitive from a film noir, reeking with fatalism and menace. His narrowed eyes devoured the space about him. James sensed an angry man spoiling for a fight. Felix swayed to and fro on his feet like a boxer about to enter the ring.

"Often wondered how these houses looked inside," he said. The disdainful tilt of his head dismissed the house and James' taste just as effectively as his comment, "I prefer open plan."

"And open minds, Felix," Claudia called out from the kitchen.

Ignoring Claudia's remark, Felix pointed to the luggage at his feet. "Somewhere safe for these?" He left the overnight bag in the hall and took his briefcase with him, as James escorted him to the dining room.

Over drinks (Felix demolished the whole jug) James adopted a receptive expression to show interest in what Felix had to say. Outside the rain came down in heavy showers, blown by an angry wind, more rain than had been seen for weeks. James pictured the river in spate at the end of the garden, all the while aware of Claudia's patient evaluation of her husband's mood. She too could not have been taken in by the bravado. Felix was trying hard to hide ... what was it, fear? Fear of them? Had he some inkling of their plans for him? How could he? James watched them both carefully.

"You look tired, Felix."

"Long day, Claudia."

James gave them an Alsatian wine and they discussed it while he tossed the salad in a pesto dressing, dropping purple and white nuggets of Cashel Blue into the seasonal melange of greenery. "Try the focaccia," James encouraged them.

Felix seemed to relax, some of his swagger returned as if he had decided that he was as much the hunter as the hunted. He drank, looking appreciatively at Claudia. "What a brainwave, this fabulous evening. And you look dazzling, my dear."

"Bravo," James interjected, glancing at Claudia whose cheeks had turned pink.

"Thanks to James, he's arranged everything." Rising as she spoke, she collected their glasses on her way to the kitchen.

"The same again, you liked that, Felix?"

"Delicious, yes." He turned to James. "Unusual combination, James. I don't think I've had Alsace with salad before. Deeply grapey, isn't it?"

James reckoned he should be dead and dispatched in thirty minutes maximum. "The conservative choice would be something white, light and dry, one of the lesser Burgundies."

"You know your wine," Felix complimented him.

"One must know exactly what the rules are before one can afford to disregard them."

Felix raised his eyes, studying his host. "Haven't I heard that before?"

James laughed, saying, "Forgive me, Felix, I can't resist quotation. Elizabeth David I believe, a woman ahead of her time, quite a stunner actually."

"Like my Claudia."

"Nobody quite like Claudia."

"Don't I know, James, that's why I value her so." Felix may have been shaky on arrival but by now James knew that his earlier assessment had been correct. This Felix was no pushover.

Claudia returned with two half-filled glasses which she set before them.

"How nice, thank you, Claudia," James said. He concentrated on Felix: venal but definitely interesting, a man he might have enjoyed sharing a dinner with in different circumstances. He found himself wanting Felix's opinion on the cooking, even as he reckoned he'd be knocked out by the time he was in a position to react to the watercress sauce. James had added a soupçon of cream and wondered if Felix would have noticed its mollifying influence on the vinegar and wine reduction. And the salmon? Could he tell it was wild? James could tell things about him: the way he let the wine swoosh in his mouth, the smack of his lips, the rakish slap of butter on bread, wolfish eyes tracking Claudia's glide around the table. A kindred spirit. Knowing the banker's fate he felt a twinge of pity. There was something else also, stronger than the fumes of fish grilling, an odour of treachery at the table. James whiffed it, presumed the others did too, feeling its responsibility, camaraderie, as if there was another guest, a late arrival with whom each of them shared an old secret.

Felix dropped his glass in mid-quaff. He squinted, stayed ramrod straight for a moment and then collapsed into his chair. James and Claudia waited in silence. Felix remained still, head resting on his chest, arms loose.

At last, after an interminable minute, Claudia whispered, "He looks so peaceful."

Suddenly Felix opened his eyes and, in a flash, they saw the truth dawn on him. His drugged gaze alighted on them like a tired bird finds a branch. Practised predator that he was, he saw through them with a prey's instinctive recognition: he had been outwitted, cheated at his own game. Claudia and this man, James, mirror image of himself. Enraged, he did what they never imagined he could do. He attacked. Enervated by the drug, breathing with difficulty, his flailing sortie in James' direction resembled the crazed effort of a drowning man. All he succeeded in doing was to topple the bowl of watercress butter sauce, scatter cutlery and glasses and spray the table with wine from an upturned bottle, coming to rest outstretched on the dinner table like the stuffed centrepiece at a medieval banquet. As James stood over him, wooden mallet in his right hand, (the one he used for cracking open boiled lobster shells or for flattening escalopes of veal), Felix smiled, a lift and opening of the lips reminiscent of a cowed dog expecting the worst. James brought the mallet down on Felix's head, forcibly, twice. There was a cracking sound of shattering bone but, surprisingly, no blood. Claudia helped drag him to the sofa. She despised him and yet, now that she was party to his undoing, she showed no emotion, watching horror spread over his features. Felix attempted to say something but all he could achieve was a dull grunt. Eyes, whirling in their sockets, bulged as if about to burst. His tongue, trapped in his mouth, prodded cheeks and gums. The blood rose from his neck, reddening as it rose. Stricken by aphasia, brain damage began to close down his senses one by one, slipping into deathly lassitude.

Coldly, Claudia asked, "Lost your tongue have you, Felix?" James could see the V of her breasts as she leaned over to inspect him. "Looks like he's had it," she said.

They managed to manoeuvre Felix's body to the back door where James had parked Pedro's wheelbarrow. The night was dark, no moon, no neighbouring house lights, rain pelting down. Drenched through, they reached the shed and with a last wrenching effort bundled the body inside. They heard a sound from Felix at one stage, a brief moan, but carried on, determined to get rid of him quickly.

Bodies distorted in death's first pose sometimes gave an appearance of life. Last minute, reflexive adjustments could make a dead body break wind, eyes might blink, muscles creak. This James knew. Claudia held the manhole open while he dragged Felix to the edge, feet first, and eased him in. There was a loud splash and they dropped the manhole cover carefully back into place. Tidying up was minimal:

little blood or disarray. All that could be heard was the rain pattering on the shed's small window as they left and made their way back to the house.

"In answer to your question, Claudia, I thought drowning the sensible option. If or when, as the case may be, the body is cast ashore somewhere downstream, the police will presume suicide after moral collapse, a reasonable conclusion considering his lifestyle."

They had showered and seated themselves before a fire, hastily lit, Claudia's statuesque profile enhanced by firelight, her white face framed by damp swirls of hair and the collar of her robe. She kept rubbing her palms over her thighs, as if some unwanted remnant of the night still clung to them.

When James knelt before her, taking her hands in his, she inched closer until their faces touched. They kissed with unrestrained passion, letting hands free to claw bathrobes away, pausing then to observe, for a moment, each other's nudity. She flailed violently as he entered her and then, with strength he did not believe possible, she pulled herself up to him in wild convulsions, scratching and squeezing, begging him to stay with her. He sank into her and felt her all over, his hands coming to rest on her shoulders, easing towards her throat. The suck-slap of bodies seemed like a distant commotion as, for one moment, he entertained the simple logic at his fingertips: he could enclose her throat in his hands and press and twist. And tighten.

They lay still for a while until James got up to go to the kitchen. She was fully dressed and glowing when he returned with a silver tray of tea and shortbread. They sat together sipping and munching without a word, prolonging the pleasure until Claudia said, "When can we meet again, James?"

He was slow to reply and when he did he was emphatic. "Not for a while, let this blow over." He had reverted to haughtiness, distancing himself.

Some days later James learned how endangered Felix was from within the criminal underworld. Claudia felt safe enough to contact him about Felix's part in the conspiracy to defraud, which Inspector Gibbons revealed to her in the course of formal notification, when the body of her husband had been thrown up by the tide. Gibbons told Claudia that they suspected Felix killed himself while in an agitated state. He said Felix had been mixed up in some very nasty business and must have been aware of the danger he was in. He assured her there would be a full investigation and, that if other parties were involved, the department would make every effort to bring them to justice.

A week or so after that the headlines proclaimed, "Banker Found Hanged!" Newspaper pictures identified a German national, Otto Frink, *a known associate of Felix Underwood, who police sources have hinted may have committed suicide about a week ago. Both deaths are believed to be connected to an FBI sting operation involving cocaine smuggling and money laundering. Inspector Taylor Gibbons, who is conducting the investigation locally, confirmed that both men were key figures in a world-wide drugs network.*

Chapter Seventeen

Compliancy is a tactic, Claudia reminded herself. In spite of herself, James' words penetrated and confused her almost as much as the sex did. Words, words, words, knitted and sown together as a throwaway cloak of convenience. Let him assume she wanted only what he was prepared to give, dole out devotion in measured portions; men are always impressed by dependence. Why then should she care about his childish games when she knew from the beginning that James Livingstone Gall was an accomplished actor, his polished irony delivering diversion as often as actuality? Sometimes the lines dried up and she caught glimpses of the child he had never outgrown, the corrupted innocence that made him capable of great brutality.

She lay on her own bed addressing the ceiling on the morning after they had done away with Felix. She allowed herself a humourless chuckle. If she had to deploy mad sex to deflect from her real intentions, she would; Jesus, why not when it was so damn good? She had done the background research, for months tracking James' magazine pieces, his radio and TV appearances, commentary by him and about him, reviews and criticisms. She traced former editors for their contributions to her so-called thesis, gave free rein to a coterie of chefs, who were only too willing to express an opinion and grasp an opportunity to garnish their diaphanous egos. Flattery, as James might well say, gets you anything. Nobody was indifferent: JLG, larger than life, grudgingly respected, universally unloved. But she now knew more than anyone how dangerous a man he was, hiding a killer's icy calculation behind the dandyism of an opinionated gourmet. Who else had he murdered as well as his own mother and Felix? Hadn't she seen the trembling lips? Barely perceptible, but she had noticed.

Her thoughts wandered back to Felix. Dead, she could despise him less. There was no sense of relief, only a hollow feeling in her stomach, as if she hadn't eaten for days. With a determined effort she called again on the memory of her father, his lilting "Claudia Cara" playing in her ears like a mantra that followed her into the shower in approval of the thorough soaping to wash off the odours and secretions of the night before. She closed her eyes, letting the water splash on her hair, pouring down over her face, shoulders, breasts, belly, thighs and for a flashing moment recalled showering together with Felix in happier times. When she switched off the water and opened her eyes again, the last swift gush drained away beneath her feet. For some reason she found herself smiling.

"Go with the flow, Felix," she said.

"Claudia Cara" breakfasted with her, receding only when she permitted Dean Martin's effortless recording of "Everybody Loves Somebody" to caress the airwaves.

A rattle and rustle signalled the arrival of the morning paper through her letter box, and she went to pick it up. *The Travel & Food* supplement displayed a smiling picture of James Livingstone Gall above his review of a Korean restaurant, recently opened. She read it, let her eyes rest on his photograph again, declaring aloud, "I could love you, James, if there was not other business between us to be attended to. And if you were not such a conceited prick!"

Chapter Eighteen

After depositing Felix in the tide, a self-pitying James found himself ruminating about life and death: nothing stood still, beginnings were ignorant of ends. We knew nothing except, perhaps, that Béarnaise sauce was best with beef and that events repeated themselves. Life was brutal and short, made up of episodes that had only one aim: to force us to re-enact them. That was the truth: repetition until repetition became the mainstream, as voluptuous and necessary as blood. The post-modern word for it was addiction, but it was far more than that; it was life's essential force. And this repetition had a price. James paused to contemplate his own suffering. The bowels: a bad bout lasting forty-eight hours.

At such times Pedro kept his distance, letting himself in and out the side entrance to the garden from which he could access the house with his key.

"Some party, Mr G!"

James had left the bed and, still smarting from sickness, was not fully attuned to Pedro's presence. "Don't address me that way!"

Scurrying about with a duster, not looking James in the eye, Pedro replied, "Yes sir, as you wish, sir."

Attempting an amiable recovery of the situation, James said

quickly, "A bit of a mess, sorry about that. Excessive resort to Alsace, I'm afraid. Sticky terrain, not for the fainthearted."

"Only two bottles, sir."

"Two, only two, could have sworn we had more. Damn guests, can't trust anybody any more."

"Left without their luggage, sir." He held up Felix's briefcase. "And another bag in the hall."

"Oh, yes, of course, safekeeping, left them here for a few days. I offered, you see. Just leave them both in the hall, Pedro." James followed him, not sure why except that he could not take his eyes off the briefcase. For a pregnant second Pedro looked quizzically, shrugged and placed the briefcase on the floor beside the overnight bag. Felix's confounded bags, usurpers in his own home. James knew he should have hidden them, disposed of them, of course he should have.

It took him half the morning to get into the swing of the day, not helped by a sky of sullen clouds looking in the windows as he dressed. Then he attended to the mail. Those damn bags worried him but he dared not go near them.

"How's the new bay tree doing?" he asked, in the hope that a reference to the garden might get Pedro out of the house.

"Coming on well, sir." And then he stopped whatever he was doing. "I almost forgot. I found this in the wheelbarrow." Dangling Felix's watch in the air between them, he said, "Can't be yours, sir, can it?" He pointed at the inscription on the back, "To F. with love, C."

"My mother's! In the barrow, you say?"

Pedro hesitated and then handed him the watch as if it were an offensive weapon.

For Pedro's benefit, James feigned scholarly detachment for the rest of the morning, writing a column for *The Times* on "Chillis: How Hot is Hot?"

As soon as he was alone, he forced open the briefcase: newspaper, dark glasses, flight tickets, John Grisham's *The Broker*, hardback notebook, condoms, three-pack, two sealed envelopes. The bulkier envelope contained cash: several thousand dollars and sterling, brand new notes. In the other, marked "Original", was a tape, which he supposed was that incriminating Sergio in the killing of a partner so many years ago. Three notebook pages listed codes and series of numbers that might have been bank accounts.

Manny Johnson was one among a chronological list of names with telephone numbers in a section headed "Business" at the back of the book. A scrawled arrow led from Manny's name to a circle at the bottom of the page enclosing another name: Claudia. James memorised Manny's number, locked away the contents of the briefcase in a drawer in his bedroom, and dialled.

"Ya, Manny here, who wants to know?"

"Forever charming, Mr Johnson."

"Mr G!" he exclaimed. "What's the story, my son, you wanna buy me a drink?"

"Several, Manny."

"Something to celebrate?"

"Mourning the passing of a mutual acquaintance."

There was a pause.

"I think I can drink to that."

He knew Manny Johnson for quite a few years now, going back to when Johnson and his chef partner had run a faux-Italian trattoria in Soho called "La Dolce Vita", an ostensibly legitimate business fronting for illegal income from prostitution and a prospering protection racket. After James gave the place a bad review, Manny threatened him. "I'll blow your balls off!" Then Manny realised that the damning critique had absolutely no effect on his real business and invited James to lunch. By some perverse logic he decided they should be friends, his decision, although James had to allow that he felt the thrill of a flattering intrigue. Hence his introduction to The Butcher's Arms. Because Manny had the habit of reminding James of the "brilliant bullshit" he wrote, James had never quite forgotten it himself:

If it's cucina rustica you're after, I suggest you give La Dolce Vita a wide berth ... Italian food is betrayed here by a profound ignorance ... Chianti bottles, nesting in cobwebs, disguise a ceiling on the point of collapse but there is no hiding incompetence in the kitchen ... my cannelloni had the colour and the texture of Tuscan hills. You can't eat scenery!

James cradled the phone with his neck. "You were acquainted with the banker chap, Manny?"

"The long distance swimmer ... maybe, who wants to know?"

"Heard you and he were ... associates."

"So, we did some business. I put him in touch with people. Who gives a shit?"

A couple of days later James called to see Manny at The Butcher's Arms, still curious about Felix, anything that might be useful to know.

Manny appeared to be quite open, explaining his deal with Felix. "He blew it and took down some good guys with him. Been interviewed myself. That cop, Gibbons, big, constipated gorilla. He's got nothin' on me. I've had an account at Bellingham ever since Felix was a cashier. Why wouldn't two old buddies be in touch now and then?" He pulled his chair close to James, his fat neck protruding above the wide collar of a piratical blouse, smelling of expensive perfume, beer and sex. "Wanted me to disappear a certain lady."

"Who?"

"I think you know, Mr G," Manny said. "My guess is she's the reason you're down here pumping your old mate."

"You could just identify her."

"She ain't dead yet." He threw his arms wide open in a gesture of innocence. "Nothin' to do with me, she's all yours now."

"If anything should happen to this lady, Manny, I presume you would be in a position to allocate blame?"

"No worries, Mr G, Felix fucked it up. Any deal we had is finito, if you see what I mean."

James bought a couple of drinks, eschewing the invitation to "dig in to a plate of lasagne, the best since La Dolce Vita."

"Verdi?" James asked, equally tongue in cheek.

Watching Manny eat reminded James of crocodiles at lunch in a tourist park he visited once in Nairobi. He tore the pasta sheets apart and blobs of meat sauce fell from his lips. Between mouthfuls his fixed smile and darting eyes regaled James with dumb eloquence; his whole frame shook with the force of mastication; the fat rolls of a spare tyre quivered visibly beneath his shirt like a shoal of demented fish. Not taken in by this Falstaffian display, James knew that Manny was a dangerous psychopath. He wiped his mouth with the back of his hand and took a swig from his beer, belching with satisfaction, speaking between belches, "What bothers me is the bastard had no guts. Felix, he didn't have it in him to top himself, not the type."

"All the evidence points to suicide," James interjected.

Manny discharged an enormous, rampant fart. "We don't have all the evidence."

"Are you saying …?"

"Guys like Felix get too greedy, Mr G."

"So, somebody killed him. Is that it?"

"That's it, he got disappeared."

James regarded Manny with suspicion. "You seem very knowledgeable on the subject. How can you be so sure?"

"Maybe I done the deed myself," he said, his slit eyes gleeful. "He owed me big time."

"You can't be serious."

"No, but whoever did him did me no favours."

Every time James entered his world, Manny conferred on him an equality of roguery and he went away feeling the deferred weight of some awful reckoning. Nevertheless James could not stifle the dangerous thrill he got from these encounters. He considered how his stock would rise if Johnson knew how Felix really died, how with Claudia as accomplice they had "disappeared" the banker. A part of James desired Manny's recognition.

James walked all the way home, his heart and senses lifted by the time he reached his own street, this wide, tolerant avenue and its little Square, a world away from the mean alleys around The Butcher's Arms. He loved the warm brush of lime trees over the Frenchy awnings of cafés, double protection against summer showers; the fashionable boutiques, the delicatessen and its omnipresent proprietor, his belly-bulge in itself an assurance of refinement and quality; the consoling predictability of Peter's Pastries, whose ovens issued day-long invitation to patisseries and coffee, lunchtime quiches, indolent afternoon teas and the promise of a takeaway pie for that unexpected supper guest. He loved letting himself in by the solid oak door of his house, the feeling of security inside as he scanned the hall and then the dining room and the white bedroom for signs of Pedro's attendance. Sitting before the drawing room fire, readied by Pedro for lighting, he gave in to his knowledgeable attachment to the painting above the mantel-piece: a Wyeth landscape with house, trees and stream, its leitmotif of veiled menace brilliantly achieved. He felt the early-evening chill and put a match to the fire. He dozed off and awoke with a start. The bags! Chiding himself for not attending to them before now, James rushed to the hall, sighing with relief at the sight of them, still awaiting disposal. The briefcase lay empty beside the overnight bag where he had dropped it earlier. Unzipped, he couldn't tell if the bag had been tampered with. All he could glean from the contents were signs of hasty packing for a short trip. Had Pedro searched it? Of course he had.

James put the briefcase in on top of Felix's clothes, zipped the bag and carried it to the shed. He reopened it to introduce a couple of weighty stones from the garden and zipped it tight again. The splash as it met the water under the manhole was of a minor scale compared to the disturbance caused by Felix's falling body.

Chapter Nineteen

James had always treated Pedro well, careful to allow him the freedom of the house and garden since he felt that, in a way, he had a claim. One could say that Pedro came with the property; James hired him a few days after he bought it. The pretence of equality appealed to him, and Pedro had never indicated anything other than contentment. They were, each of them, faithful to their roles, largely unspecified but nonetheless understood. Lately, however, faults had begun to show. His "Mr G" irritated, alerting James to further signs of intrusiveness, which, once suspected, he found. Pedro trailed a vague air of ambiguity after him, which hung about after he left, diminishing the quality of his work. Not quite insolence. It seemed to James that they had breached an imaginary line beyond which they had to find their feet again. The alternative he did not want to contemplate. Where would he find another Pedro? But Pedro would have to comply with some new rules or face the consequences. James left a message on his phone. "Livingstone Gall here, when you report for work tomorrow we have some matters to discuss."

Spirits lifted in the aftermath of action and he was suffused with resolve. He had reviewed Korea, a new restaurant purveying dishes of that country. A blurb on the menu proclaimed, "excellent authenticity for your delight". He telephoned his reservation and took himself off on foot. Good, indeed, were beef soup, pickled pear soufflé and a composition of pork adrift in a creamy, oniony broth, but squid on a risotto of millet reminded him disconcertingly of Pedro: small, tough, inscrutable.

The shot of soju, offered smilingly on the house, burned his throat and hit him like a heavyweight's illegal kidney punch. Korea's national spirit, translated, meant "burning liquor". Even without the host's solicitous interpretation, James might have divined the meaning for himself.

It was raining when he left the restaurant. Not a taxi to be seen. He walked with upturned collar clenched at the neck. The shower became a downpour, driving him to the shelter of a Tapas bar still open for business. He found a corner, hung his wet jacket on the back of a chair beside a radiator and ordered a glass of Rioja with unwanted bread and pickles. His critical eye switched on like a spotlight sweeping across the bare, wooden floor to the long bar counter, taking in the waitresses and barmen at work, the diners variously eating, drinking, hands and faces dancing with the vital stories of their day. It might have been a stage he had suddenly entered on cue: this theatrical space with such a sensitive acoustic. Kitchen congress reverberated through swinging service doors; the doggerel of a drama in rehearsal and aged floorboards lent a Riverdance echo to ordinary concourse. Something in the ambience facilitated self-absorption. Why do I do this work, he asked himself, peering into the wine glass. He took out his note book and made a list:

To record the restaurant world as it is, warts and all.

To capture the thrills of the moment: a new dish, a young chef brashly innovative.

To display my talent for all to see.

To satisfy my desire for revenge.

To challenge mediocrity, identify the charlatans.

To hold a mirror up to the industry: its ills, its glories.

To justify my failures, make up for my mistakes.

To attract beautiful women.

To tell fascinating stories.

To please my readers.

To please myself.

To forgive myself.

To escape myself.

Because the food Muse grips me.

To become the saboteur I've always wished to be.

For the children I may never father.

To survive.

To continue to believe in the pursuit of pleasure.

For redemption.

For my mother.

The writing down had always set him free, off like a hare before the hounds. He walked out of there light as a croissant, mellowed by several glasses of the Spanish wine, not yet ready for bed, thinking of Grace and how peacefully she went in the end.

Marching along, his tempo was the tempo of the street. He had the gait of a man of the area, a man who was known by this place, though he had never been on foot in this part of town before. It was very late; there were few people about. The lights of an all-night café caught his attention. It was Hopper's painting, *Nighthawks*, reincarnated before his eyes, all the shadows and tension that said something ugly's going on. Four people, replicating the painting, stood out: a Bogart figure, mean, slit eyes, stiletto fingers; his moll in a scarlet dress, cool as you like; a stout, anonymous figure in a black hat, his back to the street; and the boy behind the counter, white hat and jacket, nervous. Hopper's picture had not included the one other character in the scene that James now observed, a uniformed waitress prancing between tables.

Inside he smelled cheap coffee and rank fat, twin indicators of a mismanaged café. The clientele had an air of sleaze striving for discretion. Bowed heads, inaudible mutterings, a deviant churchiness. Except for the waitress, coquettish in a tight top and mini skirt, the place seemed choked of life, her lively attendance a rebuke to the bad odour. She came to James with an open smile, bending to take his order. The cones of her breasts pointed at him through her cotton T-shirt and he stared back. All he wanted was a stiff drink but her chipper proximity demanded more of him. "And something sweet," he said, in an undertone.

"And something sweet," she repeated, mimicking.

James believed that professional waiting-at-table required male qualities of presence that a waitress would never possess, a view he kept to himself in these days of indiscriminate feminism. Something other than waitressing know-how attracted him to this young woman, sensations enhanced by her flirtatiousness. She brought him a cognac and a chocolate éclair oozing cream. As he watched her strut about between tables, James thought he would like to hold her in his arms, dance with her. A tango, the cut and thrust of it, her long wayward legs, the parted lips, pale skin, cocked head, hair bunched and streaked. He drank the brandy in one gulp, pushed the morass of éclair and cream about until it began to leak over the rim of the plate onto the table. All the while he tracked the manoeuvres of the dancing girl.

As he left the café, she swung open the door for him, moving in and away. Touching his arm, she said, "Night darling, see you."

Hidden in a recessed doorway across the street, James waited. He hailed her as she left the café at the end of her shift. They moved into the darkness of an alleyway, out of sight of the diner, disappearing into a deeper band of dark from where no sounds carried.

On leaving the alley some time later, he saw that the diner was now empty except for the white-coated attendant behind the counter. A surge of energy sent him on his way, pulling him along like a friend in a hurry to the theatre or a train.

At home, blessed by the benedictions of Chopin nocturnes, body fresh from a shower, he opened a book on female beauty, one of those bulky coffee table volumes rarely given time: Botticelli, Titian, Vermeer and a series of harsh twentieth-century female shapes from the fractured hands of Picasso. None of them had the immediacy of the waitress in the alley, her unnaturally white skin and glinting eyes that demanded to be seen—"Look at me!" As he leafed through the book, the fingers of his right hand began to twitch and lock in painful spasms and he had to bathe them in warm water and olive oil for half an hour. His doctor had warned him about over-exercising that hand. "Expect arthritis in old age," he'd said. Preparing for bed, James caught sight of the calendar hanging by the dressing table, the day's date highlighted in red: Grace's birthday.

Chapter Twenty

Next day, Pedro's day off, James slept late, exercised his hands on the piano, flexing finger joints up and down the scales. Much as he felt confident in sorting out Pedro himself, an instinctive spur impelled him to call Theo. "Doctor Hilfer won't be in today," the secretary informed James. She was reluctant to go into detail but her tone cracked with concern. When pushed, she admitted that Theo was ill but she could not or would not be specific. That bothered James. Theo sick. A pang of anxiety, not for himself but for Theo, surprised him. For the briefest moment his thoughts were fondly for Theo.

And then, his mind filled with Pedro and his absence, he knocked over the coffee pot and had to refill it. He found himself in Pedro's room searching through his wardrobe and drawers. In a case under the bed he uncovered a lined, hardback schoolboy's writing book. Pedro's, obviously, a collection of anecdotes about his work in the hotel, lists of jobs he had to do and whole pages of detailed How To's, the chores of a junior porter's life in a grand hotel. Precise but boring. James replaced it and, as he did, he discovered another similar book. On the first page, two words in Pedro's clear but laborious hand: *The Story*. Taking it with him to the kitchen, James sat and read:

I am not Pedro. He was my twin. He died and when I came out of prison I discovered that he had left himself to me. My mother said he would have done anything for me, given me his last penny. He had no money so I took what was left, his name and his innocence. I like myself as him much more than I ever liked myself. Plain and stupid Sean.

Pedro never got caught. When we broke into the old guy's house we had no idea he had a gun. Pedro grabbed it and we both had a go, Pedro first. "Bang, bang you're dead!" He ran off and I fired twice. A neighbour saw me leave. I didn't tell on Pedro, Mum needed one of us, at least. The leukaemia got him anyway, took him along with my criminal record.

Just mum and me, nobody gave a shit. I swear. Those times, in the flats where we lived, poor, single-parent families survived, just about. Who'd miss one less from our look-alike litter? As I said, nobody gave a shit.

At this point James paused and flipped through pages of wayward description, Pedro's sometimes boring ups and downs, stopping, starting, skimming as he read.

I got into hotel work, portering, looking straight and clean in a navy uniform with epaulettes and gold buttons. Learned how to speak proper. Yessir, no sir, two bags full sir! Good? I was the best arse-licking, front-hall porter The Doncaster Hotel ever saw. Off duty I read books left behind in the hotel, even wrote little tales of my own, shitty efforts that I tore up before anyone found them but I kept at it anyway.

Mum polished those gold buttons till her fingers were raw and when I came home one day to tell her I wouldn't be wearing the uniform any longer, I swear, there were tears in her eyes.

Mr Gall's visits to the hotel put us all on our best behaviour; he was famous for the stories he wrote and talked about on radio and TV, all true from his own experience, disgusting toilets, lousy food, big-shot head waiters treating commis like dirt, chefs who tanked up all day on cooking wine. He was a hero for us young guys front-of-house and he was a big tipper. When he asked me to work for him I didn't think twice. I don't regret it because the job of running his house pays well and I have been able to cough up for mum's nursing home and he is a writer and I wanted to write too. But five years is a long time, almost as long as I spent locked up. Five years with him is a kind of prison too. He treats me fair but he's weird, talks to himself. He knows about mum but doesn't really give a shit about me as long as I do what he wants. He doesn't know how to let me disagree with him so I don't bother. He talks to me as if I was a foot taller than I am, looking over my head. Sometimes, I swear, I have to look behind me to be sure there's no one else there. *My Man* he calls me behind my back. He's so fuckin' particular about some things. Different shaped glasses for every bottle of wine; red wine at room temperature, champagne cooled not chilled, white wine chilled not cool. It took me ages to cop that rubbish. I thank my lucky stars that he does most of the cooking himself. Cooking! The guy's a fuckin' addict; I swear, it's like coke or heroin, he gets so strung out he's not at the races, in another fucking world. What he gets up to down in the garden shed? Whole dead animals and God knows what, wild birds hanging, dripping blood, deer meat, fish, freezer full of bones, Jesus, the pong some days! He doesn't want me next or near that shed. "My laboratory, Pedro, private!" As in "Private, Keep Out," like one of those top secret government no-go areas.

He throws parties for knobs like himself; I do most of the prep work, the *mizon plass* he says, which is a complicated frog way of saying set the table, Pedro. I do overtime for parties of six or more, waitering. Until midnight, no later. "You can go now Pedro, can't have you missing the last bus!" Like he wants me out of the way.

I have to wear white shirts and dickey bows. Jesus, do they knock it back! Women and men, bottles and bottles. A mess the morning after, like a bomb site some days. He has an eye for the ladies. You wouldn't believe it, what they get up to, him and those gorgeous women, model types with legs up to their necks. I see them into the hall when they arrive at the house, help them off with their fancy coats. I swear, embarrassing when they come close; some of 'em, Jesus, I swear, they'd put a horn on a hobby horse. Hot shot with the women, no doubt there but if you didn't know he was a ladies' man you'd easy think, ya, a nine pound note! Seen arse bandits in prison, eyes crawling all over you. Mr G's never made *a move on me, not so far.*

Look, if I've made myself sound like mister know-all-togetherman, no way! My prison report from a therapy woman said, "This young man lacks self-esteem arising from childhood deprivation and negative body image." Negative body image! Fuck me, James bloody Bond would have a negative body image if he looked like me: Five foot at a push, skinny, a touch of the tar on my little-boy face. And my name, Pedro, for fuck sake! How could mum have picked that mongrel's name?

Miss Franklin, my English teacher at school, said that all the best stories had a twist in the tail. The twist in my story came a few weeks ago. Mr G (I call him that now and he don't like it) had a beautiful woman to dinner and that was fine, nothing different there. Then, a week or so later, I'm not sure exactly, the same woman and another man. They made a shitty mess in the dining room, no problem there either until I found the watch in the wheelbarrow; there was blood on it. I looked around the garden; the barrow tracks led to the shed, "My laboratory, Pedro!" He don't know it but when you been inside, prison I mean, you learn things. The papers were full of the dead banker story. I knew straight off. He was here for dinner the night he disappeared. How do I know? Mr G told me himself, his own words.

"A banker and his wife, not very exciting, I'm afraid."

"To F. with love C." They were the letters on the back of the watch. In the paper they called him "Felix Underwood, who leaves behind a widow, Claudia Underwood, daughter of the deceased hotel tycoon, Sergio Catalano."

"To F. with love C." You can learn a lot from the newspapers!

Next time I went out to the nursing home to see mum I told her the whole story, every little bit of it that I could remember and when I'd done I started all over again, putting all the pieces of the picture together. Like a jig-saw. Mum nodded all the way with me. I tell her everything; she don't take anything in no more, nods and smiles in her own way. She can't hear but I can and when I have a story like that one I listen very carefully and then I write it down so that I won't forget any of it.

Prisoners brag a lot. O.t.t. rubbish about beating the shit out of coppers and all the sweet women they fucked. Most of it, forget about it but there are old lags doing time who you could listen to: the scam merchants, easy money guys, con artists. One guy I listened to, when we worked in the prison laundry together, Sam Hand was his name, pushing fifty when I met him. What a life! He worked the Mediterranean as a gigolo when he was in his twenties and thirties; he had tales, I can tell you, make more than your hair stand up. Nice, Monte Carlo, Venice, Costa this and that. I swear.

"Shitloads of rich bitches out for fresh meat like me, young and well hung," he told me, grinning with the thought of the good times he had.

"Good money, Sam?" I asked him.

"Young bull like me, I was some cut of a man them days, I could name my price. A fee for the job plus bonuses. Dab Hand, I was, Dab Hand!"

I didn't get the joke straight off but when it hit me we had a good laugh.

"Bonuses, what was that about?"

"In the gigolo trade you got into bonuses once they trusted you enough to invite you to stay with them for a few days in their villa or hotel suite."

"Then what?"

"Open sesame, cash and jewellery, old biddies with bags of dollars and diamonds. In like Quinn, help yourself, fuck 'em and fuck off!"

He told a good yarn, made it sound easy. I didn't believe it all but it stuck, the basic idea of it, making the most of your opportunity. That's what Sam said was the most important thing, when the mark depends on you then you have them by the short and curlies.

Mr G trusted me, couldn't do without me I reckon. Probably trusted me enough to think I wouldn't have a look inside the banker's bags.

James sat staring at that last line, sweat trickling off his forehead, trapped in fascination. A tremor shook him, head to toe. "Little bastard," he fumed and went to the phone. As Pedro's number rang, James, exhaling at length, thought better of it. Then he dialled Theo's number, thought better of that too, and put the phone down again.

Chapter Twenty One

"You left a message, sir."

Pedro turned up early. That and the knotted determination on his brow loaded an extra layer of tension on James' aching head. James had not slept well. He wasn't sure how to begin. "Pedro," he began as forcefully as he could muster, stretching his mouth, "Pedro, you and I have been together for quite a while now."

"Five years and five months," Pedro replied and then he paused. "On the day they found the banker, I'd been here five years and five months."

"The banker?" James stared at the fuzz of black hairs protruding from Pedro's open-necked shirt.

"In the river, you remember, not long after I found the bags in the hall."

Those damn bags. "I remember, Pedro, and it was then I decided that we had perhaps reached a new stage in our relationship."

"Yes, Mr G."

Their eyes met. James felt the distinct throb of a vein in his temples and walked to the window to disguise his discomfort. His lower lip quivered. He faced Pedro, who had not moved, the same wily assurance in his steady gaze. "I've been thinking, Pedro, that it is high time to re-evaluate our relationship and the arrangements here. You know how highly I value your services. You have been, you are in many ways my right-hand man and maybe I have not acknowledged that as generously as I should."

"Yes, Mr G." Pedro's relaxed stance seemed accepting of the compliment.

"I want to correct this, this oversight, immediately."

"How much, sir?"

"A further fifty a week."

"Thank you, Mr G. I'll clean up the kitchen shed then."

Miserable rat, he had no business in the kitchen shed. "No need, Pedro, you know I prefer to look after that myself."

On reflection, later, when the headache subsided, James began to feel a crooked gratitude to Pedro, his inadvertent teacher. He now knew he had no alternative; very soon he would have to face a future without the younger man's services. He found himself wishing for some of his mother's clarity, the tenacity of her conviction. Federico and the others. "They had to go, James, they had to go." And then, from no accountable source, came to him a vision of the waitress, two nights ago in the alley, her sudden ignited eyes. She would never know the desiccated crone that lay in ambush for her in old age. He saved her that iniquity. She screamed once, once only before he pressed all the sound out of her. Had she been heard, had somebody intervened, he would not have relented.

That evening he spoke to Theo, convalescing at home after "a sharp intimation of mortality, James." He'd had a heart attack but yes, he'd welcome a visit. Surprising, because he had always maintained an aloofness beneath his habitual courtesy.

"I'll drop by in the morning, Theo."

"A pleasure to look forward to, my boy. Come after the medic has left, ten or so."

After talking to Theo, James felt the advent of a second self, not the needy patient, though he was indeed that, but a better-half who had the potential for friendship. He wished for Theo to get better soon.

He got to work then on a speech to a local business Chamber: a critic's guide to snack culture with particular reference to sushi, tapas and Indian street food. A cloudiness dimmed his mood as he began to write. He did his very best, signed off and poured himself a soothing cognac from whose fumes thoughts of Claudia rose. He was unable to suppress a childish resentment as if he were being neglected. What was she filling her days with and, more important, her nights?

Chapter Twenty Two

Taylor Gibbons saw himself as a policeman of the old school, by which he meant that the problems of crime were solved by methodical, step-by-step detection. He believed in using all the technology available; he wouldn't deny the outstanding modern advances of DNA testing to track down murderers or the latest forensic breakthroughs.

"But at the end of the day it's all about hard slog," he explained to his wife Mabel when he arrived home at the end of another fifteen-hour shift. "There's no shortcut," he confided, in the grave tone that expected to be taken seriously, which Mabel did. Case by case she went through the highs and lows with him, listening to his daily narrative. This latest enquiry had him more upset and baffled than usual.

"Your favourite, dear," she purred, laying a plate of shepherd's pie on the table before him. He ate a forkful of mash and mince, raised his eyes to ponder the flight of a trapped fly on the kitchen window, drank a long draught from the glass of Guinness she had poured for him and said, "It's the suicide, Mabel. Twisted bugger, he was, no doubt about it. But I can't see him topping himself like that."

"The banker chap?"

"Yes, dear, up to his neck in a dozen scams. He had reason to disappear but his kind get so big in their boots they don't kill themselves. All the money makes them feel precious, up on a pedestal looking down on the rest of us."

"You said they found him in the river at low tide. Did the autopsy show anything?"

"Not much, that's what's so frustrating. He'd been in the water a week or so, body in bad shape, tossed about like a cork, stomach completely eaten away by scavengers."

"You're not giving up, Taylor?"

"You should know by now, Mabel, that Taylor Gibbons is no quitter."

"You need help, then?" They both knew exactly where this was leading.

"I could ask Jack Parfrey to have a look at it, I suppose. 'Twould do no harm, get him out of the house. We've worked well together before."

"Give him a call, Taylor. He appreciated your loyalty in the past and he has helped out before."

Consulting his former colleague only prolonged a long-standing dependency; he had for years maintained a fairly successful profile on the coattails of Jack Parfrey's legendary achievements. Parfrey, with Gibbons in tow, had brought several murderers to justice in his twenty five years as a senior investigator with the metropolitan police. Parfrey treated Gibbons as a kind of plodding son requiring paternal guidance. And, even though he was officially retired, he seemed to still enjoy involving himself again.

"You see, Rose," he told his wife when she questioned his willingness to get back in harness again. "I'm a hunter at heart."

In Gibbons' office they went over the detailed report of the investigation to date.

"It looks open and shut, at first sight, I'll grant you that, Taylor."

"It's what I've been saying from the start, Jack. Logically it's a suicide."

Parfrey released his big frame from the office chair that barely held his bulk, stretched his arms wide, bringing his interlocked palms together behind his head, holding that pose for half a minute as if to impose order on his thoughts. While a mute Gibbons watched, Parfrey deposited himself again in the chair, which protested like an abused animal. "There, you've put your finger on it. Logic, as you point out, leads us to suicide, plain and simple and yet you've had your doubts."

"Yes." Gibbons guessed that Parfrey had an idea and he was going to hear about it.

"In the hunt there is no logic, the prey does not run from the predator in straight lines and our killer, if he exists, is not playing by our rules, is he?"

"I suppose not."

Parfrey pulled himself out of the creaking chair once again and, wagging a teacherly finger at the muddled Gibbons, pronounced, "I will not be put off by logic."

"But there are facts that can't be ignored: the banker, Underwood, had strange friends. I've connected him to Manny Johnson and—"

"That creep!"

"Underwood was a closet homosexual and Johnson procured for him. Manny grew up down east, knows all the right places for the likes of Underwood."

"Could have been a lover's tiff, is that what you're saying?"

"I'm not sure, Jack, could be but with Manny involved there had to be major dealing."

"And there was, the money laundering ring that the Americans smashed; Underwood was a player, Frink and himself the European front, before they got the chop."

"Or before they chopped themselves."

"A drowning and a hanging, classic suicides, we're led to believe. I don't buy it, Taylor."

"Maybe they were out of their depth."

"Underwood certainly was!" Parfrey laughed at his own joke and Gibbons joined in, at which point Parfrey became serious again.

"Ok, ok, let's change the perspective. This banker's private life, apart from the seedy side: family, friends, golf club, did he use a gym?"

"Quiet life, fished a bit, lived in a big house by the park, shared it with his wife, the Catalano woman."

"Sergio's girl?"

"Yes, no kids and not much of a marriage." Gibbons consulted a notebook open on his desk. "He lived in the main house and she has a private apartment to the park side, her own entrance. They rarely socialised together. She does some work for the Sercat group, still on the board, travels a lot and has no close friends as far as we can establish."

"A rich, lonely lady. How does she get her kicks?"

Gibbons again consulted his notes. "Fundraising, charity work, giving her name and financial backing to charities her father supported. Works mostly with volunteers, doesn't mix much."

"Affairs, boyfriends, girlfriends? With a pansy for a husband what does she do for sex? She's hardly celibate."

"She's only been seen with one man recently."

"Who?"

"The food writer, Gall. He's on TV, talks a lot. They've met a couple of times in Sercat Central, had lunch together shortly before her husband disappeared. I talked to the hotel manager. Gall is interested in Sergio's life story, wants to write a book."

"James Livingstone Gall." Parfrey enunciated the name slowly as if digesting it. "Now there's a name to conjure with."

"He's got a website," Gibbons announced as he fiddled with a computer. Parfrey hovered behind him. "Let's see, ah yes, had his share of hot dinners; The Ritz, no less, Paris, California." Wide-eyed, they surveyed the man's exotic account of himself, the guides, restaurant reviews and sychophantic comments of noted chefs from the four corners of the globe.

Reading aloud Parfrey called Gibbons' attention to the last two entries, reviews of Korea and Le Gourmet. "You get expenses on this job?" Parfrey inquired of his partner.

"The usual, not much."

"How about a French fry-up at Le Gourmet then, my friend?"

Chapter Twenty Three

Over a week since Felix was found. Claudia wondered how soon she and James could meet again.

That morning she had awoken from a dream which had her climbing a mountain, James just ahead expending inordinate energy, hampered by a wax mackintosh, resembling a gigantic bat. Suddenly the mackintosh was overcome by convulsive spasms, flapped about violently and then dropped into a deep bog hole, taking James with it. Watery seconds preceded the appearance of another body drifting to the surface: a naked man, gliding, weightless, pulling away from her amateurish pace. Almost out of sight, his head swivelled, fixing a pair of enormous hazel eyes on her.

"Felix!"

She did not believe in ghosts, in an after-life, heaven, hell, in any of it. But that was Felix, the eyes as vindictive as ever in life.

"He's dead," she murmured shakily to herself. "Felix is dead, dead, dead!"

Why did it affect her so? The plan to murder Felix she had taken on as she would any thorny project, rationalised its necessity, got on with it and when it was done, with James' help, she had felt released. The couple of nights' jumbled sleep was to be expected. "This you wanted," she continued to reason with herself. "What's done is done. Move on for Christ's sake. Don't be such a baby!"

But after this bloody dream, those fucking eyes, she found herself gulping brandy before breakfast, half a bottle, which she threw up with the remains of the fish from the night-before's dinner. Then she collapsed on the kitchen floor, weeping as she had not wept since her mother died. The morning lost itself. At noon she managed a bowl of chicken soup, cleaned up and called James' number.

"Claudia, my dear, what a nice surprise!" James' voice, his unctuous telephone tone, consoled her. That voice flowed into her, banishing all thought of Felix and his awful eyes.

"James, I have found some pictures you might like to see. An old album, snaps of Sergio and his management team at a European conference, a few rare personal ones on holiday in Croatia."

"What good luck!"

"We could meet?" A side of her wanted him to sense her neediness, another prayed he would not.

"Tomorrow in the afternoon, I have an hour or so to spare."

"Sercat Central again?"

"Afternoon tea, Claudia, how thrilling."

She went back to bed and slept dreamlessly for a couple of hours. In the evening she had an early dinner at Le Gourmet. As maître d' Bernard fussed about she remembered how it had all began here: flirting across the room with James, the sexual innuendo that had set the ball rolling. "For old time's sake," she whispered smilingly to herself, having ordered a main course of osso bucco.

Chapter Twenty Four

James walked into Sercat Central shaking his head in disbelief. What was it about big hotels that had them in never-ending states of refurbishment, workmen in hard hats scaling a convolvulus of scaffolding, the rat-a-tat of jack-hammers, paint peels scattering on carpet and client? Tax breaks, an accountant's bottom line? Such was the racket in the lobby of Sercat Central. He and Claudia sought the insulation of a private residents' lounge to the rear of the hotel. Claudia led him there.

James had kept her waiting, another quizzing from Pedro on a trivial housekeeping matter, more of his recent petulance. He had allowed the impact of the secret notebook to mull until he felt able to be decisive, filed for future action. In a word: procrastination.

Her "You're late!" radiated disapproval, implying that Claudia Catalano expected punctuality. He attempted to placate her. "Today, Claudia, I will dine on humble pie. Forgive me, please." She shook her hair in that prepossessing way of hers. He felt corrected and forgiven.

The genteel parody of a children's play that adults call "Afternoon Tea" (cucumber sandwiches, fairy cakes, fruit cake, miniature scones, clotted cream, preserves, leaf tea poured from silver pots, sugar lumps and milk, lace-frilled serviettes), James and Claudia had choreographed for them by waiters on a table large enough to keep them modestly apart. For the benefit of staff buzzing about, they went through the motions of interview: her recollections of Sergio, the photograph album, James' note-taking.

"Don't you just adore cucumber sandwiches?" she said at one point, eyebrows arching suggestively.

Gradually the service staff stopped fussing and departed. She continued to eat indiscriminately, tempting him.

"I like a woman who is not afraid to show hunger."

She crossed her legs, leaned forward, picked up a fruit scone, busied herself with spoon, jam and cream, looked about to convince herself they were alone, ate a bite, deposited the unfinished confection on a side plate, uncrossed her legs, spread the linen napkin on her lap, raised her head to him and whispered, "I've had the most horrible dreams of Felix."

"Eating too much?"

"Don't patronise me, James!"

"You've lost your husband. Dreaming about dead relatives is not at all odd, Claudia. I dream about my mother all the time."

"This is different," she said with an emphatic shake of the head.

"And it will be different every time you dream of him. You must learn to deal with these ... intrusions as if he were alive. Send him packing!"

"You really think I can?"

He could smell her body odour through a muted veil of perfume. "Despise him in death as you did in life. The same hatred that empowered you before will do the same again."

She lifted the half-eaten scone, extricating raisins with her fingers as she spoke. "I would not wish killing to become a habit."

"Afraid it might?"

"Are you?" Claudia's eyes pierced into him.

"We all have to live with changing fortunes. The only certainty in life is that there is none … except death." He feasted on the yeasty tang of her. "Which reminds me, Claudia, I have that tape which Felix had in his briefcase." The half-eaten scone fell from Claudia's hand onto the plate. "It's in a safe place, my dear. No need to worry."

"That's a relief." Claudia bowed over the table towards him. "We must trust each other, James. Don't you think I should have the tape?"

"You will, it is rightfully yours. But there is one more thing. I'm not able to put my trust in Pedro any more. He knows about Felix."

Startled, she looked around the room again. "What will you do?"

"*We*, what will *we* do?"

"I can't … you can't drag me into this … Pedro's your responsibility."

"In this, Claudia, we are equal. He knows about the shed, found Felix's watch in the garden. Nothing explicit, but he's going to show his hand soon and we need to be ready."

"Police? He may have, has he …?"

"My judgement is that he has not confided in anyone yet. Pedro is a loner, nobody close except a senile mother. I'm not prepared to be intimidated into impulsive reaction. You see, Claudia, he fears me and his fear of me is my greatest ally."

Two polite taps on the door signalled the arrival of the hotel manager Grant Percival, apologetic "for the inconvenience in the lobby, short term but necessary, I'm afraid." He then expressed his condolences on Felix's death. "Awful business, so, so sorry."

Activated by Percival's interruption, Claudia became, with a brusque shake of the head, her father's daughter, a woman of importance. He consulted her about some business matter, after which he hesitated at the door. Addressing Claudia again, he said, "Almost forgot, I had a visit from the police, an Inspector Gibbons. Thought I should tell you. Routine, awfully polite about it, wanted to know when you and Mr Underwood used the hotel. Had to rack my brains, could not recall exactly. The last time you visited with Mr Gall … I told him you were working together, the book about your father and Sercat Hotels. But for the life of me I could not remember when you and your husband last used our services."

Claudia and James remained silent after Grant left; it must have been a minute or more before their eyes met.

She was furious. "Incompetent shit!"

"Indubitably," he said. "But the man responded as any upright citizen would to the routine questions expected in the circumstances."

"It makes me uneasy, James."

He shared her unease, but not wanting to show it, he said, "I wouldn't dignify it with another second's thought. From the police we have nothing to fear. Gibbons, the officer in charge of the investigation, is the perennial Inspector Plod. You've seen him on the news."

"You're right, James, how silly of me."

"Pedro, however, is another kettle of fish altogether. How to charm that snake, dear Claudia, that is our conundrum."

Her face registered a question and the answer, whatever it was, spread itself in a grin which widened and waned. She covered her mouth with her palms. "James, oh my God! You're not planning what I'm thinking you're planning, are you?"

Claudia rushed off to a meeting, which gave James the opportunity to find a quiet spot outside, where he could catch up on a couple of calls he needed to make regarding Pedro's mum and one of Pedro's old prison pals. "Mise en place, Pedro, dear boy," he said to himself as he put the phone in his pocket.

James went from Sercat Central to Theo's for the second time in a week. Theo was pale and drawn but chirpier than last time. "That quiche you made for me, James, rich, so much cream. You don't want to be rid of me, do you, my boy?"

James apologised. "I'm so sorry, Theo. How thoughtless. From now on it's salads, vegetables and pasta. No more cream."

As they chatted, seated on either side of an open fire, Theo's maid, Becky, served tea. Sipping, James studied Theo covertly as he smoked a cigar. He looked like an unfinished drawing of himself, his limbs disproportionately long and thin. He smelled of medicines.

"Don't disapprove, James," he said, waving the fuming cheroot about. "It keeps the smell of decay at bay."

There was something beautiful and heroic about Theo's disregard for personal illness. "I've been reading a food column of yours, that one on low standards in high places."

James chuckled. "Have a look at *The Guardian* on Saturday."

"More low-down on descending standards?"

"And the destructive influence of youth."

"The voice of experience?" retorted Theo.

James frowned. "Quite serious actually, Theo. The regression of standards coincides with a current widely-proclaimed world view that youth per se is the fount of knowledge, a world where adolescence has replaced age as the gold standard of everything."

"Everything?"

"Yes, everything, Theo. Life as a youthful game on an ever-changing screen, push-button distraction, turn off, move on."

"And what, may I ask, James, has this to do with food standards?"

"You may well ask," said James.

"I have," Theo sighed, looking weary.

"Pizza encapsulates this disconnection: flabby pastry, pock-marked with arid olives, clingingly chemical cheese, over-cured ham, tomato pulped to a paste the colour of coagulated blood; nothing that could be described as healthy or fresh, but all of it beating to the pulse of our times; individual freedom mired in a bog of dough, badly cooked and unreliable as teenagers."

"My, my," Theo sighed again.

"Please forgive me, Theo. Although I have given the matter considerable thought, I know I should not burden you with it. Enough of my sermonising. I shall depart and let you rest."

Standing gingerly, Theo accepted a hug, resting his chin on James' shoulder.

Chapter Twenty Five

E ven though Taylor Gibbons' secretary had reserved a table at Le Gourmet for Jack Parfrey and himself, they were required to wait while it was vacated and reset. They waited in an ante-room in the company of half a dozen other intending diners, reading from menus distributed by a middle-aged French woman in funereal black. Were it not for cooking fumes and the exhibition of ornately framed cert-ificates on the walls, testifying to the proficiency of the chef in thick italic, the atmosphere was church-like and the menu cards might have been hymn sheets. Gibbons longed for the comfort of home and Mabel's cooking, whereas his colleague exuded contentment. Parfrey's portliness advertised a weakness for fine fare: fat belly, the blush of wine on cheeks and nose. That he did not share this conceit made Gibbons uneasy; he could never justify expensive dinners in the line of duty. French cooking and snobbery went hand-in-hand as far as he was concerned; his plain-man-of-the-people self-image sat awkwardly in Le Gourmet.

"Relax and enjoy, Taylor. Here's to intelligent investigation."

Gibbons ran a hand over his oiled hair, stretched the fabric of his tweed waistcoat and self-consciously clinked his glass of scotch and water against Parfrey's flute of Kir Royale, feeling, as so often before, that Jack lost the run of himself sometimes. But before this resentment had any space to grow, he had already surrendered to his friend's unorthodoxy, with the help of warming whisky. Raising a white flag again in the face of a menu wholly in French, he tried to rescue some dignity. "If there's a steak, I'll have it well done."

"Hors d'oeuvre?" queried Parfrey, reading from the menu, "oeufs à la Russe, foie gras, mousse de volaille?"

"I'll leave that up to you, Jack."

Bernard took their order and hurried off to the kitchen.

"Nice to see you smile," a bemused Parfrey remarked.

"You sounded like Peter Sellars in the Pink Panther."

With a moue of pretended hurt, Parfrey said, "Give me some credit, Taylor, I speak Français, not Franglais."

Gibbons, in spite of his insecurity, began to absorb the juicy ambience to the extent that, when they sat down to eat, he was experiencing a hunger of anticipation that made him slightly giddy. "I'll have a glass of that," he said, pointing at a bottle of Côtes du Rhône between them on the table. Even as he spoke, the sommelier arrived to open the bottle. Parfrey approved, the wine was poured and they drank. Gibbons enjoyed the cuisine: very mushroomy mushroom soup, tender steak and strawberry ice cream. Parfrey was more circumspect. "Not as sure-footed as I'd expect from a restaurant of this reputation. My mullet was nice, but to tell the truth, Taylor, the fillet of beef suffered from a mugging by red wine and juniper sauce, heavy-handed herbing too; and the orange mousse, what did it remind me of?"

"Baby food?"

"I don't think we should say as much to the maître d'; here he comes," said Parfrey under his breath.

Bernard, navigating through the busy room towards their table, halted in mid-stride, his attention diverted by the arrival of a beautiful woman. The policemen watched as he devoted a performance of sedulous care to this elegant person, escorting her to a small table in a corner of the room, where the ceremony continued: seating the lady, napkin laid gently on her lap, proffer of menu, arch of back, pirouette and retreat.

Parfrey bestowed a wry smile on his friend. "In French restaurants everybody's equal. Except some are more equal than others."

"She's better looking than you are."

Bernard, on his second attempt, came directly to them. Yes, they assured him, dinner was fine, service satisfactory.

"Very attractive lady just arrived." Parfrey's comment, sounding like a prompt, elicited the response he expected.

"Beautiful woman, very beautiful … very sad." Bernard adopted a sepulchral droop of the shoulders, and when the policemen declined to fill the silence, he continued in doleful tones, "Ah oui, sad, very sad. She lose her husband, Mr Underwood, the banking gentleman, a client of us." Bernard's gloom lifted as soon as his presence was required elsewhere.

Jack Parfrey and Taylor Gibbons measured Claudia with professional detachment and the discretion that a bustling restaurant permitted. Next time Bernard came close, Parfrey summoned him with his eyes and he came over to them.

"Mr Livingstone Gall, the food writer, he's full of praise for Le Gourmet. Does he come here often?"

Bernard's eyes lit up. "Ah, oui, Mr Gall is a good friend, he dine every week, most times. Everyone know he write complimentary to Le Gourmet, no?"

"And Mrs Underwood, she's regular too, is she?"

"That I cannot say, sir. We do not excite too many questions of clients; discretion you understand."

When Bernard moved away again to bid goodnight to guests vacating tables on either side of the two policemen, Gibbons felt free to be bold, chiding Parfrey. "You didn't expect him to tell you her life story, did you?"

"No, we know a lot of that already, but it would be helpful to have a peep into her diary."

"We know she and Gall met at Sercat Central. You think they might have been here together too?"

"It's a good each-way bet." Parfrey sipped espresso and nibbled a chocolate truffle.

"Proves nothing, Jack."

"You're right, but my gut tells me we're missing something." Before Gibbons had time to react, Parfrey began again, an earnest expression on his face. "Let's put pressure on Gall, Taylor. Quiz him about the lovely lady, Claudia Catalano, lately Mrs Underwood."

"Why?"

"Because he's a damn snob and anyone with a triple-barrel name has to have skeletons in the cupboard."

"You're not serious!"

Parfrey chortled. "Of course not, Taylor, just probing aloud for your benefit ... and mine."

"Gall has nothing to do with this, Jack. We have to stick to the facts. This is no time for your academic games. We have a possible murder on our hands."

"Two, Taylor, two!"

"Two what?"

"Two murders. Underwood and the other banker, what's his name?"

"Frink, Otto Frink."

Parfrey seemed preoccupied for a moment and when he engaged Gibbons again, he said, "Three, I should have said three. Three potential murders."

"Have you gone barmy?"

Parfrey chuckled and became serious.

"I hope not. Let me explain: let's assume we're talking about murder, only assumption at this stage as we have no proof. However, the simple mathematics gives us three dead bodies on our doorstep in the last few weeks, two bankers and a waitress—"

In rising frustration Gibbons interrupted, "What does the waitress have to do with the other two?"

"Nothing, nothing that is obvious except that it is part of the total. Three dead ones."

"For Pete's sake, we're investigating the deaths of the bankers, Underwood in particular. Let's stay with that!"

Parfrey sighed, pouring the last of the wine. "You're right, Taylor. I'm getting too old for all this concentration."

Too old, my hat, Gibbons thought. Too much red wine more likely. Feeling superior, he said, "Vino loosens the tongue."

"And lubricates the brain; no harm in that, my friend."

They paid and left, seen out into the night by Bernard.

As they sped away in a taxi through half empty streets, Parfrey turned to Gibbons. "Something on the website, Livingstone Gall's, something about an article of his a few years ago, a poisoner's manual or not a poisoner's manual, something along those lines." He paused. "Do you remember that?"

Gibbons reply was succinct. "Don't be daft, Jack!"

"I'll have another look when I get home," Parfrey said.

The taxi dropped both men home, Gibbons first.

Chapter Twenty Six

James noticed that Pedro displayed a new confidence. He scoffed when taken to task in the kitchen about pots of inferior quality he had picked up at a supermarket's spurious promotion. "Pots," James declared, "should have bottoms that can bear reasonable hardship; they have to be firm to take the heat."

"Like Claudia, Mr G?"

Pedro flashed a simian smile that had James momentarily speechless. Monkeys smiled when they were angry. James was not afraid, no, but he chose to truncate the conversation, and with a shrug of indifference, left the kitchen. Pedro, trompe-l'œil that he was, appeared to be what he was not. All day James dwelled on this fact of him being there, his insinuation over the years and now, like a rash of rampant fungus, visibly malign. Sleep came slowly that night; ideas cluttered his thoughts, piecemeal and in unique formulations. Darkness had plans.

A storm was building between himself and Pedro. It had to break soon. Prudence was required. Understanding Pedro, James had sympathy for his position. The circumstances that made Pedro might just as well have been his own; pure accident that he was not servant to Pedro's master. In imaginary transpositions he put himself in Pedro's shoes, felt the burden of unfairness he must feel at his dull lot. Would he, James, take advantage of insider knowledge if roles were reversed? Without question, yes, he would. Therefore it was sensible to prepare for the inevitable.

Pedro laid the tray of morning coffee and shortbread on the table by the desk, obscuring the hard copy of an article-in-progress James had printed for revision.

"Pedro," he protested. "Can't you see what you've done?"

"I know what I've done Mr G, and I know what you've done too."

James sat back, poured coffee, offered him some.

"I'll have a brandy," Pedro said, helping himself to cognac from a decanter.

James beckoned to the nearest armchair into which Pedro flopped, attempting nonchalance.

"I know every inch of this house, Mr G, where you keep everything."

"As you should, Pedro."

"And the shed, the kitchen shed, I have a key." Lifting the glass in an elaborate arc, he drank, wincing as the alcohol hit. Then he lit a cigarette with undue care, waiting for a response, not looking at James. James drained his cup and poured another, stirring in sugar, cream, slowly lifting his eyes to find Pedro blowing smoke rings, following their flight to the ceiling and returning James' gaze. James cleared his throat, speaking slowly, deliberately. "I've been to see your mum. Poor dear, she's not quite, how do you put it ... not the full shilling, is she, Pedro?"

"What the fuck!"

"She never got used to you, Pedro, did she? Keeps calling you Sean for some reason."

Dumbstruck, bravado deserted him. Ash from the cigarette, burning between his fingers, dropped on the carpet.

"I had a chat too with an old friend of yours; fallen on hard times he has, lost his looks, not the dab Hand he used to be. He told me to tell you that, said you could have a laugh at his expense."

In spite of shock Pedro managed a slight smile, his shoulders sagged, head falling to his chest. When he spoke it was a harsh whisper, more to himself than to James. "Sam fucking Hand!"

"Nice man, alcoholic wreck, but a nice chap nonetheless. He remembers your prison days together with amazing recall; fond of you, said you had a lot of talent."

Fidgeting, Pedro reached for an ashtray. Grinding the life out of an unfinished cigarette, he faced James. "Hasn't got me very far, has it?"

"Come now, my man, you have done well, reinvented yourself and carried it off all these years."

"You going to turn me in?"

Haughtily James paced the room, paused to look out the window. He opened it a couple of inches, turned, paused once more. "Absolutely not, Pedro, why should I? You've committed no crime I need to be aware of and what would I do without you? You know where everything is, you've said so yourself. Who'd manage the mise en place? I did at one point wonder how we could continue together. But I'm inclined to think that we could still have a future, you and I."

Some tension, with dwindling cigarette smoke, seemed to exit through the partly-opened window.

"Yeah, yeah." Pedro stared at him. "I'm the only one, apart from Claudia, who knows about the banker."

"I blundered a bit there, should have expected you to find out."

"I played the tape he left behind."

"Thought as much; what did you make of it?"

"As the judge said at my trial: incriminating evidence. Her old man knocking off the opposition. She wouldn't want that to come out."

James rose, topped up Pedro's cognac and walked away from him to the window. His lip had ceased to quiver when he seated himself again. "You could destroy the tape," he suggested to Pedro.

"Yes, Mr G."

James looked hard at Pedro, saying, "You might have a copy for all

I know."

"You have a criminal mind, Mr G." Pedro had regained composure. James could not tell whether it was due to the cognac or just bravado. The element of surprise had stunned Pedro. But only briefly. Now he would surely attack.

"I like it here," Pedro said with a sigh of resignation.

Advantage James! Capitulation deserved magnanimity, James decided. "I could have the spare room done up, open up the shed for cookery classes. You have a flair for it, Pedro, I could teach you."

"I'd appreciate that, Mr G."

"If you wished I could give you writing lessons too."

"You would?"

"We should look out for each other Pedro, neither of us is getting any younger."

"Mum's on the way out. Won't see Christmas, the nice matron says. What do you say we get rid of the tapes, both copies?"

From the breast pocket of his shirt Pedro produced his copy. He extracted the plastic coil, threw it into the fireplace and lit it with a match. Facing James, he said simply, "Your turn, Mr G."

"I think this is really a police matter. Perhaps, Pedro, we ought to let them have mine to, how should one put it, to facilitate the investigation."

"Set her up?"

"It will have to be discreetly done, anonymously, parcel in the post to Inspector Gibbons, the investigating officer."

"What about the money he left with the tape, Mr G?"

"Finders keepers, take it. You do know where it is?"

Pedro had gone off, perky again, seeming pleased with their negotiation. James watched him leave the house and went directly to collect the tape from the drawer in his bedroom, transferring it to a new hiding place behind a couple of loose tiles in the bathroom. He burned the telltale notebook and disposed of the remaining items, minus the cash that Pedro had already pocketed. Out of the fumes

a picture of Claudia rose, witness, James fancied, to what had transpired. He could … should call her but no, not yet. Festina lente!
The whole business had rendered him hors de combat; he decided to
cancel his early-evening reservation at Le Gourmet.

Theo called to let James know he felt strong enough to start regular
sessions again. "What do you think, James?"

Theo requesting his opinion? "You're the shrink, Doctor Hilfer."
He could see Theo smiling at the other end of the phone.

"I believe in the value of the objective assessment, you should
know that."

Unthinking, James blurted, "And you should know I'm not objective on the subject."

Pause.

"You've been good to me, James."

"Works both ways, Theo."

Another pause.

"You'll be taking up where we left off then?"

"I depend on our sessions, Theo. Nothing's changed."

"Splendid," he said and in a lighter tone repeated, "splendid, my
boy."

The old codger, didn't he know James would be back in a flash even
as he sensed (as he suspected Theo did) that illness had overtaken and
replaced any remnant of the "professional" arrangement they shared
up to now? Analytic listening would henceforth be a two-way process.
When James put the phone down, he spoke to it as if still conversing
with his mentor. "What do I feel now? Healthy filial affection, I fancy
you'd call it, Theo."

Chapter Twenty Seven

In order that she and James could continue to meet without suspicion, Claudia suggested to Grant Percival that a review of Sercat Central's latest restaurant incarnation ought to be undertaken by James. The previous quirky café "concept" had failed: For Sale Café, its name and its meaning. Everything to go including furniture, pictures on the walls, the gold-trimmed carte, tableware, linen, glassware, the chef's hat and, as if in afterthought, food and drink. On his only visit James deduced from the restaurant manager's mincing ingratiation that he also had his prix.

Normally Livingstone Gall reviews were independent, for public consumption only. But for Grant and his usefulness, James made an exception.

Naturally Claudia dined with him, sweeping into the newly-named Café International bound in a silky, tight-fitting dress, crimson as her lips. Held by a slight sash at the waist (no zips, hooks, buttons), it was suggestive without being indecent. Puffiness around the eyes betrayed fatigue; Felix, James surmised, his ghost reappearing to sour her sleep. Yet, her femininity shone, promising that paradox of intimacy and damage that James found so thrilling.

"Tell me, James, I have to know about Pedro … haven't stopped thinking about him."

Although he demonstrated no sign of it, her vulnerability aroused him once again.

"As I predicted, Claudia, he showed his true colours. He had a copy of the tape—"

"Oh, my God!"

"We conducted a question and answer negotiation, old-fashioned barter. He told me what he knew and I paid him in kind." He paused, she lowered and raised her head, wanting him to continue. "He destroyed his tape there and then and I intimated that I would pass on the original to the police as a gesture of solidarity with him."

"James!" she gasped. She reached for a glass of water, gulping it down.

"Apologies, Claudia, my little game, bear with me."

"Get on with it!"

"You see, I calculated that in order to neutralise him, I had to get him onside, to make him feel like an insider, which he has never been. He and I together, unity of purpose, that sort of thing. I did, as is my wont, background research, enough to maintain a position of advantage with the scheming Pedro."

"You gave the fucking tape to the police!"

"Wait, hear me out. He knows how close we are. If I could appear to sacrifice you, thus drawing him into an exclusive relationship, he would be effectively where I want him." Here James paused again before breaking into a wide grin. "Of course I didn't give your tape to the police."

With that James took the wrapped tape from his pocket and slid it across the table. Satisfied that it was the real thing, Claudia put it carefully into her handbag, complaining, "You could have told me."

"Tactics, my dear, to buy time. Pedro I had to handle my way."

She was perplexed. "Pedro thinks I am now out of the picture and you and he are some sort of duet, is that it?"

"Exactly, something he's always wished for. I'm a father figure, substitute for the father he never had; his mother is in the depths of senility, dying slowly and no comfort to him. I'm the only family he's got."

"So, James, you are going to tell me what Daddy has in store, are you not?"

"I spoke to Pedro this morning, the upshot of which was that he has decided to take a holiday. He is, at this moment, visiting his ailing mother, availing of the opportunity also to acquaint the matron-in-charge of his plans. He likes her. They get on well. She will be caring in her affirmation; he needs a break."

"We have to eliminate him too, don't we?"

"Darling, Claudia, even as we speak the process is in-train. Tomorrow Pedro has one last strenuous job in the garden. He will be rewarded with a good dinner before I send him on his merry way."

"You won't be needing me?"

"Afraid not, old girl. By now Pedro expects you to be in the clutches of Inspector Gibbons. You turning up tomorrow evening would only present us with unnecessary complication. Don't worry, I can handle him."

Her half-hearted show of disappointment barely concealed relief. The rage that impelled her to murder Felix marked that as a crime passionnel; hatred and sexual jealousy intrinsic to that act could not be replicated willy-nilly. If she were to kill again, James thought, it would only be under the influence of a similar grand passion.

"You've hardly touched your prawns, James," she teased, visibly happier now.

James adopted a high and mighty critical stance, pretending to look down his nose, playing to her gallery. "Prawns awash in chilli and you: two shades of red, dangerous disharmony as close to works of art as Livingstone Gall is likely to be today. As for the goat's cheese: malodorous, magnificent."

"No kidding," she retorted and they sniggered simultaneously like giddy siblings.

In agreement that the cooking at Café International reached no higher than a notch above mediocrity, James began to make suitable notes for his report to Grant. Meanwhile Claudia went to powder her nose. When she returned she paused at his shoulder, apparently reading what he had written, pressing her breasts into his back, murmuring, "When are we going to really meet again?" She ran a limp hand along his neck and sat facing him again, stretching one shoeless leg under the table, brushing his thigh and moving upwards.

"Soon, very soon," he replied, breathless under appraisal of impertinent toes.

"I have suggested to Grant," Claudia continued, "that he ought to commission a comprehensive world-wide examination of Sercat hotel restaurants, which I have volunteered to co-ordinate. We could do it together."

"How perceptive you are. Yes, my dear, we could do it together." As he spoke, he noticed her throat elongate. She slowly withdrew her foot and threw back the last of the wine.

After Claudia left to attend to business with one of her charity project managers elsewhere in the hotel, James sought the chef de cuisine, Gunter, to give him his reaction to the food, as Grant Percival had requested. Gunter did not appreciate criticism, leaving James with a taste of his aversion and an odour, what was it, rancid butter or stale semen? Distaste propelled his thoughts back to Pedro. He went home.

James played the piano for half an hour or more, sipping wine and gradually coming to terms with the forthcoming showdown, when he and Pedro would finally part company. Later he ambled around the house humming a nondescript tune, which was how he sometimes accessed what he wanted to think about. Pedro had gone to visit his mother, giving James another opportunity to peek at his storybook. Oddly it was not stored where he had discovered it before, but instead on the bedroom floor, as if Pedro had dropped it or cast it carelessly aside.

Chapter Twenty Eight

The Story, as Pedro called it, had moved on.

Fucking nutter, Mr G wants me to move in to the house with him. What else will he want if we're sleeping under one roof, weirder he gets and he has the gen on me. He went to some fucking trouble to track down Sam Hand. We must trust one another he says, bollocks to that! He thinks it's all hunky dory. I'll say bye bye to mum and off I go on holidays and when I come back we're a fucking couple. What does he want in the garden anyway that I've not done already? He did for that smart banker, him and his Claudia woman. I may be up for a trip but not in Mr G's wheelbarrow, not bloody likely, no thank you, sir, Mr Gall. I swear.

Been to see Sam Hand myself. Poor fucker, down on his luck, pissed as a newt but still a spark of the old humour. "Sure I told your boss guy about me and you doing time together, why wouldn't I, he bought me shitloads of booze just to listen to my stories … tales of the resurrected?" He cackled, quizzed me with pissy eyes, a big fat grin on his face. "You buy me a brandy I might tell you one!"

He did, more roundabout tales of the women he conned on the Costa del Sol, big, big money and, most of all, how easy it was. "You're still young enough, you could do it I reckon, smartass darkie looks like yours."

He was drunk but he had a point. If I fucked off to Spain I could have a future. Mr G and me, the end of the line. Inspector fucking Gibbons will be fishing no river for Pedro, no way.

Mr G thinks I'm in, him and me cosying up like a pair of faggots. He's always been dodgy but lately I don't like what I see, the way his chops shake and he looks at me different like I was a piece of meat or fish he fancies for dinner. Creepy, I swear. He has to bathe his hands, worries about keeping, how does he say it, maximum digital flexibility? Walks up and down humming like you'd think the house was full of bees. I don't like any of it.

Big bloody deal handing the tape to the cops! That woman Claudia, why should she give a shit what her old man done a hundred years ago? No problem for me to burn the copy I made … only copied it to let him see I was on to him, that's all. No, no cops for me, no thanks. That's the last straw, I'm off … one long fucking holiday, I swear. One sure thing I learned in prison: if a guy gives you the heebie-jeebies get out of the road.

I gave most of the banker's money to Susan, the matron at the nursing home, said look after mum and if I'm not back before she passes on, she knows what to do. Insisted I sign a note, official like, so she has my ok to mind the money and do the best for mum, which she does anyway. Susan, she's a real brick and a looker too, well-stacked for her age. We get on ok.

I sat by mum's bed for an hour, maybe more, told her I had to move on but she was in good hands and I'd be back again soon. That was the only lie I ever told her. She did her smiley, noddy act and when I kissed her she whispered. "Good boy, Sean, tell Pedro he can come home now."

That made me cry, I swear.

Now all I have to do is get the hell outta here fast.

Chapter Twenty Nine

James trusted his imagination more than anyone or anything, sending it off to places he had never been. He'd sent it to restaurants he wouldn't be seen dead in; let imagination stuff itself and bring home the bacon, as it were. Reviews were so often works of fiction that attendance in the flesh might be counter-productive. He could tell a restaurant's quality by the facade, never mind the menu in the window. The point was that sometimes it was good to be in the dark, to be driven by instinct rather than intellect.

The spread of Pedro's toxicity had done its dirty work. He had worn James down. And so his exit excited the heart's applause. Done with him at last, departed of his own accord. Equanimity was not cheaply purchased, however. James had to admit to emotional turmoil when it was clear Pedro had cut and run: devastation, head and belly riding a whirlwind. Gone, Pedro gone, without permission, implying failure on James' part. Of course the little rat had scarpered like his kind do, gone to anonymity like an irrelevant animal. He would replace him in time. Nobody was indispensable, James reassured himself. But his determination to dislike Pedro had the strangely converse affect of accentuating how much he liked the damn fellow.

Claudia was unhelpful. "You should have done as you said you would, get rid of the blighter yourself."

Try as he might to accept the logic of the situation, rage gripped him for days on end, rage at Pedro's audacity, his own sloppiness. He considered alerting the police to Pedro's real identity; in a foolish moment he even convinced himself he could frame him for Felix's murder. He'd track him down, hire a hit man. Wouldn't Manny Johnson get a kick out of that! Eventually a better idea came to him.

A product of institutional planning, the nursing home sat modestly in a quiet cul-de-sac, half hidden from the public road by a line of adolescent willows. Patches of trimmed lawn and clearly defined parking bays encircled the customised red brick building. Over the main entrance a wooden crucifix bespoke suffering and care. The sign to the left of the front door, neatly scripted, read: *Visitors Welcome*.

James reintroduced himself to Matron, the amply built nurse-in-charge, so well regarded by Pedro. "Remember me, old friend of the family, come to see Pedro's mum?"

"Apart from your one visit, Pedro's the only visitor Angela's ever had," she said.

"He asked me to look in on her now that he has left the country."

"Ah, Pedro, a loyal son, lovely man. You know him well then?"

This mild interrogation he understood to be an expression of customary concern. "Yes, he used to work for me." On safe ground and to give her some reassurance, he added, "Last time, Angela remembered me from the old days."

The instinctive kindliness of her nature dismissed any qualms she might have had. Pointing to a corridor with off-white vinyl flooring bisected by a red line, the matron directed James to follow the red line to room twenty-one at the end. "Don't raise your hopes," she said as he started off. "She won't have any idea who you are."

Angela did not resemble her son however carefully James strained to decipher the woman behind the wrinkles that colonised her face. She slept, bird-like in a neat cot, chest heaving in small waves, mouth agape, so feeble that she could, he felt, expire at any moment. He gazed at her for several minutes until she became his own mother in that other hospital bed. He had killed Grace, undetected. Killing was concluded only when one got away with it, the act incomplete on its own. But then again, his mind argued, the survival of some depends on the demise of others. Killing, as Darwin would have it, is a constant, crossing all boundaries. We kill to eat; where would we be without the execution of chickens? Controlling one's fate is always at the expense of someone or thing.

Pedro's mother shifted to the crackle of fragile bones. She opened her eyes, looking about her, appearing to see nothing. A pillow placed and pushed, she'd be dead in a minute, less. James picked up a spare pillow from the end of her bed, held it in wordless consultation with himself and made his decision.

"Well, how did you find her?" Matron enquired when he returned to the reception desk near the entrance.

"Peaceful," he replied. "You were right, she did not recognise me at all."

"That's Angela, knows nobody. Poor dear, she keeps calling Pedro Sean."

James left the nursing home just after one in the afternoon, lighter than when he entered. In sparing Angela he let go of Pedro, the millstone he had become. An exquisite, paradoxical simplicity: saving her, expelled him.

The experience engendered a thirst. He walked a while along suburban avenues, stopping for beer at an empty afternoon pub, empty apart from himself and the owner, whose attention to horse racing on television eschewed social intercourse, demonstrating also a skill heretofore unencountered: the blind pour! He may or may not have been aware that James drank, paid and left.

By now James had a destination in mind for an early evening dinner: an Italian premises not too far from home. La Ciotola served regional Bergamasco dishes. He was an admirer of this honest cooking without pretension, but sounded a warning note to himself as a good critic should: pass on the polenta. Polenta was the overweight soprano of Italian cooking, omnipresent, worthy but forever failing to hit the high note. Was that unfair? Prejudice was always unfair.

A good dinner never satisfied, was never enough. James had felt this way before, striving to make sense of it. The better the meal the less sure one became. Art at the table was as sure to promote unsettling emotions as any other, flicking a switch that turned on the dark, decivilisation in progress, primitivism in the shadows.

He went home, filled the empty decanter with cognac and poured a substantial measure. His reflection saw him in the mirror over the fireplace, and he was stunned at the sight. He looked bloated and therefore felt it.

Outside the night was still holding its breath. James went back to the Tapas bar where the same noisy people as before, or versions of them, toasted one another. More brandy, inferior Spanish. A rumbling tummy led him to the lavatory, a constriction designed for constipated pygmies, unsuited to the call of his bowels. He extracted himself as quickly as he was able, settling his innards with another brandy, ready for the anonymity of the street. On this evening the Hopper diner was busier; Elvis crooned from an old sixties jukebox he had not noticed before: *Love me tender, love me ...*

James stood at the window and when a customer left he caught the whiff of charred meat and caramelising onions. Without thinking, he entered, found a corner table and ordered coffee. A woman came in directly after him, seating herself at the table next to his, her back to him.

"I'll have whatever he's having," she told the waiter, jerking a thumb over her shoulder in his direction. He could see the alley across the street, empty and unlit. When he turned to look at the woman she had discarded the scarf that covered the back of her neck. She was dressed in black and white. An off-duty waitress. He stared at the bare flesh above the rim of her blouse. She was very still, her white neck marred by the red scuff left by the tightness of the scarf and a scatter of moles sprouting tiny black hairs. After she finished her coffee, she draped the scarf loosely over her shoulders, stood to face him, murmuring as she went by his table, "Much obliged, I'm sure."

Through the diner window James saw her cross the street; she paused once to look back and moved slowly into the alley. He finished his coffee, paid and followed her.

When he reached home the swirl of pain in his guts had him reaching for a medicinal cognac and then another. His hands ached. By the time he got to bed, he was very drunk. Dawn found him stretched fully-clothed on the bed, bursting to soil himself, rushing to the bathroom, feeling so vile it was a mystery he was still alive. Ten, fifteen minutes later, he didn't know how long, he pulled up his trousers in a disorderly fashion, shuffled to the sink and turned the cold tap on. The full crescendo of Niagara assaulted his hung-over ears. Every splash stabbed his temples and his skin wept sweat. The sink filled and he dipped his hot head to the cold water, expecting his neck to snap. Cold water doused the fire somewhat. Feeling a fevered relief after repeated immersion, he raised his head, daring to look in the mirror. That's when he saw them: four rusty spots on his shirt, irregular circles of dried blood the size of his undone fly buttons, aesthetically repugnant like splashed paint. Then he remembered the woman from the diner and how her nose began to spit blood as he strangled her.

Chapter Thirty

His first assignment for Sercat Hotels outside of the capital took James and Claudia south to the unimaginatively named South Coast Sercat. In the car they behaved like clandestine lovers on a day out, flirting, sharing jokes, indifferent to everything but themselves, diverted from concerns that lay in wait. At one point she enquired, "Have you been to San Francisco, the most beautiful of all the Sercats?"

"San Francisco, yes, the hotel no. But it is one that Grant listed for a visit. He showed me a sample menu, overblown and wordy; seemed to me it needed an editor as well as a chef."

She flicked a sideways glance at him. "Do you ever stop thinking of food?"

"Sometimes, if the company is good enough."

"Let's go, James. California, just us, away from here."

"Yes, Claudia, though America is so medieval these days."

"Medieval should be right up your street." For a while she drove in silence, each of them lost in thought.

He thought of her and why he found her so appealing. Claudia was always herself, making up for inherited wealth, the tainted legacy from Sergio. So different to me, James thought. That and her body aroused him. He knew that she knew it, letting him stew a little, laughing, flashing her eyes as if she was nervous, which she was not.

She ground to a halt outside a roadside inn, pulling in sharply to a tarmacadamed car park. Shaken by the suddenness of it, he remonstrated with her. "Damn it, Claudia, you don't have to prove your joy-riding skills to me!"

"I know this place. Sergio brought me here for lunch shortly before he was killed."

Inside James chose a table while she wandered between the heavily-timbered recesses and alcoves of the old inn, resurrecting memories of her last visit. They went outside, strolling hand-in-hand by a stream that ran through woodland, chatting easily about nothing of importance. Back at the inn she went to the bar, telling James over her shoulder, "This is on me."

When she rejoined him she said, "You like killing people, don't you?"

James noted her habit of surprising him with questions that were not questions. He did not feel compelled to reply directly, lifting his glass and taking a long draft, replacing it carefully on the beer mat provided. "How well did you know your father?" he asked.

"I loved him."

"Did he like killing people?"

Hesitant, she looked down at the napkin in front of her, fiddled with it, allowed herself half a smile before replying, "Yes, James, I think he did."

"More than once?"

"Probably."

"Is that why you're attracted to me?"

"Because you're a murderer?"

"Because I like it."

Again she hesitated, "Probably." She moved her chair closer to his and one of her hands began to commune with his thigh.

"Because you're so incredibly rich," he said, "you think you have the right to possess anything, anyone."

She held her fork in the air, waving it about, a weapon of emphasis as she responded, "Wealth works!" He was about to offer his opinion when she interrupted. "You have private means apart from the writing and TV?"

"Some, my mother invested well, left me comfortable."

"With Sergio's money."

This was news to him. Her hand abandoned his thigh, moving away. She continued, "Yes, James, I have the bank statements. She milked him successfully and the irony is that he didn't care, he was so fucking infatuated."

"She loved him," he suggested.

Brushing her hands in a backward action through her hair, her rebuff was brief. "Love? Grace?"

Pause. He sensed there was more to come.

Dripping disdain, she said, "You should know."

James did know; she knew he knew. Conflicting emotions shut them up. Tears, hers, fell freely and he almost cried in sympathy. When their eyes met it was a kind of truce. Shouldn't they let Sergio and Grace go, leave them behind?

They booked a room and spent the afternoon and that night at the inn, not quite dismissing the ghosts that infiltrated the tousled sheets of their lovemaking. Lust let them off the hooks of reason and the deeper, telling search of each other, skating the surface rather than delving beneath shadow and secret.

Lying awake, James watched Claudia sleep, the curving swan's neck, her warm body touching his. He realised, in no apocalyptic manner, that she was far, far from him; he would never get to know her, and he too meant so little to her. Yes, she flattered him; they were equally expert at flattery which, in itself, was nothing, had no value except in the immediacy of its narcissism. They were present as audience, one to the other. Extraordinary that they had shared a dinner table, made love, killed a man, made love again, dipped into the complicated history that bound them and dipped into it once more without understanding or resolution. They could not hide who they were for long but on that night at the inn, behind the fervent pretence, their masks remained intact. At that time, in that lapse, they behaved without a hint of prescience. As dawn crept in to the beamed room, James remembered a cat his mother had and how he had cornered his prey with stunning swipes of his paws, playing with it for hours before it died of exhaustion or moped in limbo between torture and dispatch. Like the remorseless tom, James felt completely in charge. Certainty strengthened as he drifted into post-sleep doze where thoughts tumbled through realistic dreams.

Chapter Thirty One

Jack Parfrey breezed into Taylor Gibbons' office at police headquarters, sprightly and beaming. "Top of the morning, Taylor, how grind the wheels of justice this fine day?"

"You're in good form," Gibbons said, assessing his partner.

"After all these years, at my advanced age, I've discovered the secret of life."

"Porridge," said Gibbons, without raising his eyes from a file on his desk.

"Porridge?"

Gibbons looked at Parfrey. "Porridge for a long and healthy life, that's Mabel's philosophy."

"I'm sure Mabel has a point, bless her, but porridge is not in the same league as yoga for health and relaxation."

"You're not serious, Jack, with a body like yours?"

Self-consciously, Parfrey stiffened his chest and attempted to contract his bulging belly, inhaling deeply. "A body like mine benefits more than most: breath control, simple meditation, specific postures and, most important of all, spiritual discipline."

"Last time I remember you talking like that you had taken up poker."

Gerry Galvin

"That was different, yoga is not a fad." Businesslike again, Parfrey enquired. "Developments, Taylor?"

"Forensics went through Underwood's house again, found nothing of value except a hidden safe, his prints, a lot of cash: dollars, sterling, euro and ..."

"And?"

"Pornography, disgusting pictures, males, all males including Underwood himself."

"Home movies," Parfrey said grimly. "Anything else?"

Gibbons sorted papers and picked out a batch. "The bank eventually came up with Underwood's account statements, which tell us nothing except that his respectable front was no different from that of any other banker in town."

"Credit cards?"

"Usual range of purchases."

"Le Gourmet among the restaurants he used?"

They pored over the credit card statements together until Parfrey broke the silence. "Three to one Le Gourmet."

"So what?"

"Le Gourmet keeps cropping up, doesn't it?" Parfrey shifted uncomfortably in his chair, speaking as he faced his colleague. "Been through all the files on this, asked myself what's the history here? Where do these people, Underwood, Claudia, Frink, where do they come from?"

"I think we can forget about Frink, Jack, the Germans have that in hand."

"I agree. Which leaves Mr and Mrs Underwood. Who are they really?" Sure of himself, he continued. "Felix is straightforward, a career banker-cum-fraudster ever since he joined Bellingham as a nineteen-year-old. Clever, bloody clever, deceived everyone, moved up steadily until he more or less had a free rein, associated with known criminals and seemed to lead a charmed life until the FBI blew the laundering operation wide open and Underwood became a liability."

"Like Frink, he knew too much."

Parfrey nodded, proceeding with his analysis. "So they, the bank big boys, took the necessary precautions."

"To protect themselves by silencing the likes of Underwood and Frink."

Parfrey opened his palms wide. "Quod erat demonstrandum."

Gibbons appeared quizzical. "Back where we started," he said.

"Not quite, Taylor. You've been investigating this because you are not satisfied that Underwood committed suicide. Who might have benefited from killing him? Obviously the bank, someone in the underworld he may have double-crossed, like Georgie The Godfather, The Calder Gang, Manny Johnson, a jilted lover or his wife?"

"We've been over all that ground, you know that," Gibbons said.

"I've had another look at Claudia, the wife."

"And what's new?" Gibbons was becoming impatient.

"Her father, Sergio Catalano. Guess who he was having an affair with at the time he was found dead in Croatia?"

"I think you're going to tell me."

"He and his maid, found dead on a beach from some obscure food and alcohol poisoning, signed and sealed as an accident. Sharing the holiday villa with Sergio at the time was his then girlfriend, Grace Gall, mother of James Livingstone Gall, writer, broadcaster, critic, recently seen in the company of a certain lady. There's more. I discovered that Grace Gall's husband died in a boating accident not long after James was born. Old Bill Maxwell, you remember him, he was the officer investigating at the time and he told me he had his own suspicions that Grace might not have been the innocent young wife she appeared to be. Interestingly, Percy Gall's drowning was alcohol-related and he, like Sergio, had recently consumed a seafood dinner."

"You're not implying that Gall's mother had a hand in Underwood's death from beyond the grave," Gibbons said, shaking his head in disbelief.

"Talked to a few people around where she lived. She was an outrageous oddball and the local consensus is that her son is cut from the same cloth. After her husband died she had men in the house, living with them, several different guys and you know what, Taylor?"

"What?"

"They all disappeared."

Gibbons snorted in scorn. "Why don't you dig up the back garden while you're at it?"

"I would but the house and property was sold off for development a while back. Now there's a high-rise apartment block on the site."

"That's the end of that then."

Parfrey did not appear to be listening. "I've traced the sister of one of the men who stayed in the house."

"And who might that be?"

"Federico Cellini, a drifter of Italian extraction. Hung around food markets, dabbled in organic gardening, part-time cook and Romeo. His sister posted him missing after he failed to contact her one Christmas. He always spent Christmas with her family. She hadn't heard from him in six months and never heard from him again. Last seen in the Gall house."

Pause. Gibbons had given in, he listened.

"There were others coming and going, a butcher, who delivered to the house, said he remembered seeing at least three different men at different times living with Grace Gall and her son. Live-in lovers, he called them."

"You think her son James and Catalano's daughter might be able to help us on this one, Jack?"

"More feeling than logic, Taylor. Enough to require them to help us with our enquiries."

"Ok, I'll set it up."

"Get him in first."

"Remember our golden rule, Taylor. Never—" They'd been through this routine many times previously.

"I know, Jack. Never ask a question to which you do not already know the answer."

As the detectives were about to leave the office, they met a uniformed policeman on the way in. He handed Parfrey a sheet of paper. "You requested this, sir."

Gibbons watched Parfrey spread the foolscap page on the desk and asked, "Who's that?"

"The second waitress killing, you remember, a couple of weeks ago. Man seen exiting the alley around the time she was murdered. I asked for an identikit picture."

"Same guy as the first?" Gibbons asked.

"Looks like it."

Chapter Thirty Two

So far Claudia believed she had her way with James, he did her bidding. He was charming and wonderful company, in and out of bed. Useful too, still useful. Grant Percival and the board of Sercat Hotels were so pleased that the JLG imprimatur would be available. Even Sergio would have grudgingly admitted that Sercat Hotels were not renowned for their restaurants. Claudia pressed Percival to produce an itinerary for James quickly so that they might be on the road together soon.

In other circumstances she could see herself in an open relationship with James; she imagined what it might be like if they were married. They had so much in common. But the old loyalty to her father and hatred of that incorrigible woman, James' mother, brought her back to where this started. She argued with herself, feeling horridly guilty and quite confounded by opposing desires. James might be unlucky but he inherited his responsibility in the same way she had inherited hers. If there was one thing Sergio Catalano believed in it was duty. Sergio's belief was hers, whether she liked it or not.

And yet in another sense, the price for Sergio's death had already been paid. Although she would never be able to prove it, she was convinced James had poisoned Grace, dealt with his terrible mother for his own reasons. Wasn't this enough, she asked herself, almost speaking the words to her absent father. Wasn't it time now for her to have her own life?

James was no model man. Dear God, no! Quite weird really, wobbly lips and the way he kept flexing his fingers like a bookie at the races, very odd. She had watched him admire himself in mirrors, preening, gleaming. So dazzled by himself. Comical. That night in the inn on the way to the coast, he caught her giggling as he posed and he was not amused. How quickly he let the shell of charming James slip! Oh dear, she saw the change: Jekyll and Hyde. He is two persons, she thought, and I know one well, with glimpses of the other. Occasionally she thought they were glimpses of Felix.

She supposed she could get used to all that if she wanted to. If she wanted to. Jesus! They go to the extreme of dumping Felix in the river and apart from infrequent sex they behave like middle-aged marrieds in the presence of an unseen chaperone, their relationship in a suspended state of withholding, keeping commitment at arm's-length.

James' surprises were not always welcome. On the trip to the coast he had asked her, quite out of the blue, if Sergio liked killing people. She had to hide her shock and then noticed that he was so taken with the question that he failed to notice her discomfort. She blushed, which was a sign not of embarrassment but of fear. So close to the bone, that question might have indicated that James was more informed about Sergio's real record in the murder stakes. Maybe. She just did not know for sure and was not going to press him on it.

What she herself had found out about Sergio came in bits and bobs from her mother. Hints mostly, but once or twice her mother had let her guard down about Sergio after he had been really nasty, flaunting other women in public or running down her family. One day when Claudia was seven or eight, she witnessed a terrible row. He'd just spat some horrible Italian swearword at her and for once she stood up to him; one word she said, one word loud enough for Claudia to hear (she would never forget it). Mafioso! Sergio hit her mother with the back of his hand across the face, the force of it knocking her to the ground. Bloody-nosed but defiant she stood to face him and in the calmest, dramatic voice said, "Yes, Sergio Catalano, kill me too, like all the others!"

He left in a rage and didn't come home for days and, when he did, he made up to his wife with flowers and the magnetism of his personality. How Claudia loved him when he was able to turn around her anxiety and sadness. Her child's mind did not take it all in then, but it returned to remain a fixture in her memory. Much later, after her mother's death, he and Claudia became friends, so much so that she felt she could talk to him openly, quizzing him about her mother's outburst. "Was it true what she said about killing, Papa?"

"What did she say? I don't remember."

"Kill me like all the others."

"Did she say that?" He seemed surprised. "If she did, she had her reasons; your mother always had good reasons, even if she was wrong."

"She was so sure. Is it true?"

He shrugged expansively, held his head to one side and then the other. "Claudia, I do not lie to you but I cannot make accounts of everything I've had to do in my life; I am a businessman and a businessman does the business, many times nice and easy, sometimes not so nice." He gave her the benefit of his mischievous grin and she asked once again, "Is it true, Papa?"

"For your ears only, Claudia Cara, it is true."

They never discussed it again, nor did she want chapter and verse. He had murdered more than once. That was part of her heritage. If Sergio could do it and get away with it, so could she. What did she care what James knew or didn't know? She had no intention of being anybody other than Claudia Catalano. He could take it or leave it.

Chapter Thirty Three

James endured a morning full of Grant Percival's nit-picking: Hong Kong before or after Singapore, interminable questions. Argy-bargy, tedious, but James wore him down. He left Percival in no doubt that the contract with Sercat Hotels did not inhibit professional freedom. In simple terms, James had his way. The adrenalin rush of a deal well-done, could not, however, account for the disequilibrium of not being sure who he was, feeling victimised by some unidentifiable hoax.

Lunch at Joe Chang's in Warbrig Street set him up for that afternoon's appearance on a TV panel discussing current culinary waves and the chefs who surf them. He'd appeared on Maybee O'Hara's show before, knew that despite their torrid affair many years ago, there was no love lost between them. She wanted him on solely to taunt him, trap him into making an ass of himself. He enjoyed the opportunity to lead her up the garden path. Their mutual hostility produced diverting television for a bored afternoon audience. James knew what she was up to and had promised himself never again to play Maybee's silly game, but the invitation to perform was too much to turn down. This afternoon's appearance only confirmed yet again what he knew already. She had the presenter's aptitude for exciting interest rather than searching truth; completely false, but he had foolishly accepted again and felt rotten afterwards.

Thoroughly downcast, he went straight home, called Theo, whose unanswered phone rang out a refusal. The house, without Pedro, held no warmth. He lay down and tried to sleep but could not erase the TV images flickering before his eyes. He got up, showered, exercised and dressed for a night out. On the point of leaving, his hands began to shake uncontrollably and he had to bathe them for almost an hour. Shivering, he changed clothes, covering himself with an ankle-length overcoat he had not worn for some time. He tried to remember the last time but couldn't. As he left the house the sounds of the street rushed up as if they had been waiting for him. Peter from the pastry shop paused to greet him as he closed down for the night and a new moon lit up the road in a shiny grey. James hailed a cab, whose driver, intuiting ill humour, remained silent until they reached their destination.

James did not expect changes at The Butcher's Arms: same bulging barmaid, blackboard menu, the cloud of static menace above congealed odours of stale food, disinfectant, bad breath, unwashed bodies, rank clothing, urine and beer. An inner eye spied on him. Why he was here he dared not ask. He sought the darkest corner with a bottle and a glass, fighting nausea with alcohol, filling his lungs with foul air, head swimming, nostrils flaring, sweat trickling from chest to belly and between his legs. The place possessed him, easier to yield than to resist. Like surrender to a medical procedure or scientific experiment, he was traumatised by a process beyond understanding and then gradually reawakened.

The pub sprang into life: a frozen movie, reactivated. Two drunks slobbered on barstools, a brawny youth clad in jeans and cutaway vest shovelled pasta into his face; on a raised dais musicians fiddled with instruments; the barmaid shrieked an obscenity at two off-duty waitresses sitting at the counter.

"And fuck you too!" One of them answered back, kicking at a

stool and knocking it over on her way out; the other moved away from the counter and found an empty table close to James from which proximity a raft of moral flotsam floated. She had marked her territory and he was in it. He tried to be revolted. Smeary lipstick, drooping face, mouth half-open, dyed hair protruding beneath a red and white striped woollen hat. The band began to pound out hits of the sixties. The temperature rocketed. He had to unbutton his shirt beneath the overcoat.

Chapter Thirty Four

James had no idea how he got home, waking to the telephone ringing at nine o'clock the following morning. Susan, the matron from the nursing home. Took him several seconds to come to. Pedro's mother had passed away in the night. He sympathised and found himself agreeing to search for Pedro.

"You are the only hope I have, Mr Gall."

"I'll try," he said, not having the slightest idea where Pedro might be or how to track him down or why he had consented to try. Remorse or a morning-after fit of sentimentality. As it turned out Pedro was not so difficult to find. Sam Hand suggested the Costa del Sol, even supplying the name of a pub in Fuengirola where Pedro might be known. James called the pub and left a message for Pedro to contact Susan at the nursing home.

After Angela's internment, Susan took them back to the home: James, Pedro, a doctor, nursing staff and Sam Hand, looking like an emissary of death, dressed up in shirt, jacket and tie, pale and twitching for want of a drink. Death broke barriers and so it was then. James embraced Pedro and they both embraced Sam. Goodwill circulated on silver trays of tea, ham sandwiches and homemade buns. Susan made a little speech eulogising Angela, which made Pedro sniffle. Sam wept openly, cup and saucer rattling in his hands. Handshakes exchanged, exhortations and promises to keep in touch. Sam had to have a drink. James needed one too. The Butcher's Arms again. Pedro insisted on paying. Involuntarily James searched the pub for signs of his previous visit. Nothing, nobody. A barman he had not seen before greeted and served them, acknowledging Sam, ignoring Pedro and James.

Sam accepted the lacuna like a prisoner on the run, drinking steadily. In a short time he ran out of bluster, stumbling into incoherence, while Pedro and James competed, drink for drink, warily, with stern application. Their conversation softened, growing gradually liquid. Pedro let out his gratitude. "I didn't expect you to be there, Mr G. Susan told me you called to see Mum before." Shaking his head, he repeated,"I didn't expect it."

"Have you a place to stay?" James asked.

"Probably get a flight back to Malaga tonight."

He looked like an abandoned waif and all James' paternal feelings came flooding back. He found himself saying, "You *are* welcome to stay with me, Pedro."

As if it was the most obvious of outcomes, without hesitation he replied, "Sure, that would be good."

"The prodigal's return," James said, patting him on the shoulder.

Whereas Sam's intoxication disabled him quickly, Pedro and James drank on in a state of impenetrable sobriety, enabled by the enormity of what confronted them. Reconciliation, but not merely reconciliation. They got a taxi home and James cooked a beefy bolognaise, further indication of his moderating attitude. Pedro was always open to spaghettification. They had wine and cognac and Pedro asked permission to smoke. Later, having wished one another good night, they had a moment of indecision, mutually felt. After the drama, the brave face and the beaten path.

"It's good to be back, Mr G."

That was it, Pedro re-employed without formality. James no longer found his "Mr G" offensive. Rather it betokened maturity and tolerance between them.

James had let the house go. Pedro set about putting it to rights. Having cleaned inside, he turned his attention to the garden and the sheds. Both sheds.

"Your lab, Mr G, been busy, you have."

"No more than usual, why?"

"Mud on the floor, dirty knives in the sink, manhole cover out of position. You must have been in a big hurry to get out of it."

James was genuinely puzzled. He had not been in that shed for over a week and was quite sure he had cleaned up as usual. Pedro had tidied carefully, no signs of mud or displaced equipment, when James went to check, everything ship-shape. It was only when he was on his way out that he saw them: the overcoat and the woman's striped hat hanging side-by-side on two hooks inside the door. Slowly the events he had somehow obliterated from his mind re-enacted themselves: following the woman from the pub, negotiating with her. Leaving the taxi together three blocks from home, walking the rest of the way. More drink, luring her to the shed. He had been right to let the river have her. Now he lifted the manhole cover once more, dropping coat and hat into the rushing water.

"Are you alright, Mr G?" Pedro had all the silver spread out on the kitchen table and he was immersing it, piece-by-piece, in silver dip, washing, drying and shining as he went along.

"I have to admit, Pedro, not feeling too good. Too much to drink recently, old liver playing up."

"Sit by the fire and I'll get you a Bovril."

He did as bid, horror skulking behind righteousness, justifying and quaking with fear in the same breath. He had killed several times before but this was a sinister departure. If memory let him down, he was putting himself in danger. Stay sober in future; sober he would not let his guard down. Delayed shock laid him low: diarrhoea and excruciating hand pain exacerbated by depression. Pedro nursed him over three terrible days. On the fourth he recovered a semblance of normality. The kitchen, Pedro's domain, emanated warmth. They sat facing each other, Pedro poured coffee. James checked the mail and asked, "Calls, anything important?"

"Several." He consulted a loose sheet anchored by an ashtray in the centre of the table. "Maybee O' Hara would like to meet you as soon as you have a morning free; a Mr Percival said you'd know what he was calling about; Gibbons, Inspector Gibbons wants you to return his call as soon as possible, and a funny guy, called himself Manny, says it's about time you had a drink together."

"Manny, funny, what's so funny?"

Chortling, Pedro said, "When I asked, 'Manny who?' he said to tell him many's the drink he owes me."

"Gibbons, what did he want?"

He looked at his notes again. "Didn't say."

"That's it Pedro?" James asked while wondering about Claudia, why she hadn't called.

"Yes," Pedro replied with an air of finality.

James returned calls to Maybee and Grant Percival immediately, wrote a short introduction for Gunter Gruber's new book, breaking for a comforting bowl of Pedro's vegetable soup before facing up to the two outstanding calls.

Gibbons, sounding gruff, insisted that he and his partner needed to talk to him. No, he would not go into detail over the phone, but yes it was urgent. Ten tomorrow morning in his office.

James put the phone down. "Manny Johnson can wait," he said aloud, "I'll call him tomorrow."

Pedro, previously preoccupied, suddenly erupted. "Johnson, Manny fuckin' Johnson!" He looked up, eyes leaping in bemusement. "You know *him*, Mr G?"

"And he knows me." James explained the restaurant connection and loose friendship.

Pedro was unimpressed. "Bad egg, ask Sam."

"Manny has his uses," James protested.

"All bad. Guy like him has no conscience. Shot his own father, he did. Him and his brother, shot him dead, stood over him, the two of 'em did, like two rotten peas in a pod, one worse than the other. Just like me and my brother, I swear."

"I can manage Manny, Pedro. We understand each other."

"Shot him dead in a crowded pub and you know what, Mr G?"

"What?"

"Police couldn't find one witness. Dead body in the bar and nobody saw nothin'!"

"I know, I know, he's a disreputable thug but he has been helpful to me before and may be again."

"What's in it for him?"

"Maybe he enjoys my company."

Pedro looked sceptical.

"Look here," James said, "I'm no innocent abroad. I have an affinity, an empathy with Manny and his kind. He has no qualms about what he does, is completely transparent unlike so many supposed stalwart citizens." He wanted Pedro to understand him as he understood Manny. "Manny is a complete shit. Don't think I am not aware of that. But so am I, Pedro. We have a lot in common."

"He kills people, Mr G!"

"And so have I, you know that." He let that fact sink in to Pedro's consciousness, observing its assimilation. Pedro knew already but this time he heard James admit it. His cheeks puffed up, the breath of comprehension escaping in a low whistle through his lips. James continued, "Manny and I invent our own self-serving worlds and fill them up with contraband. He robs banks, shoots people and invents alibis. I'm a writer; I steal ideas and make things up. Ultimately we share the most potent trait of all: the killer instinct, which in our case is no sporting euphemism."

Pedro washed his hands in the sink. "I shot an old geezer, me and my twin brother." He went on to relate his experience of prison and how he stole his brother's identity.

Floodgates: he confessed his attempts to turn Felix's disappearance to his advantage, his distrust, fear and in the end how he had fled, dreading James and a police investigation that would surely uncover his real identity. He told how he had found that Sam Hand's rose-tinted recollections of Spanish fleshpots had no relevance in modern Costa del Sol; soft-centred sleaze had mutated to hardcore crime. Mafia types with guns in their pockets for everyday use; no place for Pedro, whose criminality survived only in the guilty crannies of his memories.

"You've paid your debt, Pedro, no need to run away any more."

"Thanks to you, Mr G."

"I'm afraid the tables have turned somewhat. I'm the fugitive now. Some day I may need your help." James stopped short of disclosing his more recent foray in the dark. Unable to comprehend it himself, he could hardly rise to the task of explanation to a third party, not even Pedro.

In the morning he'd facilitate the police. He called Claudia to alert her to this and, when there was no reply, he toyed with leaving a message but thought better of it. What she did not know would not trouble her.

As Pedro had left for the rest of the day, James treated himself to coffee, a baguette and warmed chocolate. He dipped craggy bits of baguette into the dark Valhrona and gulped it down. Droplets fell and clotted on the white table cloth. Later, showered and changed, he sat in the drawing room to read *The Whole Beast: Nose to Tail Eating* by Fergus Henderson, a book that had often provided refuge, the grounding James craved in a crisis. He read the introductory paragraph of a recipe for Duck Neck Terrine and dozed off between Ham in Hay and Rolled Pig's Spleen.

Chapter Thirty Five

Policeman Parfrey was a prime prospect for one of those instant, keel-over heart attacks that low-fat diets purported to circumvent. James was wary of his ilk; they invariably compensated for flaws in one facet of existence by dogged discipline in another. Fat policemen, he suspected, succeeded where their thinner fellows failed. Something to do with the confident course of blood through veins, fats and sugars fast-forwarding solutions to the brain. Those were his thoughts as he seated himself before the policemen. Barely able to restrain the pulse of nervous levity that pulled strings in his mind, he put on a serious face.

Gibbons played teacher while Parfrey studied James obliquely.

"In the course of our investigation into the death of Felix Underwood, late of Bellingham bank, we have had reason to research into the background of those closest to him: his wife, colleagues, acquaintances and your name has come up." He paused as if expecting a response and, when he did not get one, he stole a glance at Parfrey, cleared his throat and might have continued if Parfrey hadn't butted in.

"How well do you know Claudia Underwood, Mr Gall?"

"I have some interest in the lady as Claudia *Catalano*."

"Some interest?"

"We are engaged on a project together."

Parfrey stuck to his guns. "Casual or close?"

"I have not got round to categorising the relationship, but I would not call it intimate. We work together."

"What kind of work?" Gibbons asked.

Safe ground.

At length James described his work as writer and commentator and how, over many years, he had observed the growth, worldwide, of Sercat hotels and particularly the phenomenal energy and acumen of its founder and managing director, Sergio Catalano. Recently James had undertaken a book on the meteoric rise of company and founder, and interviewing Catalano's only offspring presented him with a golden opportunity to research the protagonist from the inside. "I regard the meetings I have had and those still to come as vital aspects of my mise en place for this project."

Together Gibbons and Parfrey parroted, "Mise en place?"

"I do beg your pardon, gentlemen, mise en place is a French culinary term to describe preparatory work, problems anticipated."

"Homework," grunted Parfrey.

"In a sense."

It went on like that, becoming clear to James that these policemen were embarked on a fishing trip, not very well planned and based mainly on Parfrey's intuitive proposition that James had some role in or knowledge of Underwood's death. Flimsy, hit and miss. Obvious too was that Parfrey didn't like James, his moral nature instinctively at odds with the ambiguity James represented. James had to admire Parfrey's honest uprightness but saw also that such earnestness was no match for a chameleon like himself. In brief, Parfrey and Gibbons played by rules he would never be bound by. All their accumulation of information regarding Grace and Sergio, Grace and her men, all to no avail. They hunted ghosts and ghosts did not willingly line up for scrutiny. Fortunately his indisposition of the three days previously had passed, and in the hour or so with the policemen his old assurance asserted itself. James denied knowing Felix Underwood or having any connection with his bank, and when Manny's name came up he outlined his marginal professional association with the Italian and his former restaurant. James knew what they were at, making him aware of the direction of the investigation, the thread of slack connections between Felix, Claudia, Manny and himself. There was no point in protest. If he was innocent why would he be intimidated?

Gibbons terminated the interview briskly, as if authority was his. "Thank you for coming in, Mr Gall."

"Delighted to be of assistance, gentlemen."

There was a knock on the door. An officer in uniform entered, flourishing a black and white drawing, holding it in front of his chest for all to see. Crude, James thought, yes, crude but a likeness nonetheless of someone familiar. Parfrey thanked the officer, handed the drawing to Gibbons. "Better, that's better, Taylor. We're getting closer." Turning to James, he said as he gestured at the drawing, "Mise en place, Mr Gall."

James had to walk through a working, open-plan office to get to the entrance lobby, where another uniformed policeman was tacking notices on a wall already festooned with posters and pictures of the lost and wanted. Among photographs of missing persons he recognised the woman in the striped hat from The Butcher's Arms (head and shoulders with her name, Magda Reborov), and next to that a copy of the identikit drawing he had already seen. James didn't have to give it a second glance to know why it looked familiar. The face in the drawing resembled Grace. He looked away lest he appear unduly interested. When he did steal another glimpse, it was not his mother he saw but himself.

Chapter Thirty Six

When James admitted he had read the story in Pedro's black book, Pedro looked at him in wide-eyed surprise. "Ah, so I left it behind me."

"Yes. Careless of you, Pedro. I found it on the bedroom floor."

"No problem, Mr G. I bought another one at the airport." He hesitated and asked self-consciously, "Can I write, Mr G?"

James was surprised by Pedro's need for approval rather than embarrassment at the notebook's disclosures. "Beautifully, Pedro, I can't wait for more."

Beaming with pleasure Pedro ran to his room and returned with his new journal, handing it to James, who felt compelled to read the next installment there and then, Pedro peering over his shoulder.

Spain. Disaster. I swear.

Sam Hand gave me phone numbers, the name of a pub and filled my head with notions. The Merry Ploughboy, that was real, all the rest bullshit. The landlord needed a barman and I got the job. At least I had money coming in and a room over the pub. Fuengirola is like Brighton with sun, everything else is the same, fights after closing time, Chinese restaurants, vomit. Couldn't take it.

Guy comes into the pub for a morning cure, has a yacht, needs a cook.

I told him I cooked for a famous food writer and he says, "Week's trial, mate, if you don't cut the mustard, you're fish food."

"Fish food?"

He squinted at me, eyes like pissholes in the snow. "Yes," he said, "shark meat!"

I got the message and another job I could have done without. Sailed to North Africa, Morocco or some place, never landed nowhere. Two black fellas in a dingy delivered canvas bags like coal sacks and we sailed back to Marbella. Never found out if my cooking cut the mustard. We were all arrested for drug trafficking. Word came that mum had died and they said ok I could go.

Susan told me Mr G was the main man, he visited mum, kept in touch, tracked me down. Gobsmacked, couldn't believe it. I swear. The man had a heart. I know what side my bread's buttered on. I know, I know, he's a crazy guy. Two guys really. He was very sick for a few days, like an old man, no life in him and then he gets up and he's big-mouth, action man, lordmuck all over again. But different this time. No more keep your distance, my man. He needs me and says as much and what do I get? A lot. I swear. I reckon I have a real home now and I don't have to watch my p's and q's as long as he can have his own space for his writing and reading, guests coming for dinner when he wants to talk posh all night. I know when to back off. Most days we eat in the kitchen. Sometimes he cooks and I do my bit if he's off-colour.

Want to know a secret? Mr G is not a well man. Can't say no more at this stage but he loses it. I might have to talk to Susan. She'd know.

James read Pedro's up-to-the-minute record, heart touched by his concern. Somewhat exaggerated perhaps, but concern nonetheless.

Chapter Thirty Seven

James was wrong, Claudia thought. Those policemen were on to us. They had her back for questioning, pointedly informing her that her friend, James Livingstone Gall, had already been most helpful. James, what had he told them? She had her lawyer, Greg Sinclair, with her this time. Greg's father, Ian, had been Sergio's lawyer and a close friend.

Questions, questions, questions: about Felix and Sergio, and Sergio's relationship with Grace Gall. She had to bite her tongue when Grace's name cropped up; all her fucking fault. When they pressed Claudia on her father's death, she let herself sob unashamedly. Greg intervened, and the older policeman gave her a hanky. He seemed kind enough.

How well did she know James Livingstone Gall? She was quite open about it, as James and she had agreed. The policemen were able to tell her that James conveyed to them his familiarity with Sergio's story, that he was currently researching it in some detail.

"Impressive man, some story," Parfrey commented at one stage, to which Gibbons nodded his agreement. Between pregnant pauses they swapped knowing looks. There was no order to their questions, jumping from one thing to another; one of them quizzing her about

Sergio and Sercat Hotels and then, for no apparent reason, the other wanting details of her charity work. It went on for a couple of hours.

Greg requested a break. Inspector Parfrey replied, "Just a few more questions, Mrs Underwood."

How she hated *that* name.

"You must have hated your husband," he said, implying in a caring voice that any reasonable person would understand if she did.

"He was not a husband in any meaningful way."

Parfrey hesitated, leaning towards her. "You would have been better off without him?"

She waved Greg's protestations aside. "I knew very soon after we returned from the United States. It was common knowledge that he fucked young men. Ask me was I upset, damn sure I was. I was furious and cut him off immediately. We never lived together from then on. We were utterly separate and he had no influence on me any more. I had no reason to kill him, Inspector, I was rid of him already." The room seemed to take an inclusive pause for breath.

"You had dinner together at Le Gourmet shortly before he disappeared."

"I chose to discuss personal business, our shared living arrangements, ongoing financial matters, in a public place rather than intimate surroundings. A restaurant is neutral territory and I happen to like Le Gourmet."

"Yes, a very pleasant venue it is Mrs Underwood, fine cooking and Bernard is a mine of information."

So, they had talked to Bernard. She cast a help-me-out-here eye at her solicitor. Greg stood and Claudia followed suit.

"A moment please," Parfrey controlled the situation, addressing her again. "Do you hold Grace Gall responsible for your father's death?"

"Yes, Inspector, I have not changed my mind. She murdered him."

In the car, as they sped away from the police station, Claudia felt surer and surer that these two investigators were not going to let up.

Parfrey in particular exuded a canny wisdom. His questions had an unsettling effect, as if he knew the answers already.

From Greg's next contribution it was clear that he shared her unease. "A few things, Claudia. I want you to listen carefully." He glanced at her as he drove. She nodded and he continued. "Three things to be precise."

"Ok, Greg."

"One: you must not see Livingstone Gall again."

"What?" she asked, the thought of not seeing James again hitting harder than she cared to admit. "Don't you think that is being a little overly cautious?"

"You have to think about protecting yourself now," he told her. "Rest assured James' main concern is James."

Claudia sighed, knowing he was right. "Fine, what's two?"

"Two: find yourself a male escort, anyone of your own circle and socialise."

"Socialise?"

"Exactly, Claudia, get yourself a respectable man and have him take you to dinner, to the opera, to Berlin or Budapest for long weekends, house parties in the country."

"I may as well get married, Greg."

"Now, there's a super idea," he said with a smile.

"You said there were three things."

He pulled in at Sercat Central, turned off the engine. "Number three: make certain you can account for every detail of the period before and after your husband's disappearance, up to the day his body was found."

As they headed into the lobby, he took her arm and whispered in her ear. "Parfrey, don't let his softly, softly tactics deceive you. I know him of old. He's ruthless and clever and he's acting as if he suspects you of something." Greg waved her protestations of innocence aside. "You don't have to explain yourself to me, Claudia. I'm on your side."

Back at the hotel they had a short lunch. When it was over,

Claudia asked Grant Percival to join her. As Greg walked away, he gave Claudia the thumbs up. This upset her; thumbs up from her solicitor could only point to his lack of confidence and by extension the fragility of her position.

"I had a call from Mr Gall and stalled him as you requested," Grant reported. "Those reviews we had arranged with him, I've found a more suitable journalist, the TV woman, Maybee O'Hara. High profile, terribly keen."

"Splendid, Grant, you have been busy," she complimented him and then, with a conspiratorial grin, asked, "have you ever been to Berlin?"

Chapter Thirty Eight

Jack Parfrey left headquarters feeling satisfied. He and Taylor Gibbons were not yet in a position to charge anybody with the Underwood death, but they were moving gradually in the right direction; no doubt in his mind that Gall and the Catalano woman were implicated. They had been on more than speaking terms before and after Underwood's death, witnessed together in Sercat Central and undeniably connected retrospectively by Sergio and Grace Gall's affair: the strange circumstances of his demise in Croatia, Grace dubious liaisons with former lovers, all unaccounted for. Only a matter of time and intelligent detection. No panic. Loose ends had a habit of coming together eventually. Claudia's apartment had been searched immediately after Underwood's body washed up but it might merit a revisit at some point. Tomorrow he'd request search warrants for Gall's place. He'd have both their telephones tapped. No more pussyfooting. They were now approaching endgame, a stage eagerly anticipated and one which thrilled him still. As he had explained to his wife, Rose, there was nothing to match the electrifying buzz of the chase. Suddenly pictures flashed across his mind of James Livingstone Gall and the identikits of the waitress' killer. The smile on his face as he walked to the train betrayed his assurance.

It was good to be working with Gibbons again. They were, he thought warmly, more than the sum of their parts and that made him smile again. He'd suggest to Rose that they should invite Taylor and Mabel to dinner when this was all over; the women got on well and Taylor, whatever else he might be, was a good friend. Taylor would be retired like himself soon, so this was probably their last case together. By the time he bought his ticket and strolled to the platform to await his incoming train, Parfrey had envisaged an agreeable scenario in Le Gourmet in which he, Taylor and their wives enjoyed Bernard's hospitality and a slap-up dinner, courtesy of the department. What was that wine he had, Côtes du something? A Burgundy was it or Bordeaux? This was his small preoccupation as he saw the lights of an approaching train. A gaggle of fellow travellers gathered and jostled around him. The usual assorted commuters: suited men with briefcases and umbrellas, women laden with shopping bags, giggling teenagers on the way home from school, tradesmen carrying bags of tools, secretaries and youngsters switched into musical ear plugs or mobile phones. A cursory assessment of the crowd told Parfrey he'd have to stand. He was tired, could do with a seat. The train kept coming, growing larger as it exited the tunnel into the main concourse. Suddenly it came to him: Côtes du Rhône, a red wine from the Rhône valley, and he remembered the sommelier's amusing comment. "Grapey," he'd said in heavily accented English that sounded like ropey. Taylor had reacted with rare flippancy. "In my book all red wine is ropey."

The waiting crowd surged forward, Parfrey held his ground. The train kept coming.

Someone, something struck him forcibly from behind, propelling him forward. Instinctively he reached out for support. But there was no barrier, nothing to stop his propulsion outward and downward on to the tracks.

Chapter Thirty Nine

Witnesses to Parfrey's fatal fall at the station presented a united front, as if anything other than an accident might implicate them in dark deeds. Reading newspaper reports, Pedro pointed to their unanimity.

"He just tripped and fell on to the line."

"One minute he was right in front of me and when the crowd moved towards the train he fell off the platform. It was awful."

"Yeah, I'd say it was an accident. Who'd want to kill him?"

"Accidental, absolutely. Sure there was a crush, there always is at rush hour, but I didn't see anyone push him. An old guy like that must have lost his footing. Sad but horribly simple."

James didn't believe a word. Gibbons was on the news. He looked, sounded broken. The investigation into Felix's disappearance, driven by Parfrey, would flounder without him. Parfrey had been the central figure and with him out of the picture, Gibbons wouldn't have the tenacity to continue. That's how it appeared to James and, as the days passed, it became less and less likely that Gibbons or his colleagues would bother following the tentative, circumstantial case that had little credibility outside Parfrey's head. Available, documented police files concluded that Felix Underwood had, in all probability, killed himself while of unsound mind. The file would remain open as a matter of course unless compelling new evidence materialised. All most agreeably convenient for James. And for Claudia.

Parfrey died on a Wednesday. On Thursday James had a letter from Claudia, delivered by courier. In stilted lawyer-speak she advised him: *I won't be meeting you again nor do I wish you to make contact with me. I have decided that any further consort with you is not in my interest at this point in time. Whatever transpired between us I have consigned to the past and I would suggest that you do likewise. Some things are best left behind us and there is always a time to move on. That is the healthy option.*

Signed sparely: *Claudia Catalano.*

Next day was Grant Percival's turn, equally cold; his letter informed James that his services to Sercat Hotels had terminated forthwith and requested the furnishing of an invoice for fees to date.

Throughout the weekend James fumed and schemed, schemed and fumed. "The bitch, the bitch. She can't just discard me like some unfashionable accessory. I won't let her away with it; I could have her killed. I could do it myself." In sustained fury he wrote hateful replies belittling her self-importance, her father's questionable pedigree, her sexual inadequacy; on and on, spiteful, nasty harangues. And one by one he shredded them, burning the odious confetti in a fit of fevered helplessness, reaching a state of burn-out, through which his faculties stuttered and reasserted themselves, ultimately facilitating the following reply:

My Dear Claudia,

I suppose I should be grateful for the warning. Jack Parfrey was not so lucky.

James

To Grant Percival he wrote in syrupy appreciation for relieving him of the most boring assignment of his life. He demanded three times his normal fee, confident that the gutless Percival would pay up.

Whatever passing satisfaction he got from those letters, resentment towards Claudia simmered on. The poisons he concocted for her never left his head, stagnating to a foul pool that contaminated nobody but himself.

And then Maybee called for no other reason than to gloat. "I'm so excited James. Grant Percival of Sercat Central wants me for a mega review series of all, all James, every one of their restaurants worldwide."

"Yes, Maybee, I know all about it."

"He said you had been considered but the Board wanted a fresh, modern vision."

"How kind of you to let me know."

"Another matter, James. I won't need you for the panel on next week's show as your last appearance did not go down well."

"Is that all, Maybee?" he snapped.

"That's all for the moment. See you around, James."

This was all Claudia's doing. Perhaps he should be grateful she had not arranged to kill him off anonymously, like Parfrey.

Within a week of the exchanged letters, he rose one morning glowing with certainty. He knew then without question that he would have to see her again; no plan of action, simply an overwhelming impulse to face her facing him.

The main bar at Sercat Central had a raised area from where there was a clear view of comings and goings through the lobby. Wednesday mornings she had her charity meetings. James ordered espresso and cognac and waited. When she reached the revolving doors she seemed to hesitate, raising her head slightly, glancing right and left. A barely discernible twitch of the nose. Sensing his presence? Dressed to kill in brushed blue velvet jeans, black top and denim waistcoat, her blonde hair bullied into a tight bun, she might have stepped from an early nineteenth-century, patrician family portrait: stiff, upper-class, makeover for a new century. Her eyes remained hidden behind designer sunglasses.

Whatever James might have done was thwarted by the arrival of

Claudia's charity committee. She greeted them individually and then they moved as a group to the lift, chatting vociferously. James watched the lift door close, drained his espresso and left the hotel. By the time he walked all the way home, his head cleared and he was grateful that he had not given in to the vindictive impulses that had led him to the hotel that morning. In a way, just seeing Claudia was enough for now.

Chapter Forty

James stripped and subjected himself to an hour of physical routines before a shower and the consolation of laundered underwear, starched shirt, bowtie and tuxedo. He had dined in the highly-rated Les Hirondelles once before but had not yet reviewed it. Now, with journalistic opportunities in decline, seemed as good a time as any. A venue to dress for. He knew no better example of appetising titillation than the pike quenelles at Les Hirondelles, where the staff pretended not to recognise him but treated him as if he was somebody. The maître d', Salvatore, an Italian of the old school, inhabited that graceful space, neither intrusive nor aloof, in which only masters of the craft officiate. A cut above friend Bernard at Le Gourmet. Bernard gushed and whined; Salvatore straddled understatement like a ballet dancer. And one knew he was watching. It was that feeling of being under scrutiny, however unobtrusive, that led James to question what he himself did for a living. At its self-regarding heart, criticism was a mean career; meanness its raison d'être. Kind criticism was paradoxical and, more to the point, bad copy. On the contrary, arrogance, certitude, an eye for Achilles' heels and the cutting coup de grâce slinked on to newsprint with reptilian ease. Food critics perfected this low art.

Plucked from reverie by the sounds of a piano and cello duo in the bar, James listened uncritically: two young musicians, refugees from some symphony orchestra, making gentle love to their instruments, sharing their intimacy with strangers. The piano, tinkling counterpoint to a plaintive cello, the generosity of the players, their responses to each other, captivated him so that his mood lightened. Somehow, it may have been the pianist's skill, he began to hear only the cello: moans of painful pleasure from the oversized instrument, replicated in the closed-eye tension on the cellist's brow. Even when the cello went silent an aftermath of beauty stirred, discernible in the musicians' empathy, one to the other; not sexual but respect and the warmth of human collaboration. A restaurant with music like that would entice anybody back for second helpings.

In spite of all his sessions with Theo, James' obsessions sustained him, goaded him on. He was the kind of man who rode the rocket of compulsion, hanging on for dear life. That night in Les Hirondelles he ate caviar on bite-sized disks of lobster afloat on chlorophyllous dollops of rocket purée, spiked with ginger. He pictured it as still-life on a gallery wall: background herbal green, obsidian Beluga roes, pink and white shellfish, fodder for a Dali or a Miro. There was an element of reward about an unfilling soup between courses, which Les Hirondelles achieved in a demi-tasse of ethereal parsnip foam, subjected to the slightest acquaintance with black truffle. Sentimentalists and food critics were suckers for suckling pig. He had it with crab-apple jelly and baby roast potatoes. Having helped himself from a sublimely reeking cheese board, James then returned to the bar, the music and a second glass of vintage Port (Croft '63). What an oddly happy grouping: replete with James, the Port, musicians serenading for their supper, Salvatore pulling the strings. He would of course write about it, one of those experiences that required the passage of maturing time.

What happened next was surely a fluke of fate: Claudia, alone, led by Salvatore to an unoccupied snug where she was obscured from view. The shock of her theatrical entrance made James gulp. Tipsy rashness dared him to swagger up to her. He thought better of it, sat still, waiting. If she saw him he would acknowledge her. Would she, him? When the man joining her turned out to be Grant Percival, James paid and departed, his mind's eye rotating artlessly in pursuit of the complexion and extent of her entanglement with the hotelier.

Chapter Forty One

The only way James could relieve his obsession with Claudia, the fool's paradise that he had let himself into, was to pay his respects to Theo. Yes, Theo could be unsparing of overfed ego, but he was always altruistic. Theo's frailty and repetitive heart problems limited his psychiatry practice to theoretical papers and editorial work, which he did at home. Theo needed looking after now. Sessions with him were no longer the counsellor-client kind. Their equality had become one of friendship. James, privately acknowledging the element of turntable in their relationship, visited him for dinner with dinner. Theo's appetite was poor but he still liked a couple of glasses of claret and a liqueur or two. Becky reheated some simple low-fat dish à la Gall, which they scoffed with a bottle from Theo's cellar, and a digestif. No more cognac for Theo, doctor's orders. Discussion was wide-ranging, both their interests weighed and distributed one to the other. This did not come about overnight. But gradually. Theo began to talk about himself with increasing openness, showing a side of wistful retrospection. James had been slow to probe Theo about his life and family, and when Theo displayed this new willingness to reveal himself, James had the temerity to encourage him.

"I've always been curious about you, Theo, your background, your life before I blundered into it."

Theo rearranged himself in his chair, coughed a couple of times, looked at James, looked away and then back again. "You know, James, I've spent many hours listening to you speak. I've admired your frankness. Perhaps it's my turn now."

"To be frank, frank about what, Theo?"

Theo paused once more and then, leaning forward, stroking his beard, replied, "The story of my life, Mr Gall!"

James, taken aback, said quickly, "Theo, please you don't have to—"

"But I want you to hear it, James."

James sat back as Theo began to speak.

"My father never recovered from the shame of collaboration with the Nazi regime in Krakow, where he lived all his life. I grew up feeling sorry for him and begged him to forgive himself. After all, his job as a tailor making obligatory uniforms for occupying officers of The Third Reich was a pardonable offence under the circumstances. No, he did not see it so and berated himself for surviving when others, family and friends, went to the gas chambers. His melancholia affected us all; care for him became my mother's main purpose in life, to the detriment of my sister and me. To send us off to my aunt in London was an act of monumental love and treachery. He talked her into it, convincing her, I think, that this sacrifice was demanded of them: let the children escape, that was the duty of failed parents."

"Such a harsh view, Theo."

"Harsh, horrible times, James, and they knew that as Jewish children at that time during and after the war, our future in Poland was bleak. It took me years to forgive. Jess, my sister, never did. She suffers in the contrary way of families, just as my father did. I am the lucky one."

"You must have suffered too."

"Emotionally yes, but we were fortunate that my aunt and uncle cared deeply for us, loved us as if we were the children they never had themselves. They were both practising doctors and well-off. The bourgeois comforts of London almost erased the earlier deprivation until I went to university. Suddenly I became an angry outsider."

"Ah, we have something in common at last."

"Rage is a negative asset, as you know, James. It has to be tamed, the alternative I don't like to contemplate."

"Please do."

"Rage, if discharged rather than treated, will undermine you more than any of its intended victims." He delivered this with the blunt severity of old age. The excruciating irony of his situation! There he was faced with his own fragility, while so many erstwhile victims of breakdown he had helped repair bestrode a state of rude health.

James bridled. "You've got a cure?" He sensed Theo's eyes on him.

"It's so simple, love and forgiveness, James. You have to find someone to love; love and intimacy and having found it, sustain it."

It's alright for him, James thought to himself as he pondered the precarious balance of his own mind. Theo had dealt with his demons, whereas he sat there ambushed by the unnerving presence of his gorgonian mother and, of course, Claudia. He was not aware that Theo had continued speaking "… the illness usually begins and ends in the heart."

"You fell in love?"

"Head over heels, love at first sight. I fulfilled the clichés when I met my wife, Eleanor. We were married a month after we met, two poor students. All we had was potential. She was dead within a year …" At this point Theo fell into silence, taking a handkerchief out of a pocket to dab his forehead. "She died giving birth to our son, who died with her. I graduated and learned slowly, painfully, to forgive her."

"Forgive?"

"She left me, James. I had to forgive her in order to get on with myself."

"Did you?"

"Eventually." Here he stopped, looked about him. "Not quite happy-ever-after, but her spirit lingers. Odd isn't it how we can manipulate the psyche to face any challenge, move in any direction we chose. I chose to let Eleanor return, and she has not abandoned me a second time."

"You believe she's with you still?"

Beaming, he said, "Look around you, James. Can't you see the feminine touch? This is no bachelor pad, is it?"

James looked around. Theo was right. There was a female warmth in the house and, with Becky in the background, it was easy to succumb to it. It was something his own house lacked. No wonder Theo exuded acceptance, physical limitations notwithstanding. The wisdom of the man still shone.

James was shamed by obscured predilections. But lately he concluded that Theo knew anyway. What was it he said the other day? "I respect what you don't tell me as much as what you do, my boy."

Another evening, after Becky had cleared away their empty plates and lit a fire in the grate, Theo reached for a box of chocolate wafers, offering it to James before taking some himself. James reacted. "Come, Theo, chocolate is off limits, you know that!"

Letting a grin grow, he faced James, nibbling mischievously. "You must be familiar with Brecht, my boy." James was not. "Brecht said food comes first, then morals." The neutral tone, which Theo used to convey this aphoristic nugget, made it impossible to judge what was in his mind. James had the distinct impression that Theo was letting him know indirectly that whatever he got up to he was not judged.

"Therapists," James said. "You are so damn clever!"

"Repeat the word, James."

When he did, Theo said, "Again, break it in two."

His tongue played with it, "Therap ists, thera pists, the rapists."

They exchanged glances.

"Hardly matters, Theo. It's only a word."

At this point Theo winced visibly. "Too close for comfort," he replied.

"What is it, Theo, you're in pain?"

Smiling through the pain, whatever it was, he was quick to dismiss James' concern. "Pain is a constant companion, these days, I'm afraid. One gets quite used to it and then I do have all that medication I'm supposed to take."

On the way home James reminded himself again how deeply he cared for Theo. All it required of James was to be available. In this frame of mind he remembered what Theo had once said on the subject of caring for others, "Negligence is a crime, one of the most serious perpetrated by man. It's a killer." James recalled how he kept his response to that wisdom with thoughtful nods, while privately thinking how little Theo knew about killing. As for the condemnation of negligence, was this a plea? Did Theo fear that James would abandon him? As he drove across London, tears fell freely down his face and he made no effort to stem the flow. He had not cried for years.

Chapter Forty Two

J ames' seven o'clock radio alarm woke him to the news.

"Reports are coming in of the discovery of a woman's body in a lane off Sandycourt Road in the Riverwell area. There are no further details at this time."

He took startled stock. Yes, he was in his own bed and there hanging in the open wardrobe the clothes he wore the previous night. He leaped from the bed, tore the shirt from its hanger, laid it flat on the bed, turned it over. No blood. He dressed and ran to the shed, hands shaking so badly he had difficulty with the lock. Relief again, no signs of disturbance. Except in the bowels, thirty minutes painful evacuation.

At eight he barked across the table at Pedro. "Turn that rubbish off, I want to hear the news." There had been a development. "... a man is helping police with their inquiries ..." James sighed audibly.

Pedro, looking at him strangely, poured coffee. "Bad dream, Mr G?"

"Nightmare, Pedro."

His day broke up in hourly segments, punctuated by news bulletins. TV showed only a picture of a man with an anorak over his head and a phalanx of policemen obscuring him from view. He had given himself up, admitted to strangling the waitress. There was speculation about other recent killings; was this man responsible for all of them?

At six o'clock an urbane newsreader reported.

"A thirty-six year-old man identified as Saul Cooper of no fixed abode has been found hanged in his cell at Riverwell Police Station. The authorities are tight-lipped but sources are suggesting that, before he took his own life, Mr Cooper admitted to three other recent murders of women in the same area, a notorious red-light district."

Pedro hovered all day long, saying nothing. Although James was aware he was being observed, he said nothing either. As the News at Six began they sat down together.

"Poor bastard," Pedro said when the news ended. "You know what they did, they beat the shit out of him. He'd admit to killing his mother and grandmother, anything to get 'em off him. Cops, they go too far. Poor homeless guy, he wouldn't be able to take it. Pushed him, broke him, that's what they did. They beat the truth out of him whether it was the truth or not." He looked at James closely as he spoke in an explanatory monotone, as a father might speak to a son. "Guys like that don't have any chance. They're set-up from the time they're born." Pedro took a deep breath, shivered perceptibly, letting his anger out. "It could have been me, that poor bugger what's-his-name could have been me, I swear." Pedro had begun to speak again before James was fully aware of it. "My mother used to go to confession to have her sins wiped away." Pause. "Confess the bad things and you can forget about them because God has taken them to Heaven to give them a good cleaning. She believed that and, you know, I kinda do too."

"You think there's hope for me, Pedro?"

"That's another thing my mother said, there's hope for us all, Mr G."

Another long pause that led James down a path of wondering. Who am I? Why am I here? What is the point?

"To hell with it, James," he heard Grace pronounce after another one of her misfortunes. "Let me cry for a while and then let's dress for dinner."

James knew that Claudia would arrange his demise if it suited her purpose and that he must not forget that he would always be a target as long as they both lived. Lack of reason and logic in her persistent, unexamined sense of loyalty to Sergio drove her still. An abiding passion. Felix, also, floated permanently between James and herself, their version of deterrent. She could have Grant Percival but he was no Livingstone Gall. Pedro would call him "a fuckin' poof". An inexhaustible supply of snow-white shirts, silver hotelier ties and the pong of twice-daily shampoo suggested a meticulous man. But James' observation had uncovered Percival's darting animal eyes and a lack of symmetry in the swing of the buttocks, as sure a sign of defeatism as his flabby hands. He was Claudia's short-term replacement therapy. Percival might not know it but his time as her man-of-the-moment was already ticking away. "Why do I bother?" James asked himself. "He's such a twit. Percival has the potential of blankness; she will make something of him, patchwork but quirky. She will have him service her (some use for those flabby hands), but she will be guarded, never revealing the wild, anguished emotions that I, James Livingstone Gall, had begun to explore."

Chapter Forty Three

Manny called in exasperation mode. "I called you, Mr G, left a message with your boyfriend."

"Not boyfriend, assistant, if you don't mind."

"Whatever, you not talking to your old mate no more?"

"I owe you an apology, Manny, so much has been happening. I seem to have forgotten."

"Nobody forgets Manny Johnson."

"Not really forgotten. There will always be a corner of my mind reserved exclusively for you." James pictured his sly, chuckling face and the accompanying frolic of fat cheeks.

"You still in the rip-off business, Mr G?"

"If it's consultancy you mean, yes. I make myself available for certain projects dependent on a variety of factors."

"Such as?"

"No negatives in your case, Manny. If you have a proposition, I would consider it without question."

They set up a meeting at The Butcher's Arms in spite of James' attempts to divert to a less intimidating venue. "You don't love The Butcher's no more, Mr G? Bullshit, you're crazy about the joint."

Manny awaited, a bottle of cognac and two empty glasses on

the table in front of him, the same table at which James sat the last time he was here. Manny eyed him closely before leaping to enclose him in a bear hug. If it were possible, his girth had expanded since their last meeting. A tailored, cobalt blue suit flapped about him like a tent. "Did I ever tell you I own this place?"

"But of course you did, Manny. It is so you."

"Yes," he said, waving his stubby arms. "All mine. Have to keep my eyes open, some fuckers don't know how to behave, no finesse, know what I mean?" James knew what he meant. "Cops all over the place last week." He paused to pour both a drink. Their eyes met over the rims of lifted glasses. "Romanian gypsy woman, part-time waitress."

"What woman, Manny?"

"Magda, scrubber who snuffed it. You know the one."

"Oh, yes, I saw her photograph."

"Yeah, yeah, you saw her photo, pretty as a picture."

"Didn't pay much attention."

"Yeah, you wouldn't, would you?" James guessed that Manny, a believer in the scenic route, would make his point at the end of sweeping meanders. "Last seen at The Butcher's Arms, Mr G."

"Really?"

"Yeah, sat over there. The point is ..." Here he stopped, put both arms on the table, leaning closer to James. "The point is he couldn't have done it, the Cooper bloke. Raving lunatic, made out he was Jack The Ripper. All in his head. He couldn't have killed Magda because he wasn't within an ass's fart of the place."

"Are you sure of that?" James asked as casually as he could.

"Bloke I know, landlord of a pub in Midlington, tells me Saul Cooper spent that night sleeping off a piss-up in an outhouse behind his pub. He remembers it well because it was his daughter's birthday. They had a party and Cooper was such a fuckin' nuisance he turfed him out. He was still in winkle-land the following morning. Shat himself he had. Benny, the landlord had to hose him down and put the skids under him, told him to fuck off and not come back."

"Interesting. You do have interesting tales to tell, Manny."

Manny emitted a porcine, snorting sound and cleared his throat. Then he pulled a yellow handkerchief from a front pocket, spread it wide between outstretched palms, spat onto it a blob of greenish phlegm, which he studied carefully before continuing. "It's only interesting if you have an interest in it, Mr G."

"The man's confession and suicide have put an end to speculation, I would have thought."

Manny laid the soiled handkerchief on the table, folding it carefully before rearranging it in the suit pocket like a buttonhole. Fiddling with the yellow sprouting linen, admiring his handiwork, he said, "If you were a ship, Mr G, I'd say you were headed for the rocks."

"And Manny Johnson's lifeboat has just appeared on the horizon."

"All hands on deck." He topped up James' drink and ordered fish pies for both of them.

"What's the fish?" James queried.

"You're the expert." Manny was stuffing himself with his usual gluttonous disregard for table manners.

James dug into the carapace of arid mash, picking at fishy globules in the viscous liquid beneath. "Mostly shark, Manny, some eel, cod, traces of something else. My guess is a bottom feeder."

Manny laughed, shaking all over. "Men of taste, you and me, Mr G. We should work together again."

"You're not thinking of another restaurant venture?"

"What I have in mind could make us very rich."

"Restaurant ruled out then."

Manny's circuitous excursion, packaged in euphemism and allusive language, was at last nearing an end. He hailed a barman to clear the table, rose, gesturing to James, "Follow me."

James had always looked on Manny with smug superiority. His impaired snob's vision, despite former experience of the man, allowed public buffoonery to cloud his complexity. Now for the first time in Manny's private office, James realised he was in the presence of an able businessman. All the trappings: computer, telephones, fax, shelves full of files, bookcases, a pair of leather sofas and workaday office chairs. The main man, transformed in these surroundings, presided behind a raised desk. Manny directed James to sit with one hand, the other engaged with a telephone, making calls that amplified his importance: he prescribed, minions took note. This power display may or may not have been a show. Either way James was impressed and distinctly ill-at-ease. A dart of pain ran down his right arm to his finger tips.

"Coffee, Mr G?"

Recollection of Butcher's Arms' coffee made James wince. "Strong and black, if you please."

Manny pressed a button somewhere to the left of the desk. James heard a whoosh of air behind him, towards which he turned to see a fully-stocked bar where bookcases had been. Manny made his way to the bar, conjuring two espressos from a machine behind the counter, which he delivered on a tray, one to James, the other to his desk. "Like the best women," he said. "Black and strong."

"You haven't brought me in here to discuss coffee or women, have you, Manny?"

"No, not today. Today I'm gonna show you how to hit the jackpot." He pressed another button and a cinema screen unfurled before them, the lights went out and the screen was suddenly alive with footage of James in The Butcher's Arms; Magda seated close by; Magda leaving the pub; and a tunnelled shot of Magda walking away followed by a man in a long overcoat. Then the film faded and the screen went fuzzy. The lights went on. Manny, standing behind the desk with hands in pockets, went straight for the jugular. "You fuckin' killed her."

"Nothing I have seen or heard here incriminates me. You'll have to do better than that."

"If it looks like a duck, Mr G, then it's a fuckin' duck. This is no court room but I have you by the balls and you know it."

James badly wanted to flee, escape from what other traps Manny was about to spring. He could be home with Pedro within the hour.

Bovril and a book. Not to be. He was up to his neck in Manny's mysterious stew. Pragmatic fear dictated that he listen.

"No worries, keep your shirt on. I'm not in the business of shopping my friends. I deal with things my way. No cops but the law according to Manny Johnson!"

Pregnant pause and Manny a picture of smugness.

"You're going to make me rich instead," James replied, unable to hide the sarcasm in his voice.

"Right on, Mr G, you and me in line for big bucks." He moved to the front of the desk, hoisting his backside on to the document-strewn worktop, from which perch he informed James that they were about to kidnap one of the wealthiest women in the country, demand a ransom, arrange payment and walk away with a fortune. Irony and bonhomie set aside, this was Manny Johnson, businessman-cum-gangster.

"Why me, Manny? I have no expertise in these matters. You don't need me."

"Wrong, sir, you have what's called credibility."

"Credibility?" What was he talking about?

He shifted his weight gingerly, a sly smile playing on his lips. "When you invite Claudia Catalano to dinner, she'll come running. That's credibility."

"No, no, I can't. No, no Manny," James stuttered.

"Fuck you, Mr G, you'll do as I say!" He continued to play a version of good cop, bad cop: all pals one minute, threateningly aggressive the next. "All you have to do is get her to meet you. She's not going to know you're in on the job; we'll grab the two of you, let you go, set up the ransom. Her people will pay up and we'll let her off. You'll get your cut and the fair lady will go home with a headache and a less padded bank account. Just like that. Her ex, the brave Felix, took me to the cleaners. Now she gets to do the laundry." He anticipated prevarication with a steely gaze and a chilling warning. "If you don't do as I say, there'll be a couple of nasty accidents: goodbye Ms moneybags Catalano and goodbye Mr G."

Chapter Forty Four

James did not enlighten Manny how his credibility rating with Claudia had plummeted recently. For her to comply with an invitation he would have to provide the perfect pretext. Their let's-have-dinner days were over.

Nothing for it but to confide in Pedro, who delivered James' handwritten note to Claudia's home, dropping it in her letter box. He then rang the doorbell and retreated behind bushes, from where he witnessed Claudia collecting the envelope marked for her attention only. She was on the phone to James before Pedro returned and they agreed to meet in the Palmyra Hotel car park near Heathrow at nine o'clock on Thursday evening, two days hence. It would be dark.

James took a taxi to the Palmyra. Claudia had driven herself. He joined her in the front of the Jaguar. Looking straight ahead, she said, "This better be worth my while. You have five minutes."

There was no time for explanation. Both car doors opened simultaneously, gloved hands held guns to their heads and ushered them to a waiting van, where they were bundled into the back. Then the van took off at speed. Thrown together, their heads banged in the dark. If there were any windows, they had been blacked out.

"This was not my idea," James protested.

Claudia acted coolly at first, breathing deeply, taking stock of the situation. An involuntary shudder made her hug herself; she stared at James as if he were a complete stranger. The swaying van threw them together again and, as they disentangled, she peered at him, recognition slowly dawning in a mixture of terror and fury.

"You bastard, what is this? What's happening, where are we going?"

"We've been kidnapped, Claudia."

"James," she shrieked in disbelief. "Have you gone totally insane?"

To no avail he tried to explain how he had been coerced, that Manny and his gang had threatened to kill her if he didn't do as he was told. She wouldn't listen. Waves of invective alternated with gasping and mewling, culminating in silent withdrawal. He had little sense of time but guessed that they had been travelling for less than an hour when the van slowed, rattled over a grid of some kind and came to a halt. It was too dark to assess surroundings as their captors dragged them from the vehicle, across cobbles and down stone steps to an unlit basement. Without a word they left, enclosing them from above. James heard the grating of hinges, a muffled conversation and the sound of retreating footsteps. James and Claudia were left trapped in an eerie silence.

Gradually he found his bearings in the unaccustomed gloom, almost tripping over a mattress. In the only light, a shaft of moonlight through a crack in the trapdoor that had been bolted from above, James identified two chairs and an antique wooden beer barrel, adapted to look like a table and set sparely with two plastic mugs and a jug. He had seen a match of those chairs in Manny's office. They were being held in a cellar beneath The Butcher's Arms, a discovery that made no practical difference except that he took some small solace from knowing where they were.

Claudia curled up sullen in a corner, eschewing his offer of the mattress. He tried to reassure her that this was all Manny's doing, that far from colluding with his machinations, he was a victim too. When he attempted to lay a conciliatory hand on her shoulder she snarled.

"Fuck off, James!"

Privately he had concluded that Manny had no intention of setting him free and the promise of shared riches was another fiction. It was absolutely vital to get Claudia on his side; if they were to survive this they had to work together.

James' efforts to cajole her into conversation met with hostile stares and stony silence. In the circumstances he surprised himself. His hands ached and he feared for their lives; Manny would kill them as soon as the ransom was secured. Yet he managed to survey the captive space in the limited light, concluding that the most likely escape route was the way they had come in, through the hatch in the ceiling, rather than the sealed steel door at the rear of the cellar, which probably led into the pub itself. For a weapon of sorts he broke off the remains of the wooden mattress frame, determined to use it when one of Manny's men came to check, as they surely would.

Ready for action James turned his attention to Claudia, fretting in her disturbed half-sleep. Carefully he nestled beside her on the cellar floor. Involuntarily her hand moved to find his, clasping it. Opening her eyes some time later, anger moderated by the warmth of their bodies, she whispered, "When is this going to end, James?"

"Soon Claudia, soon," he said, holding her closer, even as fear thumped unabated in his chest. "We'll get out of this," he assured her, affecting optimism. To keep her calm and onside he'd have to sustain this pretence.

Asserting mistrust again, she stood, stretching and pacing as if the beat of her feet might empower her. "We bloody well better, James." His attempted hug met with a withering, "Don't you dare touch me!"

Dankness rose like bad breath, holding them in anxious deadlock until their ears pricked to the sound of voices. James rushed to the hatch, cudgel in mid-swing, only to be overpowered from behind by two of Manny's heavies who, with Manny, had entered through the door to which James had turned his back. James was thrown to the ground and held down. Manny ignored him, striding to where Claudia cowered in a corner. Grabbing her right hand, in a tone of ingratiating menace, Manny said, "I'll take that, my dear." Claudia unclasped her gold bracelet and handed it over without a word. Manny held the bracelet, evaluating the weight of it, noting Claudia's inscribed initials before wrapping it in a handkerchief and pocketing it. "A little token, my dear, proof of the pudding as Mr G would say. Your Mr Grant Percival will want a good look at this, won't he? You know he fancies you enough to make me a sensible offer for your safe return. A dip into Sercat Hotels' treasure chest. Only a dip, I'm a reasonable man." He turned to go, halted as if he had forgotten something and turned towards Claudia again, extending a hand to her, mockingly. Claudia took his hand and stood trembling before him. He shook her free, saying, "Another time dear, another time for you and me." Glancing at James he snapped, "Now you know, Mr G, you were never cut out to be a hero." He hailed his henchmen and they left hurriedly through the steel door leading back into the pub, Manny's laugh echoing through the pub's underground as they went.

Claudia ran to James.

"If there's a way out of this Claudia, we'll find it," James said, holding her.

"I so much want to believe that," she replied.

The banging of doors reverberated above them. For minutes they held each other. Eventually they sought the small comfort of the old mattress, sitting side by side, holding hands. Claudia nodded off and James sought again to discover any means of escape. Testing the security of the hatch from below was hopeless. He could not exert enough pressure to make any impact on it. And the door, through which Manny and his men had entered and exited, was thoroughly locked. In desperation he ran at it with his shoulder. No go, not a budge. A stabbing pain ran the length of his arm. Wincing, he fell to his knees. He shut his eyes tight and forced himself to breathe deeply, slowly, relieving the pain and retrieving some modicum of calm. It was at that point Claudia called out, "James, what's that sound? Something buzzing, can you hear it?" He listened. She was right, there was a sound. He looked about him, tracking the source of the buzzing. A phone, he thought, just as Claudia joined him and simultaneously they both spied the on/off light of Manny's mobile lying to one side of the door where he had dropped it. Dumbstruck, they peered at the twinkling mobile like two children in awe of magic come miraculously to life. They both reached out to grab it. James got there first. "I'll text Grant," Claudia whispered in disbelief. Equally stunned, James handed her the phone and she texted Grant, warning him not to call back. Likewise James texted Pedro with the same warning and with undue care replaced the phone on the cellar floor. Now to wait and to hope.

They continued to search for some flaw in the cellar's security, Claudia, now as committed as James. An hour, more, passed. Claudia struggled to retain confidence. "Grant will surely do something. He's used to reacting in a crisis." James was about to comment when the cellar door burst open to reveal a rampant Manny, on his own, jacketless, his pot-belly preceding him like an intimidating animal.

"Where is it?" He roared at James and then at Claudia. "Where the fuck is it?" Their silence increased his fury. "The fuckin' phone!" Fist clenched, he cornered James, who pointed to the mobile where it lay, stopping Manny in his tracks. As Manny bent to retrieve the phone, several policemen charged through the open door behind him and simultaneously through the hatch in the ceiling. Manny, mobile in hand, was led away, threatening, "I'll be on your tail, Mr fuckin' know-all G. You just wait and see."

Afterwards in the plush surroundings of the Da Vinci room in Sercat Central, Grant outlined how he had already received the ransom note by special courier, Claudia's gold bracelet enclosed. "I contacted the police immediately. Then I got your frantic text and have just now given the police that horrible note and the bracelet too. They require that for prosecution purposes. You'll have it returned in due course."

He paused, straightened his silver-grey tie and affected his most caring pose. "You'll have tea, Claudia?" In afterthought he turned to James. "You too, Mr G. How do you like it?"

Claudia thanked Grant and looked across the table at James. An upward wave of his free hand acknowledged her while pursuing his phone conversation with Pedro, who had also contacted the police as a result of James' text for help. Call concluded, he faced Grant as if he had only then become aware of the hotel manager's presence. "Tea," he said, visibly composing himself. "Tea, capital idea! Earl Grey if you'd be so kind. Black, no sugar."

Chapter Forty Five

Claudia couldn't face going back to an empty apartment. She took one of the suites in Sercat Central, wallowing in the care and service while she worked out her next move. She relived the kidnap and her incarceration under The Butcher's Arms. Now that it was over all she could do was smile. In that horrible basement she had what James would probably describe as an epiphany. Looking in the full-length bathroom mirror confirmed it: there she was, smiling an all-over-smug-face-consuming smile when she should have been still shivering in shock. She didn't care, loving the feeling and where it came from. "It's you, James, you bastard," she told her reflection. "It's you, isn't it?"

Dallying with Percival had only added to the slow burning tension that had James as its source. Strange and unbelievable as it seemed, fucking Percival affected her in an unexpected way. She recalled his flabby hands flapping at her breasts, his erection pushing into her and after sex the two of them lying like dead plants starved of sun. That was when she started to laugh. She mounted him, exciting him again and she laughed, rising to hysterics as she rode him, because she couldn't stop thinking of James and how jealous he would be. She laughed until she cried, long after Percival had left her bed with his tail between his legs. James made her feel like somebody rather than somebody's daughter. She'd tell him that too. Catching sight of herself, snow-white and fluffy in a Sercat bathrobe, she evaluated her reflection, addressing it. "You are a devil, James. A dangerous devil, I know it. But you're the devil I want to play with." She started to laugh at the absurdity of it, throwing her head back, gradually calming through fits of coughs and splutters. When she faced the mirror again, the same mirror reflected her favourite photograph of Sergio on a bedside locker. She ran across the room, picked it up and pleaded childlike, "Oh Papa, don't look so sad. I don't want to let you down. But James took care of Grace for us. Isn't that enough? I'm enjoying myself. Let me have my fun with him."

On impulse she called James. His mobile's answering service clicked in immediately. Her sensible self chided: "Not now, Claudia, let's see this awkward business out of the way. When Manny's locked up I can see James again after a few weeks, without fear of Manny or anyone else. See, Papa," she said, turning to Sergio's photograph. "You can be proud of me. I know how to handle myself."

Chapter Forty Six

Like an actor, James always carried an awareness of calamity waiting in the wings. In ways it served him well, keeping him on his toes, alert to the world around him. A tyranny too, in the felt presence of his judgmental mother. "Let your performance sag, James, and you're finished!" A hierarchy of assessors judging him: not only Grace but Claudia, the women in the alley and Magda from The Butcher's Arms. All but one of them were dead. Claudia had become more desirable. Would she be amenable now? Or would his part in Manny's kidnap plot go against him?

After the last day in court, Claudia left with her "no comment" legal people and was driven away at speed. With the media in hot pursuit of "Hotel Tycoon's Daughter in Kidnap Drama!", James slipped away after explaining to journalists that his involvement was purely coincidental; his work-in-progress on the Catalano Hotel Empire necessitated regular meetings with the heiress, Claudia. James went home, reasonably confident that Manny had not said a word about the video of Magda to the police.

Later that day Claudia called. "Look at the news, James."

James turned on the TV to see Manny in handcuffs on his way to prison. James' inclination was to laugh out loud. At the same time

Manny's parting words echoed in his mind: "I'll be on your tail, Mr G."

James noticed that for Pedro the episode had become a cause célèbre. Pedro insisted he wanted all the details before and after James' text for help. James devised a soufflé for the occasion; soufflé, symbolic of new beginnings, phoenix arising amidst the pure aromas of ginger and blood orange.

Subsequently, in an attempt to put the kidnap, court commotion and Claudia fantasies behind him, James laid down a new house rule, forbidding references to her and The Butcher's Arms' affair. Pedro devoted his days to the garden, leaving James the freedom and peace in the house to edit recent reviews and begin work on the book that had been in his head for years: the story of a serial killer chef, an amalgam of his sundry familiarity with the field. The hiatus due to Sercat Hotels' cancelled review project and fewer television commitments had created a working space he could allocate to the novel. He welcomed the creative immersion, beginning with the not unpleasant task of collating texts, information, data accumulated haphazardly over many years, sifting and filtering. Rather like the time-honoured culinary practice of sauce-making, separating out extraneous solids in the process of refinement.

Strict working routine, daily walk in the park, no television, radio news at midnight. He made exception only for Theo, a weekly dinner à deux, after which he'd read to him until he dozed off. Weeks passed; a productive time in which the structure of the novel took shape. Pedro kept his distance, spending more and more time with Susan, which he presumed James did not notice. James noticed but made no comment. Work absorbed him, but then one day life intruded when he least expected it.

If James had grown sure of anything it was that the Catalano-Gall connection had been well and truly severed, but once again he was mistaken. Claudia called. She wanted to meet at Sercat Central. He felt confused and elated, resentful and grateful, delighted and suspicious; he could have cheered and cried at the same time.

"Indubitably no, Claudia."

She was in high spirits. "Indubitably, James, you are a dear. Nobody but nobody speaks like that."

"I seem to have missed something, Claudia. The circumstances of our last meeting were not pleasant. I have to accept my part in that distasteful episode—"

She cut him short. "James, everything's different now. We need to talk."

"You could come over here," James suggested without thinking.

She uttered a yelp and breathed into the phone. "The call of the wild. Shall we say seven, seven-thirty?"

Distrust rose up and lingered. His rational thinking brain advised against haste; be wary, it said, be extremely wary. He listened, briefly acknowledging the sound advice with no intention of acting on it. His heart recognised an irresistible opportunity.

James stood at the window, looking out at the street with the tense expectancy of a child. He watched Claudia park, the flash of thigh as she eased herself from the front seat, the spreading smile when she looked up and saw him at the window, the dismissive flick of a key switch in her hand. Oddly, she chose to encircle the car, surveying it, stroking the bonnet lovingly as she might a pet. The gesture incited a rush of jealousy, which James shrugged off as her long body swaggered up the steps to the hall door. He opened the door to a jubilant grin. In the hall she leaped into his arms.

"How are you?" she said, in a voice full of meaning.

He was red in the face from anticipation. "Delighted to see you."

She would not let him finish, drawing close, putting a finger to his lips. "But how are you deep, deep down, James?"

"I'm working, Claudia, working very hard and loving it."

"Never mind the work, are you happy?"

"I love my work. Happiness, what's happiness?"

Gerry Galvin

Stepping towards him again, her fragrance enveloped him. "You're looking at it. I'm happy, James, and you should know why."

What *was* she getting at? By now they had moved into the drawing room, her arm linking his.

"Your Sercat shares are over the moon?"

Ignoring his flippancy, she went on. "I've been doing some very serious thinking. Do you remember the cellar, James?"

"How could I forget it?" He pulled her close.

Trembling, she responded. "I hated you at the beginning in that horrid place, hated you so much I couldn't talk. Do you remember?"

"Vividly."

"Do you remember standing under the trapdoor with that big plank in your hand, when Manny's thugs attacked you from behind?"

"I must have looked very stupid."

"No, James, no, you were heroic. That was the moment when suddenly all my hatred of you began to turn full circle."

"So?"

"For valour above and beyond the call of duty, for reminding me how much I missed you, for making me see sense, James ..."

James' doubt leaked from him. "Grant Percival, he's no longer in the picture?"

She had moved close again; he could feel her breasts heaving. "You can forget about Grant. I've had him transferred to Moscow. He made me realise how much I do care for you, James."

They tottered, half-carrying each other to the bedroom where they made frenetic love. In the middle of the night they made love again, slowly and easily, as if their minds as well as their bodies had reached an intimate agreement.

Next morning she said, "When we're together for a while you'll learn to love me too."

"Together?"

"Yes, James, I'm moving in with you."

"Shouldn't we discuss this a little first?"

"What's to discuss, James, are we not quite the perfect pair?"

He knew that any argument he had would not convince himself, never mind Claudia. "Let's call it an adjustment exercise, trial period, if you like."

"I like that very much indeed, Mr G," she said, throwing playful kisses at him as she hopped out of bed.

James' trepidation at Pedro's reaction to Claudia's presentation of a fait accompli was, like other recent fears, unfounded. If anything, Pedro showed a respectful compliance to the new matriarchy that was positively Victorian. They slotted into their roles with untroubled aplomb, leaving James floundering until he understood that the relationship existed independently and changed nothing between Pedro and himself. There *were* changes, all of which Pedro took in his stride. He remained unfazed when Claudia declared the breakfast room exclusive, consigning Pedro's dining arrangements to the kitchen.

As Claudia breezed through the process of moving in and transforming the musty maleness of the house, her decorators modernising the place in a matter of days, Pedro danced to her tune. An unlikely trio they were, joined together by much that was bewildering: declared love, loyalty, possessiveness, self-interest and a clinging whiff of deceit. There were moments when James saw the fabric of his life torn down around him and all his instincts cried stop. Coming to terms with disruption was helped by Pedro's ease with Claudia. He traipsed after her, engrossed, as if she were an exotic entertainment, even to the extent of bringing Susan along one after-noon to witness the transformation: the inspired conversion of the house and the blossoming of James' love for this unconventional invader.

Love, yes. A bemused selflessness enfolded James, disorienting but tinglingly alive. All he had to do was reach out to each passing moment, capture it and reel it in, feel that it was all, all his. In such a state of elevation, everything Claudia wished for he agreed with. Almost everything.

There was one row, a difficult impasse around the future of the lab shed in the garden. She wanted to knock it, dispose of the equipment and use the space in some other way.

"Something beautiful and imaginative, James dear, rather than this monstrosity."

Pedro nodded his approval. At that moment James could see that they had been in cahoots behind his back and he resented it. His shed, his guilt, his decision! He stood his ground and would not have budged had Pedro not intervened. "Evidence, Mr G, you should always destroy the evidence."

They eventually decided on an ornamental fountain, using the underground water source; a fountain that might settle into the landscape like one of those post-war monuments to the dead, about which his nose would one day no longer detect an accusatory reek. The old cooker, Hobart mixer, fridge, cold room, sinks and shelving would be sold off soon to a second-hand catering equipment company. His precious set of Sabatier knives? Not for sale.

At that time, no more than a couple of months, they were a happy family. So much so that there was little time for Theo. A few calls, gifts by courier. Claudia consumed time and attention: dinners at Le Gourmet, trips to the country, theatre, galleries and prolix plans for the house. A merry dance. James could not bring himself to tell her about Theo. Something stopped him: divided loyalty and some visceral incapacity. The easiest option was to long-finger the predicament. Theo would understand. Theo was a respectful presence even when they were not in touch. Distance of space and time didn't matter. Whenever James wanted to feel good about himself, he turned to thoughts of Theo, not only for fatherly inference but also an uplifting fellow feeling.

Chapter Forty Seven

Claudia wanted an engagement bash at Sercat Central. Chef Gunter, James' former friend-turned-foe and back again, promised her an überbanquet, to which she intended to invite a cross-section of local society, political and commercial bigwigs. James wanted no public mobfest, not at this stage, perhaps later. Banquets? He'd attended his share in the line of duty. Boredom on a plate. They sought and found a compromise. In return for his agreement to consider a Sercat banquet some time in the future, she accepted his invitation to dinner in a restaurant of his choosing. He had already, in private conference with Salvatore at Les Hirondelles, made preliminary arrangements for a truffle-based extravagance to mark their engagement. In one of their private salons, just the two of them.

To get in the mood he skimmed an old newspaper column of his.

Truffle, testicular fungus ... parasite living off other organisms ... worth its weight in gold ... deformed like knobbly avocados ... the village idiot who turns out to be a genius, his bizarre bearing masking distinction.

It was a pleasant interlude, if somewhat subdued. Their muted spirits suffered, perhaps from fin-de-chasse fatigue, perhaps also in tune with the understated opulence of Les Hirondelles. James could not shake off a feeling of unease. Commitment to coupledom after a rocky journey introduced inevitable deflation. In retrospect, a lovely unthreatened moment, as close as they would ever get to being settled, content with the hum of charged silences.

Halfway through the park on the way home Claudia instructed the cabby. "You can drop us here," she said, exiting the cab, leaving a bewildered James to pay the fare. Snuggling up to him, in a push and cuddle manoeuvre, she jollied him along the moonlit pavement. "Gimme the moonlight, James."

If somewhat bemused by this distraction, he allowed himself to be carried along by the spirit of it. "I could show you the nightingale in Berkeley Square." At home Claudia's merry mood continued. James opened a bottle of chilled Heidsieck. "Join me in a toast," he intoned with faux gravitas, "To happiness!"

They drank and Claudia declared, "What about absent friends?"

They drank to happiness and absent friends and to their future. Then Claudia, tipsy by now, raised her glass once again. "Last but not least, James, I want to congratulate us."

"Us, why?"

"Because we're survivors." They drank to that. Then she said, "James Livingstone Gall, you will please join me in one final, ultimate, very last toast to the memory of those who cannot touch us any more. To Felix and Parfrey and Manny Johnson."

James raised his glass a little uncomfortably.

She had not finished. "Forget Felix," she said, slurring her words. "Forget Parfrey too. But never forget that fat bastard Manny Johnson, who thought he could cross swords with us and get away with it." Pause. "Did you see his ugly face when they nabbed him in the cellar?" She began to laugh, inwardly at first, breaking into a disjointed chortle. The emotional release seemed to drain her of energy. She slumped into an armchair and fell swiftly into a deep sleep. James sat beside her, aware of the metronomic rise and fall of her breasts as she slept.

Chapter Forty Eight

Several days went by. Claudia had commitments with one of her charities, which took her to Paris. Pedro and Susan had gone off somewhere together. "Big decisions, Mr G. Susan wants me to herself for a few days."

"May I conclude that the sentiment is reciprocated?" James asked.

"If you mean do I feel the same way, you're right."

James had his own work: the unfinished novel which was presenting predicaments. He was happy to be alone, occupied with nothing other than his own concerns.

Pedro returned to report that he and Susan were now definitely an item. James shook Pedro's hand, Pedro beamed. James was all business. "Get that woman over here tonight. Claudia will be back, we should all drink to this."

"No fuss, Mr G. Susan is no—"

James put his foot down. "I take some credit for this affair, Pedro. You and the lucky lady will do as I say. Drinks at seven. No further questions!" In retrospect James recalled that cocktail hour for its light-hearted transparency, two couples happily at one. Pedro and Susan left before nine. Claudia and James settled down to watch an old film, *Rear Window*. It was James' favourite Hitchcock. Menace par excellence.

The film had begun to roll when James' phone rang.

Pedro, deadly serious. "Sam Hand's just been on, Mr G." James waited for him to continue. "Manny, he's out, escaped from prison. His brother, waiting in a car, picked him up and he's gone. Sam said something else, Mr G. He said to get the fuck away from here as fast as you can."

James was nodding gravely. When he told Claudia that Manny had got away, she held her breath. "Will he come after us, James?"

For maximum appreciation of the peril Manny now represented, James called everybody together after breakfast. Pedro and Susan arrived with hungover Sam Hand in tow. James wanted Sam's knowledge of Manny's threat to be disclosed in person. He had no doubt about Manny's capacity for violent revenge. Nor had Pedro, but it was essential that Claudia and Susan fully understood what real danger they were in. All of them. Brandy-laced coffee eased Sam's shakes and enabled his tongue.

"Seen him first hand, I have, slash a guy's throat at the back of the Butcher's. The guy done nothin' more than skedaddle with two hundred nicker. Had him dumped in a truckload of concrete out in Croydon. He's part of the foundations of a supermarket now."

"How can you be so sure he's after us?" Claudia enquired almost disdainfully.

Sam slurped coffee, peering at her. "Seen him do a woman too."

"Do, what do you mean?" Susan turned on him, revealing her aversion to his type.

"Stuffed her gob with her knickers and sliced her tits before—"

"That's enough," Claudia remonstrated, looking to James for some sign that this was nothing more than drunken bravado before susceptible eyes. "Why should we believe this?" she demanded.

Sam held up his left hand, spreading the fingers. "See," he said, "no thumb. Manny done that to me when I tried to chat up his dolly."

Susan paled visibly, reaching for Pedro's arm.

"So," Claudia said, tossing back her hair. "What do we do now?"

Sam clearly enjoyed the effects of his little show. "Word is Manny has the hots for you guys. I'd be checkin' my passport if I was you." With that he threw back the last of the coffee, stood shakily, saying, "Me, I'm off, can't be too long before Mr Emmanuel Johnson Esquire is headin' in this direction."

After Sam left they sat silently for several minutes until Pedro spoke up. "We could take a break together, Susan."

"We?" she said, looking about her.

"You and me," said Pedro. "I've been to Spain, could show you the sights."

Susan's blush showed through her pallor. Pedro turned to James. "You, Mr G, what are you going to do?"

James had been thinking. "Manny is bent on revenge and I am number one on his wanted list. Indubitably. Each of you is guilty by association and no one more so than you, Claudia. I was to deliver you into his clutches along with a substantial ransom. That I failed him and that we tricked him is unforgivable. Manny takes no prisoners. You and Susan going to Spain is very sensible, Pedro. Claudia and I will have to devise our own way of dealing with this."

That evening Pedro entered James' office rather shyly, a parcel under his arm. "I've something I want you to have, Mr G. Something Sam gave me a long time ago."

James was taken by surprise. "Something Sam gave you, Pedro? What on earth would I want with something Sam Hand gave you?" He eyed the parcel but had no idea what it could be.

"I don't feel happy about running out on you now, Mr G. But this might be a help to you." With that he unpacked a clumsy vest from the parcel. "It's bullet-proof. Don't know how it really works. Sam swears it does. Never got to use it myself."

"Not quite Saville Row, is it?" James laughed as he tried it on.

"Might save your life."

"It makes me look quite bulky, don't you think?"

"No joke, Mr G, you're gonna need it when Manny comes after you."

James had another good look at the vest, turning around and feeling it with his palms. "Quite so, Pedro, quite so."

The following day Pedro and Susan left on a flight to Carcassonne, planning to make their way by car over the Pyrenees through the Basque country into northern Spain, guessing that Manny's tentacles were most pernicious on the southern Costas. Susan had friends in Pamplona, which could serve as a base while they considered their next move. They promised to keep in contact.

With Spain in mind James acted on a whim. He wrote a long letter to the famous chef, Ferran Adrià, at his restaurant El Bulli, north of Barcelona, proposing a visit to the great shrine of Spanish cooking in order that he, James Livingstone Gall, might endow it with his imprimatur before it closed its doors for the last time. He called Theo to tell him that they would one day soon, just the two of them, fly to Barcelona and dine as Theo had never dined before. "That's a promise," James said.

Chapter Forty Nine

Claudia prepared to attend a meeting of one of her charities at Sercat Central, despite James' opposition. Her determined mood carried its own language of emphasis: the words "fuck" and "bastard". She strode about like a caged thing and when she faced him, James felt hypnotised by the sheer focus of rage. "That fucker is not, not, James, going to put me off. Do you understand?"

"Be careful," he told her as she sailed through the hall door. He would have to be careful too. Of Manny, yes, perhaps of Claudia too. What her rage might make her do.

Alone in the house he tried to summon reserves of courage and common sense, imagining what Grace would say at such a pass. "Gather your thoughts, James. Plug in to your resources."

Resources? He felt bereft, his hands hurt and a cool draught had him searching for its source, turning this way and that until he found a partially opened window in the drawing room. He closed the window and drew the curtain but still felt a chill. Manny in his bones. He pulled back the curtains, checked each of the windows, locked them, locked the hall door and went through the back door into the garden. Pedro's bay tree was thriving, the sheen on new leaves attested. Two black-birds, long term residents, ignored him as he ambled about. The

lovage plant spread unfettered in pungent admonishment of his
inattention; he should have cut it back, candied the stalks and dried
the seeds. Fondling it now with both hands, the wafts of celery and
yeast rose around him, a cordon sanitaire protecting him from evil
influences. He reached the door of the lab, still standing despite the
plans for its destruction. It seemed to say, *I'm here, James, present and
ready, awaiting instruction.* His lab, his resource! "Of course, Mum,
right again! I *shall* use my resources," he declared loudly to nobody.
If Felix Underwood ended up in the lab, so could Manny Johnson
and anyone else deserving of such a fate.

Claudia returned, rage unabated, flaring nostrils, florid language.
But there was an Amazon behind the anger and vulgarity. Fearlessness
flowed from her, electric emissions that set off reactions in his belly
and crotch. "I'm going to seduce the bastard." This she uttered without
irony.

"Fuck Manny Johnson?"

"Yes, fuck him, James."

"Don't play with words, Claudia, this is not trivial pursuit."

She smirked. "Not trivial, pursuit yes."

Testing, he said, "We could always seek police protection, our old
friend Gibbons …"

"No, no, no. You must be mad." That smirking certainty still played
around her mouth. "There's only one way to get away from him and
that's to go after him."

"You'd really have sex with him?"

"If I had to, James, but with your help it should not come to that.
I can entice him, lure him, call it what you like, just get the bastard
alone and we could see him off permanently."

"The lab," he said, taking her in his arms.

She kissed him with such force he could taste blood on his gums.
"Genius," she shrieked and they kissed again.

That evening Pedro called from Santander, where he and Susan had rented an apartment. James told him they were in fighting mood, not prepared to cower in the hope that Manny would forget about them as he evaded capture himself.

"Don't be stupid, Mr G," he replied. "Manny has a small army." Pedro ended the conversation with a warning. "Claudia, Mr G, be careful of her. You know I like her but I don't trust her."

They were cut off before James could let him know that according to the morning news Manny's brother and two close associates had been apprehended on the M4 in Buckinghamshire. If Manny had a small army, it was smaller now.

He could hear Claudia in the bedroom. When he got there she lay on the bed naked on her stomach, buttocks raised, head turned to greet him, simpering.

"Help, James, help me. I can't do this on my own."

Chapter Fifty

The police search for escaped prisoner, Manny Johnson, had been frantic at first, reacting to sightings in diverse locations hundreds of miles apart. A cabby in Liverpool led them to a pub near Anfield football ground, where he had just dropped off the escapee. "It's him, fat Cockney in a Chelsea shirt!" It wasn't. Nor was he in the departure lounge at Gatwick, on a boat in the Lake District, or on the Glasgow train. In a couple of days the search petered out, as other more urgent matters demanded police time and energy. Manny Johnson had disappeared.

James had a mobile number for Sam Hand, which he tried repeatedly. It rang out each time. On the third day Sam called. No, he would not come to the house; yes, they could meet somewhere big and anonymous. Trafalgar Square.

Sam looked out of place in the Square, unnerved by camera-toting tourists, the pigeons, the wide open space. He led James to a public house down a side street off Tottenham Court Road. No, he had no idea where Manny was hiding. "Might be in fuckin' Argentina by now."

It took an hour of persuasive brandies before James could get him to think straight and even then all he'd promise was to keep his ear to the ground. He handed Sam two fifty pound notes as they separated.

"To cover your calls."

Sam phoned that evening. "Could be in deep shit for this, Mr G." His voice shook, "The Collingdon Motel."

Collingdon, about ten miles north of Oxford. James knew it, had a bad meal there once. He pictured Manny in the down-at-heel motel pigging out on beer and bangers, keeping his head down when all his instincts cried out for mayhem and revenge.

Claudia's plan of action was simple: she would go to Collingdon, sniff around the motel, get the room number and make direct contact with Manny. "Yes, James, sure there's an element of danger. He's bound to be armed and on edge. But I will have what he wants most of all."

"Which is?"

"You," she said. "I can lead him to you."

Daring, James thought, but he had reservations. "You think you can handle him? You know he's mercurial at the best of times. On the run he'll be very unpredictable."

"I'll be irresistible, James. I promise." She hesitated, looked away sharply as if stung by a dark thought she did not wish to share. Seconds only, hardly noticeable. When she faced James again it was with habitual irony. "Don't worry, darling, you of all people should know how convincing I can be." Ogling, she leaned in to him, licking his right ear. "I'll tell him how much I have hated James Livingstone Gall ever since I discovered you were the son of the woman who killed my father. I'll explain how I've tricked you into trusting me and that all along I've been biding my time, awaiting the best opportunity to do to you as we did to Felix. Only this time Manny will be my partner, you the victim."

"You do rather terrify me, my dear." James wondered if she realised how seriously he meant what he said.

"Oh James, you do know how to make the most wonderful compliments," Claudia countered. "But from experience I know you do not terrify easily."

"Indeed." James' answer was succinct.

"But it is not about us just now, James. It's about Manny. He will take some convincing, that's obvious, he's no born-again believer. But he's on the run, moving all the time, constantly looking over his shoulder, suspicious of everybody. He's tired and running out of options. I'm banking on his vulnerability and the old reliable, an offer he cannot refuse."

"Sex?"

"Sex, implied, yes. But primarily, James, your head and his freedom. I'll be able to show how I can bring him to you, and for afters, as you might put it, I'll give him the ransom you failed to deliver and the means to flee the country. As you know there's a Catalano yacht moored in Buckler's Hard, used mainly nowadays by executives of Sercat Hotels. The skipper is always on hand for sudden outings to Brittany or the Scillies."

"Brilliant, brilliant," James repeated.

She stood before him, legs apart, eyes flashing, beads of perspiration on her upper lip, breathing slowly through her nose like an athlete in the build-up to competition. She was right, he knew it. She would march into Manny's lair, stroke him into submission and he would follow her to wherever she wished. "I just sit here and wait?"

"You need to make the necessary preparations, James. Do you understand me?"

"The Felix treatment," James said, chuckling at the audacity of it all.

"Exactly. The same again, Mr G. This is urgent, James. Manny is not going to hang about. We have to strike quickly. With luck I'll have him back here, well-softened tomorrow evening. All ready for you."

James felt a strange on-the-outside-looking-in feeling; this was his narrative, she the interpreter. It excited him.

That night James saw his mother sitting by his bedside. When he nodded off, she kept prodding him into dopey wakefulness, sniggering. "Now who do you trust, James, ha, ha, ha?" Someone, another woman's fuzzy figure, stood behind Grace. As he fell into unconsciousness, she seemed to emerge from the fugue and before the image drifted from him he recognised Claudia.

Chapter Fifty One

After Claudia left for the Collingdon Motel, James ordered a taxi for himself. The cabby shrugged his shoulders in response to James' request. "I'd appreciate your assistance in a little subterfuge, which may mean extended hire, quite possibly all evening. A trip to the country and back, expense not an issue."

"At your service, guv'. You call the shots. As long as no law's broken," he added in afterthought.

"A private domestic affair but entirely legal," James assured him.

He nodded a meaningful affirmative. "You got my sympathy, guv'. Name's Terry. Been through the mill myself. Women, trouble and strife!" Thus their journey began in the spirit of male bonding, strengthening as they waited within sight of Claudia's apartment; watching her emerge and drive off in her Jaguar; following her out of the park to her Knightsbridge bank; waiting there for a twenty-minute transaction, while a bank porter sat in charge of her car; then along the Cromwell Road and into the country past Heathrow. Terry kept their quarry in sight from a safe distance, turning off at the sign for Collingdon, a couple of vehicles behind Claudia. He parked across the road from the motel under an umbrella of mature sycamores and the darkening night.

James watched Claudia alight from the Jaguar, head and chin up, thrusting upper body, striding coltishly from the well-lit car park to the bright spacious lobby, where two large dark-suited gentlemen with pale sombre faces and eyes hiding behind dark glasses awaited. From the back of the taxi, window down, James had a clear view. The two heavies showed no surprise at her arrival. Then, on her instruction, they moved like a pair of decanted jellies either side of her, wobbling in tandem out of the lobby towards a terrace of cabins adjoined in one block at the rear of the car park. Through a pair of binoculars James kept the trio under surveillance. Claudia was clearly in charge, striding ahead as the minders shuffled to keep up with her.

Manny appeared in one of the cabin doorways, and before ushering Claudia inside, took her hands in his and kissed her on both cheeks. A shudder passed through James' body as everything became clear. Manny had been tipped off. They were coming together to get him. He would have to be ready, prepare accordingly. He told Terry to take him back to London, where he paid him with a generous tip as Big Ben sounded midnight.

Indoors he made himself a broth of potato and onion with a fistful of chopped lovage from the garden. He swallowed each mouthful with angry resolve. How to deal with this dual threat; images of poisoned bangers for the bastard Manny; Claudia filling his head with confusing concoctions of vengeance and desire. It took an effort to restrain these runaway thoughts. Above all, clarity of purpose, mise en place! Cognac and a pill. Then he called Pedro in Spain.

"Yes, Pedro, Claudia has located Manny. She's in control of the situation." He didn't want to spell it out for him. "I expect I'll be seeing both of them soon."

"She's not working with Manny, is she, Mr G?" Pedro asked matter-of-factly.

"It's a possibility I must definitely take into consideration."

"I should be there with you, Mr G. I owe you that."

"Mise en place, Pedro. I'll be prepared for them."

"You'll wear the vest, Mr G. At least promise me that."

"It's damn clumsy, not very comfortable, but I do understand your concern. Must take every precaution, mustn't we?"

For an instant the idea of calling Theo came into his head. But how could Theo help, he asked himself? Theo was not well. Anyway it was too late in the day to drag him into the Claudia affair. Perhaps he should have confided in him sooner. Instead he went upstairs and tried on Pedro's vest again. He ran his hands over the vest, testing its texture. Would it do the trick, he asked himself? It had to. There would be no second chance with Manny, whatever chance he might have with Claudia. Fighting back a wave of resignation, he removed the vest and hung it on a rack in the wardrobe along with other waistcoats. Then he went to bed.

James tossed and turned, thoughts rushing through his sleepless mind. Claudia and Felix in Le Gourmet; Claudia in The Butcher's Arms, Manny's pub. How much had been coincidence, how much Claudia's plan? As he fell into a restless sleep, the picture of Manny ushering Claudia in at the motel replayed in his head.

Chapter Fifty Two

After a delivered supper of pasta and wine Manny dismissed the bodyguards, telling them to check in with him at seven in the morning. They stole looks at each other as if inclined to say something. One mumbled, "You sure, Manny?"

"Get the fuck outta here," he barked.

When they had gone, Manny turned to Claudia. "On the phone you said you could take me to Mr G, pay the ransom and get me to France, just like that." Claudia assessed him: wine and food had slackened his features, mouth half-open, eyes flickering. Life on the run had taken its toll on Manny. She flashed her broadest smile, handing him a small velvet pouch tied with string, saying, "Diamonds valued at fifty thousand pounds, downpayment. More to come when the job is done."

"Bona fides," he said, pocketing the diamonds with one hand, producing a gun to her face with another. "I could kill you now," he hissed.

"And draw more attention to yourself when you have managed to evade the police for so long? I don't think you can be so stupid."

"Len and Harry know all about removal and disposal. All I have to do is say the word and they'd have you outta here like yesterday's garbage."

"Len and Harry are no longer employed by you, Manny. They've had it living like gypsies. I've paid them off."

Like an awakened bear Manny growled, lumbering to the wall between his cabin and number eleven. He looked out the window and called their names. No reply. Shoving the gun in his trouser belt, he turned to Claudia. "Seems you have all the cards, Claudia. But here's one you haven't seen. Your lover-boy James hates women. Something to do with his weirdo mother, who you told me did the job on your dad. But that's not my business. Has a liking for dead waitresses, does our James. Strangles them in dark alleys."

Claudia looked at Manny with cautious eyes, taking it all in. She was on the point of speaking when Manny again cut her off. "Magda, the strangled waitress, you've read the paper? That was a James job. Got it all on CCTV in The Arms. Not his only victim." He reminded her of other killings, the similarities between them. "He got away with it because some poor bastard got done over by the police for it. Would have admitted to killing his mother, he would, after they were through with him. Hung himself, you'll remember."

Claudia hardly moved as he rummaged under the bed for a suitcase, from which he produced still pictures of the incriminating footage: Magda, leaving the pub and James, or someone very like him, wearing a full-length overcoat in close pursuit. She asked herself why she felt no surprise. But James' predilection for killing was nothing new to her. It was part and parcel of her fascination with him.

"That's a lot for me to take in just now," she said eventually. "Or do you have any more surprises for me?" Manny grunted some kind of negative. "I need to sleep on this," she continued, "let things settle. I think we both could do with a good night's sleep, separately, in preparation for our meeting with James." She moved to the door, where she paused and turned to face him. "You'll need that gun tomorrow night. Take care it doesn't go off prematurely."

Claudia lay awake in her cabin, number ten, two doors down

Gerry Galvin

the block. During the night every sound was a gunshot and, when a group of drunken revellers fell about in the car park shouting obscenities, she imagined a murderous James descending on her. In the most vulnerable hours before dawn, James seemed as present to her as if he shared her motel bed, engendering the same cocktail of fear and attraction that drew her to him from their first encounter in The Butcher's Arms. As sleep eventually claimed her, the seriousness of the cat-and-mouse game she and James were caught up in came home to her.

Awake again at seven she showered and made herself coffee before summoning the courage to call James. Fifteen further preparatory minutes at the dressing table helped. By the time she called, her resolve was absolute. With sugary Italian amorousness she greeted him. "Come va, lover. I miss you." Then, businesslike, she gave a quick update on satisfactory progress. "Not out of the woods yet but looking good. You were right, he's very edgy, so treat him with care. I gave him diamonds, he liked that. I'll have him delivered tonight. Do try to greet Manny with surprise. You are not supposed to know he's coming with me, are you?"

"Don't you worry, my dear. I'll be the soul of pleasurable delight at his unforeseen arrival. What's more I will prepare some gastronomically-challenged sausage-surprise for friend Manny. Being the glutton that he is he will find them irresistible. No sausage for you, my dear. We can celebrate together later with osso bucco."

"James, food is not exactly high on my list at the moment. I'll be happy to watch Manny digging in."

Manny could not be persuaded to travel into London in daylight, so after checking out of the hotel in the afternoon, Claudia drove them to a farmhouse in the Chilterns where an old jailbird pal provided a short-term safe house for London criminals, a kind of temporary refuge. If Manny required confirmation of his pariah status he got it; supposed friend, recognising his visitor, held both his palms up. "No way, Manny, you're in too deep this time. No way you can stop here."

When Manny explained that he wanted to get in touch with colleagues, the riposte was even more emphatic. "Don't you know you got no colleagues no more? You're on your own, mate."

For the rest of the day and on the final run into London, Claudia fanned Manny's dejection into resentment aimed directly at James, the source of their joint misfortune. She kept him at simmering point, hinted at favours to come, even as her own personal detractor questioned her ability to see this collaboration through to its logical end. Was Claudia Catalano really capable of being party to the cold-blooded killing of James Livingstone Gall?

When they reached the Square and approached James' house, the scent of cooking through an open window drifted in the air. Manny's nostrils itched. "Typical, James and his fuckin' food. Always makes me feel peckish, he does. But this is no Mayfair dinner party. We're here to terminate Mr G." Manny rubbed his nose and, reaching for the gun in his belt, he felt it and readied it. "You and me, Claudia."

Chapter Fifty Three

James had never waited like this before, isolated and lost in a wasteland of the imagination, oscillating between expectation and fear. At our very best, Theo had said, fear is replaced by euphoria. Guided by Theo's insight, bordering on transcendence, James put his mind to the preparation of the evening's special for his guest.

In the lab James lifted clear the sisal mat and the manhole cover, the sound of water beneath hitting his ears in a rush. He refused to entertain any more than a shudder at the spectre of Felix ghosting through the gurgling river. Kneeling, his right hand sought and removed three loose bricks immediately under the manhole. From a cavity, which had been concealed by the bricks, he removed a sealed wooden case. Then he returned the bricks to their former position, closed the manhole and slipped the mat back into place. The lid of the box responded to the manipulation of a sharp vegetable knife, opening to reveal six airtight capsules, transparent and full:

Pomegranate and passion fruit pulp

Liquefied liver of Vietnamese panga fish

Mulched bark of an elder willow

Crushed sorghum cereal

Dried vanilla pod and deep-fried kelp

Molten lead.

Precise proportions. Alchemy by his own hand. A fast-acting, deadly dosage. He mixed the potion and poured it into a syringe like the one he used on his mother in the hospital. He then took three rings of uncooked sausage from the cold room and injected them with the poison.

Indubitably Manny food, he thought: bangers of venison and sweet pepper, beef with horseradish and anchovy, a bulging Cumberland. James knew that everything hinged on Manny's predilection for eating.

A film of sweat basted James' brow. He dabbed himself dry, carrying the plate of sausages on a silver tray through the garden to the house, with the measured tread of a landlord on home ground. In the kitchen he moved the pot of long-simmered osso bucco to the back of the stove, then fried the poisoned sausages in goose fat. The caramel tang of cooked meat enveloped the kitchen, spreading fumes of temptation throughout the house.

All in order, James went upstairs to put on Pedro's bullet-proof vest, concealing it beneath a button-down shirt and a loose cashmere cardigan. He contemplated his image in the bathroom mirror, letting his hands glide over the shirt, feeling the vest underneath. "Yes, I think I'm dressed for the occasion, Pedro," he said aloud to himself as he went downstairs to await Claudia and his "surprise guest".

James watched from the drawing room window as Claudia and Manny parked and made their way towards the house. A grim-looking duo. He felt a roiling in the bowels. A stiff cognac, deep breathing and the feel of Pedro's protective vest, righted him. "Ready," he assured himself, "ready for anything."

When he opened the door to receive them, he had regained the actorish buoyancy with which he was determined to control the situation. His rehearsed expression of feigned surprise for Manny's benefit had already formed. But any platitudes he might have uttered were truncated in the fierceness of Manny's entrance. Gun drawn, he forced James back into the house. Claudia shut the door and stood watching as Manny pushed James towards the kitchen, away from any would-be witnesses, the prying ears and eyes of passers-by.

Stunned, James attempted to placate Manny. "Come, Manny let's, let's just talk—"

"No more talk, Mr G," Manny said, and just for a second James saw him eye the pan of sausages. "No more fuckin' talk," Manny repeated and then grabbed a sausage with his free hand and shoved it into his mouth.

In a despairing attempt to divert Manny, James gestured to the drinks cabinet. "A drink, Manny, at least have a …"

Manny, sausage gristle dangling from his mouth, lifted a bottle of red wine, glancing at the label, his gun hand steady, pointing at James. "Bull's Blood." The words shot out of him. "Bullshit, Mr G," he smashed the bottle of Hungarian wine off the corner of the sideboard.

Claudia stood by the entrance to the drawing room, transfixed. James sought her eyes but she did not respond. Rivulets of red wine began to run across the kitchen floor. Manny moved closer to James, who backtracked towards the garden exit, reaching for the doorknob. Before he could manage to open the door, Manny fired. Claudia screamed.

"No way out now, Mr G. Not any more."

The impact of the blast thrust James backwards. He tried to make it to his feet but they wouldn't support him. As he fell, his failing awareness registered Claudia's horror and Manny, grinning above him, chewing sausage. His last sense was of the smell emanating from Manny, a not unpleasant commingling on the nose: garlic and vanilla, passion fruit with grace notes of a metallic fishiness. His last faint thought, the hope that Pedro's vest would do its job.

Chapter Fifty Four

Claudia was petrified, eyes glued to Manny standing over James, who did not move.

"Job's done," Manny stated matter-of-factly. As he spoke he waved his gun hand in the direction of the kitchen table, indicating that she should sit. Like a zombie she did as she was bid. Manny had reverted to type, brash and sure of himself. He had taken off his jacket, exposing his shirt, mapped with sweat stains. She could smell him.

"Sausage for moi. How 'bout you, Claudia?" She shook her head, mumbling something unintelligible. He helped himself to more sausage and filled a soup bowl with osso bucco from the stove, which he plonked in front of her. "Eat," he said sharply, "I like company at dinner time."

She lifted her spoon and made a hesitant show of eating while Manny took another look at James' prone body, poked him with his foot and grunted in satisfaction. He was half-way through the batch of sausages before Claudia managed to force herself to swallow a mouthful of osso bucco. She ate a little as Manny laid into the remaining sausages. He farted, wiped his mouth with the back of his hand and raised a forkful of sausage to Claudia's face. "Give the man his due. He cooked a good banger." He was talking too loudly, rhetorically, as if to a captive audience. Claudia held her peace, her eyes on the gun, which lay on the table beside him.

Suddenly Manny darted from the table to the drinks cabinet, lifted an open bottle of Bull's Blood to his lips and drank copiously. He began to spit and belch, tottering back to the table, bottle in hand. "Fuckin' thirsty," he managed to declare between gulps of wine. "Fuckin' thirsty." He nursed the bottle, drinking and eating, keeping an eye on Claudia, reciting an incoherent monologue, to which he did not appear to require reaction. She let him ramble on. He had almost finished the bottle when she detected a change, his eyes squinting, no longer focused on her, the poison beginning its work.

"What the fuck, Claudia. What is this?" He rubbed his eyes, bits of Cumberland falling from his perspiring palms. He seemed to collapse into himself, head drooping. His breathing was laboured and he became uncannily still.

What she did next she couldn't explain. An inner power took hold of her. Rising slowly, she tip-toed to Manny's side of the table. In a calming whisper she laid a hand on his back, reassured him and put a glass of wine to his lips. "You'll be alright Manny, drink this. I'll get something for your eyes." Unseen, she lifted the gun.

"I can't see," Manny called out. "Help me Claudia, please. I can't fuckin' see."

"Okay, Manny, I *can* see. Hold still. This will help."

Holding the gun with both hands, Claudia pulled the trigger. The wine glass exploded in Manny's face. He fell off the chair, red wine mingling with blood dripping from his body. He shuddered violently for a moment and then lay apparently lifeless. As Claudia stared at him, the gun became a hot coal in her hands and she flung it away. Then she fled to the bathroom, where the distraught image of herself in James' full-length mirror sent her headlong through the house and out into the London night.

Chapter Fifty Five

When James came to through thunderous chest pain and headache, he found himself alone. Claudia and Manny nowhere to be seen. He remembered Manny, gun in hand, standing over him as he fell, and Claudia fearful in the background. Rising shakily, he surveyed the reeking kitchen, puddles of wine and shattered glass on the floor and on the table an upturned bottle beside the empty sausage pan. If Manny had eaten all that sausage, he'd be dead by now. The scrunch of broken glass underfoot led his eyes downward. Manny's gun lay in a blood-red pool, from which a custardy trail led out the rear door to the garden, down the path and slathered over the lovage plant. James felt his gorge rising and yielded to a bout of dry retching. Cold water from a tap by the back door revived him. He went back to the kitchen to retrieve the gun.

Where the hell was Manny? One of Pedro's garden cupids, knocked off its plinth, lay smashed on the lawn. The spattered trail continued in a crooked line towards the lab. Then, within feet of the lab, James came across Manny's body, face up, neck and chest covered in vomit and blood, right leg twisted grotesquely beneath him like some lifeless marionette. Claudia had proven herself. She had given Manny what he'd deserved. This waxworks Manny, in a nadir of abasement, was radiant with a naïve wonder that in life he never possessed.

James knew he had to get to work before rigor mortis set in. He shoved the gun into Manny's trousers. Relieved that the bullet-proof vest had done the trick for him, that all his faculties were in working order, he knew too he did not have the strength to move Manny to his final destination. While contemplating his options, he noticed the diamond-filled pouch protruding from one of Manny's pockets and removed it. "Pay day, Manny. Never look a gift horse et cetera, et cetera. You've outlived your uselessness, time to apply your devilish talents in a suitable elsewhere. Would anyone want you? No, no future romance at all, I fear, dear boy. Quite ugly in fact, putrefaction and the revolt of odours. Downhill to where you belong." Talking relieved the pain and enabled thought. "Manny, old chap, I would give you to science were it not so inconvenient. Can't be done, no alternative; it's the watery grave and sausage hell for you, I'm afraid. First the little matter of disposal, what to do with you now, immovable object and all that. I'm not feeling the fittest myself."

As the thoughts coursed through his head he remembered how Claudia helped him carry Felix. "But where are you, Claudia, now when I need you? Left me for dead, have you?" Once again his head reminded him of its pain. He would have to make do without Claudia. He began to calculate how Pedro would cope in similar circumstances and his eyes were drawn to Pedro's shed. "Don't move, Manny, back in a tick."

The shed was locked and James did not have a key. He returned to the lab, stepping over Manny, and emerged with a heavy meat cleaver, with which he broke open the lock. Pedro's sack truck stood shining, oiled in readiness inside the shed door. "Pedro, reliable as ever!" James rolled the truck across the lawn to the lab and man-oeuvred it under the dead body. With the lab door open, James slowly guided the loaded truck inside. Gasping, he took a breather and then opened the manhole. Again he addressed Manny. "I could hack you to manageable pieces, stew you, liquidise and pour you into Hades. But no, my friend, not up to that at present. No, has to be the bum's rush this time round." James inhaled deeply, mustering diminished strength, pondering Manny's remains. "Body disposal is murder's most difficult art, Manny. Can't have your bloated evidence floating to the surface too soon. No Manny, no room for error."

With that James picked up two heavy iron weights from an antique weighing scales in the lab and tied them securely around Manny's body. "Mat, manhole and splash," he intoned and, with one last strained lift and push, he dumped the weighted corpse into the water.

Attempts to call Claudia's mobile at intervals throughout the following days were unsuccessful. Her phone had been switched off. Eventually James phoned Sercat Central and elicited the number of Claudia's main charity administrator, whom he called, introducing himself as Ms Catalano's close friend, James Livingstone Gall.

"Ms Catalano is not available at present, Mr Gall. But if you wish we can pass on a message as soon as we are made aware of her whereabouts. I do know that she is not in the country at the moment."

"Tell her James called."

Chapter Fifty Six

At the time James left down the phone, Claudia Catalano was eating strawberries at a table for two in the Romanoff Restaurant of the Moscow Sercat Hotel. Other diners noted the pale, lone woman rapt in recollection, oblivious of the attention.

She recalled the insanity of that fateful evening in James' house, from which she had not yet recovered. Would she ever? She shivered at the thought. And yet some trace of the empowerment in that moment remained with her. A kind of memento to cling to, as she wondered about James and what might have been. She had to get away. In the panic that took her from the house, she could not be sure if Manny was dead. Had she really killed him?

When the hotel manager joined her, heads turned. Questions to the maître d' about her were shrugged off in a non-committal manner.

Claudia excused herself to take a call. She listened carefully to the message, pausing with a sharp intake of breath. "Thank you, thank you so much. Good of you to let me know." Bending down, she replaced the phone in her handbag, seemingly impervious.

"Anything important, Claudia?" Grant Percival queried.

"Nothing that concerns you," she told him with a curt shake of the head. "Just a message from someone I thought was dead."

Chapter Fifty Seven

Recent events took their toll on James. His solid ground of certainty and expectation became a marshland of insecurity in the absence of Claudia and Pedro. On his own, irritations grew into a violent emptiness. His lip quivered, arthritic spasms attacked his hands and every bowel movement presented unbearable cramping pain. On top of that Manny's bullet had left a tender bruise on his chest, despite the protective vest. He took painkillers. Too many. His nights were shrouded in sleepless dreaming and nightmares. Would they find Manny's body and trace it back to the garden shed? Worst of all were his mother's spectral intrusions, always chiding.

"For God's sake James, pull yourself together. Don't be such a cry-baby. You didn't fret so much when you saw me off."

Pedro would have provided company and restorative soups. And Claudia, what now? Grace's voice was quick to answer any lingering doubts he had. "James, James, you're free of that woman. Cut her out of your life, as I did her father."

There was some relief when Pedro called. James told Pedro the latest on Manny and Claudia's disappearance.

"If it's any help, Mr G," Pedro told him, "I've been learning a lot from Susan since we came to Spain. How to come to terms with the past. I wasn't able to accept things as they are and move on."

James paused before replying. This was not the Pedro he knew. "Sounds like therapy-talk, Pedro. A bit too much for me at this point."

"Yes, Mr G, that's it. Susan's done all that for me. She's something else, Mr G, believe me."

"I am inclined to believe you, Pedro, and I assure you I am truly envious." The conversation inevitably led to Claudia.

"I think you have to get her out of your system, Mr G. Claudia is one of those rich bitches who can't be satisfied. I never really trusted her."

James sighed audibly. "Ah, Pedro, dear Pedro, one wishes it were so simple."

"But it is that simple, the secret is change. With Susan to help me I've changed for the better. You could do it too."

James let a moment pass, in which his silent wish was for Pedro to change as much he needed. As for himself, he said, "Changing for the better, Pedro, presumes there is a better to change to."

The next day James was surprised to receive a letter with a Spanish postmark. Could it be from Claudia, Claudia in Spain? Some remnant of hope wished it could be. He opened it, pulse racing. It was not from Claudia, nor Pedro, but his reply from Ferran Adrià, an invitation to spend a week with him at El Bulli on the Costa Brava. James was thrilled. This was his chance to make good the promise he had made to Theo. He couldn't wait to tell him the good news. Together they would find out if Ferran lived up to his reputation.